She had no name for this feeling

Yes, she did. She had several. *Hi-s-ki-ti-hi*. Five Killer. Robert McLarn.

It was incredible to her how strongly she needed to be with him, she who had always been so careful, worked so hard never to need anything beyond what life had given her. But now she needed this man. She had to breathe his breath. Her soul had been put into the center of his soul. And for a brief moment, perhaps, she could lead him away from his sorrow.

Hannah *did* long for him, and would for the rest of her life. Now she gave herself up to him completely. She could wrap herself around him and never let go.

"Hannah!" he whispered, and she looked at him, into his eyes.

And saw herself there.

I will forget all that I was, and I will be his…!

Dear Reader,

Spring is in full bloom and marriage is on the minds of many. That's why we're celebrating marriage in each of our four outstanding Historicals romances this month!

Award-winning author Cheryl Reavis brings us a powerful story about a second chance at love and marriage with *The Captive Heart*. Known for her dramatic tone and outstanding characterization in both her historical and contemporary romances, Cheryl once again delivers. Amid the backdrop of the early frontier, a British officer has his wife imprisoned by the Cherokee. She is rescued by a Native American/Scottish slave who is trying to save his own son, and the two discover a love that knows no bounds.

Tanner Stakes His Claim by the ever-popular Carolyn Davidson features a marriage of convenience between a squeaky-clean Texas sheriff and the new gal in town, an amnesiac—and pregnant—saloon singer he can't stop thinking about! In *The Bride of Spring*, book two of Catherine Archer's terrific SEASONS' BRIDES miniseries, a noblewoman desperate to marry orchestrates her own wedding, unaware that the man she has chosen will be her true love.

There is a most *unusual* arranged marriage in *My Lady's Choice* by the immensely talented Lyn Stone. When an English lady miraculously saves King Edward's best knight, the king grants her a boon. Her choice? Marriage to the semiconscious and oh-so-handsome knight!

Enjoy! And come back again next month for four more choices of the best in historical romance.

Sincerely,

Tracy Farrell,
Senior Editor

CHERYL REAVIS

The Captive Heart

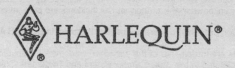

HARLEQUIN®

TORONTO • NEW YORK • LONDON
AMSTERDAM • PARIS • SYDNEY • HAMBURG
STOCKHOLM • ATHENS • TOKYO • MILAN • MADRID
PRAGUE • WARSAW • BUDAPEST • AUCKLAND

ISBN 0-373-29112-4

THE CAPTIVE HEART

To Pookie,
with thanks for all the times when
I needed a friend.

Prologue

August, 1755

He is a wild thing.

She knew that with great certainty, but she still sat alone and motionless on the flat boulder near the water's edge. She could feel the sunlight on the top of her head. She had been here for some time, long enough for the sun to finally breach the tall trees and shine down on her, long enough for her stepmother to worry.

But she made no attempt to leave. She kept listening to the silence that was not silence at all, but filled with the persistent buzz of insects and the birds singing, the quiet rush of the water over the rocks and the wind in the treetops.

Perhaps he is too wild to understand, she thought suddenly. *Perhaps he won't come. Perhaps he'll see me still here and he won't leave anything...*

There was a faint rustling in the underbrush off to her left, but she took great care not to turn her head in that direction. She had never seen him, not even once, though she had sensed his presence many times. It was a skill she had acquired since her father had moved her and his second family to the very edge of the frontier, and one she could not explain.

She wasn't lonely here—it was her nature not to require the company of others—but she was indeed very alone, in spite of her stepmother and the little boys. It was the profound solitude of this place, she supposed, that made it possible for her to recognize so acutely when another human being came near.

But this human being must have been watching when she was not so aware. He must have seen her father's anger at her wasting time and precious paper on something so frivolous as making watercolor sketches of flowers that didn't exist here in the wilderness and only served as sad reminders of a way of life now lost to them—when she should be attending his emotionally fragile young wife. He must have seen her when she defied her father and hid the satchel with the watercolors under a nearby rocky ledge, because he had taken one of the sketches—just one—and left a necklace made of braided rawhide and a single piece of decorated, triangular-shaped seashell she now secretly kept in her Psalmody as a bookmark.

And he must have seen her growing hunger as well, because more of her watercolors disappeared, but instead of necklaces small, intricately woven baskets filled with dried corn or hickory nuts or squash were left in their place.

She heard the noise in the underbrush again, and she fumbled for her leather satchel and carefully removed the only watercolor she had. There was great irony here. Before her father had gone on his journey, he had once again forbidden her to waste her time in such a frivolous manner, not when his young second wife needed her so. Three children in as many years. Three children who would be dead now if not for what her father considered her shameless self-indulgence.

She could feel her anger rising. Her father had been gone much longer than it should have taken him to ride his circuit to preach the sermons and perform the marriages, baptisms and burials his flock required of him. He should have made better arrangements for his family even if it was so incidental to his calling. He should have sent them all to the Lower Settlement on the Saxapahaw or to the Moravians until he returned. At the very least, he should have asked someone to come see if all was well with them.

But he hadn't. There was no flour or corn left, no money to buy any if by some miracle she and her stepmother could carry the children and walk to the nearest settlement without being kidnapped or murdered or eaten by wild animals. The baby cried pitifully at its mother's breast. The little boys were hungry. They were *all* hungry. She had neither the weapons nor the skill for hunting, and only the barest knowledge of what plants and berries were safely edible. Her attempts at fishing in the fast running stream had been ludicrous.

She placed the sketch on her lap, and she wondered as she always did, why their benefactor would want these small artistic efforts of hers. She was no great talent certainly, but she had been adequately taught, and her subjects were recognizable. Perhaps he simply liked the novelty of seeing what must be strange flowers blooming on paper even in the dead of winter. Perhaps he traded them for something he desperately needed, just as she did, though her "trading" had hardly been voluntary.

But this time she would not simply allow him to take the sketch and go. This time she wanted to see the person to whom she owed her life. She wasn't afraid exactly. He could have killed her a hundred times by now if he'd chosen to do so. It was a risk she had to take. If she was ever to see him, to thank him for what he had done, then an actual meeting had to be now. She had but one last, hastily completed watercolor to give him.

A bird suddenly took flight in the underbrush, making her jump. She looked in that direction, straining to see something—someone—in the gloom, listening hard.

But there was nothing now.

Nothing.

She was completely, utterly alone.

Chapter One

May, 1760

Hannah Elway struggled to step over the furrows in the newly plowed field, making her way in the hot sun to carry a bucket of water to the Cherokee slaves her new husband had bought after his recent military victory against the French. The gourd dipper bobbed soundlessly inside the bucket as she walked, and if she had ever wondered what the price for two living human beings might be, she now knew.

Two hundred and four pounds—and ten shillings.

Vanquishing French soldiers had the blessing of both Carolina governors, and any Cherokee taken prisoner while in the service of the French could either be killed for the bounty on his scalp or sold to the highest bidder. What surprised her was that Morgan would have paid such an exorbitant fee for them. He was nearly always at Fort Dobbs or on yet another campaign into Cherokee lands and therefore too occupied to see to the stewardship of his own acres. That responsibility fell to his aged father and his two, newly-arrived male cousins— none of whom knew the slightest thing about managing a hundred acre farm in the wilderness.

In actuality, the burden was hers and supposedly that of the seven indentured servants Morgan had also acquired. But why he thought bringing Cherokee prisoners in among them would be helpful, she couldn't begin to say. She was already anticipating his ire when they escaped—as they surely would. She was no jailer, nor was anyone else here save the bondsman, Hatcher, who obviously enjoyed whatever cruelty he could inflict upon those in an even more lowly position than his own.

He enjoyed having dominion over the Cherokee, but he would never risk life or limb to detain them when they made their attempt to go. Hannah had dared to speak to Morgan about Hatcher's brutality but to no avail. There was nothing she could do for the prisoners—slaves—save whatever small mercies—like a dipperful of water—she could get past Hatcher.

The Cherokee were hobbled, then tied to each other with rawhide nooses around their necks, their hands tightly bound in front of them in order to allow them to better serve as oxen for Hatcher's plow. They seemed docile enough now, not warrior-like at all. One of them was hardly more than a boy, and neither of them looked at her as she approached.

Mindful of the hierarchy, Hannah offered a dipper of water to Hatcher first. If the truth be told, Hannah was as much afraid of him as of the savages. He drank his fill, then handed the gourd back, hanging on to it a second longer than was necessary, his eyes falling to her breasts as he did so.

She moved quickly away from him to the nearest prisoner. His hair hung loose and down to his shoulders. She could smell the pungent odor of the bear oil and powdered roots he'd used on it. She could smell his sweat. He wore a homespun shirt and a breechcloth. The leather leggings he'd arrived in had been discarded in the intense heat.

He had gunpowder tattooing around his wrists and down his arms, and in a line on his chest that disappeared diagonally under his shirt. She wondered idly where he would have gotten such a shirt, who would have made it—or what man or woman he'd murdered to get it.

She might as well have been invisible, so unmindful was he of her offer of water. She knew from her father's travels as a frontier clergyman that great endurance to these people was a sign of courage and that they would bear the most heinous of tortures without making a sound. But she still waited for him to take a drink. When he didn't after a long moment, she turned away.

''The boy.''

The words were so soft that it took her a second or two to realize that he had spoken—and in English. She looked at him, and this time his eyes met hers—briefly—and slid in the direction of the young boy next to him. The boy was unsteady on his feet, his body weaving in the hot sun.

She moved to him, but he, too, ignored the water-filled gourd.

The long-haired man spoke to him, commanded him, his voice still soft, but no less filled with authority. The boy replied, and while Hannah didn't understand the words at all, she still recognized young male stubbornness when she heard it. She'd certainly witnessed it often enough in her little half brothers.

"Drink this before you get your ears boxed," she said in much the same way she would have spoken to one of them. And when she lifted the gourd for him, this time he took a drink, his first sip unleashing the thirst that must have been unbearable. She held the dipper with one hand and reached into her pocket with the other, her fingers closing around the pellets of cornmeal rolled in honey she'd brought. She removed one, and in a quick motion popped it into the boy's mouth. His eyes widened in surprise, but he gave no other indication of what she had done.

She stepped back to the man. This time he drank the water. He even accepted the cornmeal and honey, and without giving her away to Hatcher. She offered him one more swallow from the dipper before she turned to go, and once again their eyes met. She noted this time that his eyes were hazel.

One of the so-called princes? she wondered. One of the offspring of a high-born Cherokee woman and a white trader whom the British prized so highly as negotiators when they wanted more dead Frenchmen or more land? Perhaps that was why Morgan had bought him. Morgan was an ambitious man. He had already risen to the rank of major, and to have in his possession something—someone—his superiors needed would surely—

"Hannah! We have a guest!" the younger of the Elway cousins—Doyle—called from the house, and she had to fight down her intense inclination to ignore him. She found him foppish and nothing more than a wastrel content to ride Morgan's coattails as far as they would take him. His wife Sibyl was no better. Nor was the other cousin, Hugh or his wife, Charity. Hannah suspected that some serious problem with English creditors had brought the foursome here to the Carolinas. And if she had thought that having two more Elway wives in the household would lighten her workload, she had been sadly mistaken.

She sighed inwardly, and instead of leaving the bucket for Hatcher's convenience, she doused both of the Cherokees with what water was left. Then, without a backward glance, she made way to where Doyle waited with their guest, Colm McLarn.

"Mistress Elway," the Scotsman said to her when she reached them, and with great formality bowed at the waist.

Hannah accepted both his gesture and his salutation with some awkwardness. She had been married less than six months, and she still thought of herself as "Hannah Albrecht." Indeed, save a hurried and drunken bedding on her wedding night, she could hardly tell a difference in the days when she lived single in her father's house and her days here. They were all filled with nothing but backbreaking work and a complete lack of authority.

"You are indeed Jacob Albrecht's daughter," McLarn said, glancing in the direction of the Cherokee prisoners.

She made no reply to the remark, primarily because she wasn't certain it was her father's charitable example that had prompted her action so much as her desire to behave like a recalcitrant child.

"Welcome, sir," she said instead. "I trust your journey has given you an appetite and you will stay for supper."

"That I will, Mistress Elway. I am sorry to have missed Major Elway—I had heard on very good authority he would be here. Duty is a jealous mistress, is she not? But I heartily accept the hospitality of his lovely bride. I will make great effort to do my best by it. Is your father well? Is he still riding his preaching circuit?"

"He is."

"He knows there is great danger in doing that now?" McLarn asked.

"He does. But as long as he has a choice, he'll never stop."

"And your father-in-law—how does he fare?"

"Well enough, I believe. He doesn't often come down from his rooms and his manservant forbids most visitors."

"Does he now?" McLarn said. "Perhaps he can

be enticed into making an exception on my account. Tell me. Shall I be able to entice *you* into singing for me again this evening?''

''Did you have a particular song in mind, sir?'' Hannah asked, trying not to smile. She knew perfectly well that he did—the ''code'' song she'd learned from one of her father's church members when the family still lived in the settlement. To her impressionable young girl's heart, it had seemed a wonderfully sad, lover's lament. But her father had teasingly explained to her that it was in actuality a passionate yearning for a Stuart king on Scotland's throne. She had impulsively sung it for McLarn the last time he was here. It was subtle enough to entirely escape the Elways, and she should not have enjoyed their private joke so heartily.

She led the way into the house—a fine house by wilderness standards, two stories, a barn made of natural stone and a large, wooden lean-to wing at the back of the house for the four female indentured servants. Hatcher and the rest of the bondsmen, and now the slaves, stayed in the barn.

Hannah didn't tarry with her guest. She left the job of hostess for the cousins' pretentious wives to squabble over and went straight to the kitchens to help with the meal. She wanted to hurry things along so that it wouldn't be dark when they finally sat down to eat. Candles were too precious—much more so than the Elway in-laws realized—and Hannah wanted to conserve them by hastening the meal enough to catch some daylight, if at all possible.

And if the truth be told, she was much happier

before the hearth preparing a good table than sitting in the parlor in the company of people who looked down on her for being born in the colonies and for having a father and a mother who were not English.

She gave a quiet sigh. In all fairness, she supposed that the Elway cousins had to forgive her Germanness somewhat—in light of the succession of Hanovers occupying the English throne. Morgan must surely have done so, or he would never have come to her father's house with his offer of marriage. Hannah had no delusions now about why he had. He needed a firm tie to the colony to give him an edge over his rivals for promotion. By marrying the daughter of a colonist, he would seem more firmly committed to protecting King George's new lands.

But the countryside here was not exactly overrun with females who were both eligible *and* suitably English. Hannah was educated. She could read, and she could write a good hand. She could draw and paint, sing and play the clavichord. She could speak French and German and embroider. And she could work in the house or the fields or the kitchens as hard as any human being Morgan might call a slave. Indeed, she was such a catch and so accomplished that her husband rarely bothered to come home to see about her.

Hannah wondered idly if Morgan knew that her highly respected father had been an adult convert to the faith he now served so steadfastly. Had she understood what Morgan was really about before she married him, she would have made a point of telling him about her father, the ex-priest, who had given up his celibacy and his allegiance to Rome and had come to this rough and dangerous country in order to prove his new faith by serving as a circuit-riding clergyman—in which case, she wouldn't be here in Morgan's fine house now, unless he could have hired her as a scullery maid.

She could hear laughter from time to time in the parlor. Aside from being rich and acquainted with any number of the colony's governors, past and present, McLarn was a jovial and witty man—nothing of the dour Scotsman one might have expected. But Hannah still looked upon having to join them with pure dread.

Unfortunately, there was little to do in the kitchen and nothing that required her supervision. The day's bread had already been baked, and Mary Kate and Eliza, the mother and daughter bondswomen, had already seen to the making of various boiled puddings—one of them sweetened—and were now simmering the salt out of the strips of dried venison to make shepherd's pies. They both had their skirts hiked up and tucked into their waistbands to keep them out of the hearth fire—a fact that would likely draw Hatcher in here the first chance he got.

To the obvious relief of the two women, Hannah left them to their tasks and returned to the parlor. She found both of Morgan's cousins partaking heavily of the peach brandy and no sign of McLarn.

"If you're looking for the Jacobite," Hugh said, "he went for a walk."

Hannah glanced at him. There was just enough of something in his voice to make her dread of the situation intensify. Surely Hugh had enough sense not to insult a guest in Morgan's house, even if he did consider him a "Jacobite."

"Actually, I believe there is some problem with the slaves," Doyle said. "He's gone to see about it."

Hannah looked at him. "*He's* gone to see."

"Well, of course. He quite understands the grunts and belches that pass for a language out here."

"He's also a guest. You can't expect him to—"

"My dear Hannah," Hugh interrupted. "There's no point in Doyle going. Or me. It's hardly *our* concern. Or perhaps you think Sibyl and Charity would be a better choice."

Both wives, who were playing whist in the corner, laughed heartily at his wit.

"If anything happens to Morgan's property, it will be your concern," Hannah said. "Or at least Morgan will think so."

His smug smile faded abruptly. She didn't wait to hear whatever remark he would feel bound to make. She stepped out of the front door. The plow was still in the field—with the Cherokees tied to it. Hatcher had disappeared, and McLarn stood nearby.

Hannah began walking in that direction. As she neared them, she could hear McLarn, earnestly speaking to the long-haired Cherokee man.

She could tell nothing from the prisoner's face.

He looked neither disturbed, nor defiant, nor indifferent.

The boy was not nearly so unaffected. He kept looking from one man to the other, and he was clearly worried—perhaps afraid.

Hannah stopped short of joining them, waiting while McLarn kept talking. The old man was so intent, too intent to even know she was there. And she realized suddenly that the Cherokee prisoner was not so dispassionate after all. She realized that, for all his stoic demeanor, he was weeping.

Chapter Two

"McLarn!"

Hannah looked sharply over her shoulder. She could just see the horse and rider through the trees, galloping along the split rail fence on what passed for a wagon road.

Morgan. McLarn's information as to her husband's whereabouts had been correct after all.

"Will you find Hatcher, Mistress Elway?" McLarn asked abruptly. "I believe he has taken himself to the kitchens. Hurry, lass," he added, when she hesitated. "Don't worry. I will keep these two from bolting."

Hannah stood a moment longer, looking from McLarn to the seemingly passive Cherokee man and still trying to understand the situation. Had McLarn deliberately sent Hatcher away so that he could speak to the Cherokee?

Yes, she decided. He had. And now he wanted to save Hatcher some undeserved trouble from his master. But she still didn't understand what McLarn was about, and she had no time to sort it out. Morgan was here, and there was much he would require.

She picked up her skirts and hurried away, and she didn't have to hunt for Hatcher. She met him coming out the kitchen door, anxious to get back to the plowing before Morgan discovered him where he should not have been. She expected that Morgan would enter the house by the front door, but he didn't. He came riding around to the back. He looked quite splendid actually, in spite of being mud-spattered from the journey. He cut a fine figure on a horse. She had been so impressed the first time she saw him, so willing to give him her heart—until she realized that what she had mistaken for courtesy and respect were in truth complete indifference.

He said nothing at all to her as he rode past. He was intent on getting to Hatcher and discovering what the Scotsman was doing with his most recently acquired possessions. But Hatcher didn't tarry to explain. He scurried along ahead of him, as if haste on his part now would somehow negate the fact that he had left his charges essentially unattended.

"McLarn!" Morgan called again.

"Ah! Major Elway!" McLarn said as if he'd only just noticed him. "'Tis good to see you again, sir—and so fit and hardy after your recent fray against the King's enemies."

The conversation continued, but Hannah couldn't hear them now. She looked over her shoulder again as she went inside. As expected and in spite of McLarn's formidable presence, Morgan was doing all the talking.

Six more soldiers arrived, on foot and out of breath from trying to keep up with their mounted officer. They stood in the yard waiting for Morgan's attention, all of them wearing approximately the same pained expression. When he finally took notice of them and dismissed them, they congregated in an exhausted heap on the ground around the back door.

"Do we have enough food prepared to satisfy them all, Mary Kate?" Hannah asked.

"There isn't enough food on this earth—nor anything else for that matter—to satisfy a British soldier, mistress," Mary Kate answered with the surety of an Irishwoman. "But we'll do the best we can."

And doing the best they could took every pair of hands. Hannah worked alongside the bondswomen, ignoring the distasteful duties of hostess until Morgan himself came to fetch her.

"Make yourself presentable and come see to our guest," he said without prelude. "I'll not have the Scotsman thinking I've wed a drudge."

"It's not the way I look while I'm about my work that will have him thinking that," Hannah said quietly, regardless of the audience.

"Am I to take some meaning from that remark?" Morgan asked.

"Only that if you ever want the meal served, you had best send Mr. McLarn out here."

"I expect food on the table within the half hour."

"You may expect whatever you like, Morgan," Hannah said. "But I can assure you, it will take as long as it takes."

Morgan stared at her. He had a great deal he wanted to say to that, but for whatever reason, he didn't. He left abruptly.

"Mistress," Mary Kate said after a moment. "The meal is all but ready to—"

"Yes," Hannah interrupted.

"But we can have it on the table in no time at all. Should you not go and tell the master so?"

"No," Hannah said, removing her apron.

"But he's angry with you, mistress—"

"I said no."

Hannah hurried up the back stairs to her chamber to fetch a clean apron and cap, leaving Mary Kate to make whatever she wanted of Hannah's refusal to get back into Morgan's good graces. She didn't know why she felt such a need to thwart her husband—the recalcitrant child rearing its willful head again, she supposed. She knew perfectly well how a wife should behave. She knew that she should never make Morgan think she was being deliberately disobedient, particularly in front of servants. She had stood before God and promised to obey him. And she would. It was just that she had crossed some boundary in her heart and mind where his good opinion no longer mattered to her as it had before. She was his wife, but she was done with all the mental and physical scurrying for fear of his displeasure. She would be a good helpmate, but in her own time and in her own fashion.

Mary Kate and Eliza had the puddings in the serving dishes and the shepherd's pie in the hearth oven well ahead of Morgan's deadline. Hannah appeared in the parlor just in time to take McLarn's arm and be escorted to the table. The fare was simple but delicious, and McLarn made up for Morgan's silence with a constant stream of praise for the household's culinary skills.

Hatcher and the rest of the bondsmen were fed by the back door with the soldiers. When the Elways and McLarn had finished eating and returned to the parlor, Hannah managed to get what little pudding and bread was left to the Cherokee prisoners in the barn, all but running the distance from the house so that she could be back before Morgan missed her.

The barn was dusty and quiet except for the occasional movement of the horses and oxen in their stalls. The two Cherokee were kept in a stall as well, one that had been completely closed in as high as the loft, until it became more accurately, a cage. The man and the boy were both crouched by the far wall watching her as she quickly pushed the food she'd brought through the slats as far as she could. She had no idea whether they were tethered, whether or not they could reach it, and she didn't take the time to see. Morgan, in his current mood, would be apt to make them go hungry if he decided that she had once again ignored his authority.

But when she reached the barn door, she suddenly looked back. The man was standing now, his hands gripping the slats. He made no attempt to speak, and neither did she. She slipped outside and back up the path to the house.

The sun had gone down. She could hear music from the house—Charity or Sibyl playing the clavichord very badly.

"Mistress," the soldiers said respectfully as she passed.

She only nodded, uncertain as to what exactly her demeanor toward Morgan's men should be. The only thing she knew for certain was that he would surely find fault no matter what manner she assumed. When she was barely inside, one of them made some remark, one she couldn't hear and one which made the rest of them laugh heartily. She stopped long enough to turn and look at them, as if she had heard, and from their sudden discomfort she could only suppose that the remark had been made at her expense.

She left them clearly worrying about whether or not she would tell her husband and entered the kitchen in time to keep Hatcher from cornering Eliza in the pantry.

"I don't believe you are needed here, Mr. Hatcher," she said.

He almost, but not quite smiled. He didn't quite dare to be disrespectful, but she feared that the time would soon come. Hatcher would take his cues from Morgan, and if Morgan had no regard for her, then why should he?

Much to Eliza's obvious relief, Hannah waited

until she was certain Hatcher had gone before she went to join the others in the parlor. She stood for a moment outside the door to shore up her courage before entering the room. She did dread this so. She had no ally in this house, and she hated the strain of pretending she didn't mind.

"It's too bad you were second choice," she heard someone—Sibyl—say, but her voice didn't come from the parlor. It came from outside the house, through the nearby open window.

"Sibyl, I am in no mood for your conundrums," Morgan said.

"Are you not?" she said, laughing softly.

"No," he assured her. "I am not."

"Oh, too bad. I did so want to comfort you."

"Am I in need of comfort?"

"Indeed you are, Morgan. No man likes to be second best."

"What *are* you talking about?"

"I'm talking about your lovely wife, Hannah— and her...admirer."

"What admirer?"

"Well, perhaps 'suitor' is a better word."

"Sibyl, I don't—"

"Hannah's Cherokee suitor," Sibyl said, carefully enunciating each word as if Morgan might not understand her otherwise. "I heard about him the last time I went to the settlement. And what an amazing story it was, Morgan."

"Indeed."

"Oh, yes. As I understand it, this *savage*—one like those smelly things in the barn, one can only think—had the audacity to approach Hannah's father and ask for her hand in *marriage*. Can you imagine?''

"Sibyl, you are being ridiculous," Morgan said. "I'm sorry to disappoint you, but I'm not as much in ignorance as you'd like to think."

"Meaning?"

"Meaning, my dear, you aren't giving me any information I'm not already privy to."

But Sibyl clearly was not deterred.

"Whatever do you suppose made him think such a thing was a possibility?" she continued. "I mean really, Morgan. There must have been *something*. He must have had some reason to suppose that his suit would be welcome, some...encouragement on Hannah's part, perhaps? Was she a virgin bride, I must wonder—where are you going?"

Morgan suddenly appeared in the open doorway, and it was all Hannah could do not to bolt. Perhaps she would have if there had been any place for her to go. There was nothing for her to do except escape into the parlor and assume her long neglected duty as hostess. She didn't want Morgan to know that she'd heard. She supposed that she should count herself fortunate that Sibyl's revelation of an alleged Cherokee suitor had been made in some degree of privacy rather than in the middle of the boiled puddings.

Hannah realized suddenly that she couldn't really deny the gist of Sibyl's gossip. It could very well be true. Jacob Albrecht was a well-known figure among the Cherokee. It wouldn't be that unlikely that one of them with whom her father had established a certain harmony and understanding, might ask for a marriage to his daughter—out of respect for *him,* not admiration for her. But if it had happened, her father had never told her, wouldn't have told her, just as she suspected he had not told her of other suitors who had come to him for permission to court her. She had only the covert looks and glances from the men who grudgingly attended her father's church services or who hung around the many settlement taverns or the fort to base that opinion upon, but she was no less convinced that Morgan Elway hadn't been the only one who'd sought her hand. He had simply been the only one of whom her father approved.

She gave a quiet sigh. Even respected clergymen could be wrong.

Charity was still torturing the clavichord as Hannah entered the room. She intended to take a seat in the corner of the room out of the way of any conversation, knowing that it would eventually be devised to insult her and perhaps McLarn as well. At least two of the Elways had had a head start on the peach brandy, and she worried that the cousins would lose what little control they had over their snobbery. She expected Morgan to be on her heels, and she kept glancing at the door, but he hadn't followed her. She moved to the window. She could see him in the yard still, now talking to Hatcher, but she didn't see Sibyl.

"Well, Mistress Elway," McLarn said when she was about to take a chair on the sidelines. "I have partaken shamefully of your excellent hospitality and now I must trouble you further. Will you accompany an old man on a short walk around the place before he retires?''

Hannah looked at him, surprised that Morgan had invited him to stay the night. Though times were too precarious to send such an influential man on his way when the sun was going down, Morgan was not known for his hospitality. She wondered if McLarn knew how much she welcomed him giving her the opportunity to escape the society of her in-laws.

"With pleasure, sir," she said.

"I thank you, lass," he said as they walked outside. "I fear I have enjoyed all the music I can."

She smiled, but she gave no critique of Charity's playing. And she decided as she walked that whether she was "Mistress Elway" or whether she was "lass" seemed to depend on whether or not an Elway was within earshot. McLarn seemed to have a definite idea as to which direction he wanted to go—away from the house and toward the stone barn. She would have chosen another direction herself; she didn't like to encounter the soldiers again, regardless of the fact that she was accompanied now. One of them was singing, in a fine rich baritone. The song was plaintive and filled with longing, and it was definitely not a "code" song about an exiled Scottish king. McLarn abruptly stopped to listen, his usually animated features gone quiet.

"Long have we parted been..." the soldier sang. "Lassie, my dearie... Now we are met again, lassie, lie near me. Near me…near me, lassie, lie near me…''

Hannah listened with McLarn, acutely aware suddenly of how little she knew of love's hunger and joy.

'''Tis been a long while since I heard that sung,'' McLarn said after a moment. ''Not since…'' He cleared his throat. ''What were you saying, Mistress Elway?''

Hannah hadn't been saying anything, and she thought that her theory regarding McLarn's ever changing titles for her must be mistaken—until she saw Sibyl on a stone bench in the fledgling rose garden. Sibyl sat there like a venomous spider, waiting, no doubt, to pounce upon Morgan if he came near enough to give him the rest of her gossip. Hannah nodded to her, in spite of the anger she felt, and began to walk on. McLarn joined her, but she could almost feel the effort it took for him to tear his attention away from the song—no, from the memories it conjured for him.

They had gone only a short distance when he stopped again.

''I fear I'm more tired than I thought, lass. I'll take my leave from you now.''

''Then I'll show you to your bedchamber—''

''No, lass,'' he interrupted. ''I may look soft to you, but I've lived hard in this land. I'm rarely comfortable in houses, even my own and particularly when I'm so close to the wilderness.'' He looked past her into the darkness of the forest that surrounded the clearing. "I swear I can hear her calling me."

"Sir?" Hannah said, not understanding.

McLarn smiled. "I have said 'Duty' is a jealous mistress—but she's no match for 'Adventure.' Now there's a she-devil who will never let a man be. Even your father, the reverend, knows her well. Be glad you're a lass and immune to all that."

"The guest chambers are small, but you would have your privacy—"

"Thank you, lass, but no. I'll find my own accommodations. I've my good blanket with me. I'll bed down in the barn where I can cosset these old bones a bit but still feel the earth and sky about me."

And where the Cherokee man is, Hannah thought. She had a lively imagination, and her curiosity had been piqued, but she couldn't begin to guess what McLarn wanted from him.

"Then I'll see you at breakfast, sir," Hannah said, and she left him there.

Sibyl was no longer on the stone bench, nor was Morgan anywhere about. There was no one in the parlor, either, except Hugh, who snored loudly in one of the chairs, his head thrown back and his mouth open, a perfect example for one of her father's temperance sermons.

Hannah snuffed the candles. There was no point in wasting them on someone who was asleep. She went to check the kitchens, crossing the open space between the main house quickly in the event

Hatcher was loitering about or making a nuisance of himself with Eliza and Mary Kate again.

The women were still working but nearly done scrubbing out the pots and banking the fire on the hearth. Hannah wished them both goodnight and returned to the main house. She climbed the back stairway to her bedchamber, wondering if Morgan would find his way there or stay down in the parlor with his drunken cousin. He was still annoyed with her, but the real truth was that he would likely ignore her even if he weren't.

She didn't light a candle but sat in the dark by the window, listening to the noises in the house. Charity began playing the clavichord again, and Hannah could hear laughter coming from the parlor from time to time. The Elway cousins were apparently all present and accounted for and once again enjoying their own wit.

She moved to another window, where she had a clear view of the barn. In the waning light she could see Morgan near the barn entrance. He was talking to Hatcher again. Hatcher stood listening, looking down at the ground in deference to his better. At one point his head came up sharply at something Morgan said. Then, after a moment, he disappeared into the barn.

Hannah watched as Morgan crossed the distance to where his men had set up camp. He spoke to them briefly, his hands authoritatively behind his back, then returned to the house. She could hear the front door close, and then she heard his boots on the stairs.

She didn't think that he realized she was in the room at first, not until he lit a candle.

"I...didn't expect to find you here," he said after a moment. She watched as he carefully moved the candle from the mantel to a small writing desk in the corner and began to search through it. He was fair-haired and blue-eyed, and his skin was always ruddy from too much sun. He was still handsome in spite of the perpetually vexed look marriage to her seemed to have inspired. She had come to him with her father's blessing, wanting so much to please him, but how could she, when one day's pleasure was the next day's complaint?

"Where else would I be?" she asked quietly.

"There still seems to be a good deal of society in the parlor," he said. "Music. Pleasant company. You know you are very standoffish, Hannah."

"And you know that my stepmother and the little boys were my only company for months on end. You witnessed her melancholy first hand. She was rarely given to conversation. I'm not used to talking to people."

"Perhaps you should make some effort to remedy that. You certainly won't get over your reticence hiding up here. But how very amusing that you choose *not* to talk to people—in several languages—"

"Morgan," she interrupted. "I heard what Sibyl said to you."

He barely glanced at her. "Listening at keyholes now, Hannah?"

"It was hardly necessary. Morgan, I—"

"I don't want to talk about this."

"I came to you chaste, Morgan," she said anyway. "You know that."

"Do I? To tell you the truth I remember little of the wedding night. A cunning woman could have—"

"Ah, but I am *not* a cunning woman," Hannah said. "I'm too slow, too unsophisticated, too provincial. As you have taken great pains on many occasions to point out."

He ignored her remark completely, and he ignored her.

"Am I allowed to say nothing in my own defense?" she asked.

"I have things to do," he said. "And so do you. Pack your belongings. You will be leaving at first light."

"Leaving? For where? Why?"

"There has been an increase in hostilities all along the frontier. It's not safe here. I'm sending you to Fort Dobbs. Hatcher will take you."

"Hatcher? But—"

"You are my wife. It is my duty to preserve your well-being."

"The rest of the family—"

"They will come later. My father and the cousins' silly wives can't be hurried. You will go on horseback with only what you can carry, so that the trip can be made quickly. I need to stay and see that the house is made as secure as possible. Meanwhile, I want to know that you are safe. I will take care of everything here, and then I and the others will join you at the fort. You don't have to concern yourself. We will bring whatever is necessary for your comfort on the wagons.''

"I don't care about my comfort. Hatcher is—"

"Hatcher knows the country," Morgan interrupted. "He will be aware of alternate routes if you should encounter any signs of trouble."

"Please, Morgan, I would rather wait for you—"

"For God's sake, Hannah, will you never obey me!"

A capricious evening breeze found its way into the room, and the candle flickered. She didn't say anything else, but how reassured she would have been if only he had looked at her—at *her*—just once.

Chapter Three

Hannah forced as many clothes as possible into one linen sack, then added her Psalmody and her apothecary jars, some dried apples and a few candles—and some soap as an afterthought—and tied it shut. Then she waited for the sun to come up. So much for packing her belongings.

She couldn't sleep, and there was no point in trying. She felt so uneasy. She simply did not understand the urgency of her departure—and with Hatcher, of all people.

But Morgan's word was law, and there was no one here with the authority to object to his edicts. Perhaps if she'd been beloved—or even respected—she might have cajoled him or reasoned with him until he agreed to let her stay. He had not returned from whatever things he had to do, and after a time, Hannah took up the linen sack containing her meager belongings and went downstairs. No one else was stirring, and no Elway snored in the parlor.

She went to the back of the house and crossed the open space to the kitchens, finding her way in the darkness and finally sitting down in a makeshift chair near the hearth. The chair was too big for her, and she pulled her feet up into the seat and rested her head on her knees, the way she used to when she was a little girl. She had no idea how long it was until dawn. She closed her eyes. A remnant of the soldier's song drifted through her mind.

Lassie, lie near me...

She gave a quiet sigh, and she must have slept. When she opened her eyes again, the night had gone a soft gray.

"Mistress?"

She looked around, startled. Hatcher stood just inside the doorway.

"What is it?" she asked, getting up from the chair so that he wouldn't be looking down on her.

"Your mare is lame, mistress. The major said to see what other of the horses you think you can handle."

"Lame? But she was fine yesterday."

"Maybe so, mistress," he said. "But she is lame *now*."

Hannah wasn't about to take his word for it. The little bay mare had been a gift from her father when she married, one of the few he'd ever given her. If she had to leave like this, she did *not* want to have to travel on a strange mount.

"I'll see about the mare myself," she said. "You needn't come with me."

"You'd best tell the major that, then. It's not what he wanted—"

Hannah didn't answer him, and she didn't go asking for Morgan's permission. She left Hatcher standing in the kitchen and hurried across the yard to the barn, entering quietly so as not to awaken McLarn. She thought that he must be in the loft, because she didn't see him anywhere nearby. The mare whinnied a soft greeting as Hannah approached. Even in the darkness of the stall, Hannah could see the swelling just below the right knee. She opened the gate and spoke to the horse gently, rubbing her hands over the mare's neck and shoulder before she finally attempted to touch the swelling. The leg felt hot, and the mare shifted nervously at Hannah's exploration.

"Easy, let me see—what is it? Have you hurt yourself?"

But she couldn't tell in this light. After a moment she led the horse out of the stall and into the yard. The sky had grown lighter but there was a fine mist of rain. This would not be an auspicious day for traveling.

It was obvious from the short walk outside that the mare was favoring the swollen right foreleg. Hannah gave a quiet sigh of disappointment that abruptly gave way to a small hope that she wouldn't have to leave today, a hope that died all too quickly.

"Hannah!" Morgan called from across the yard. "You have no time for dallying! What are you doing?"

"I am taking care of my horse, Morgan," she

said. Without waiting for more questions she went back into the barn to get the small wooden box of remedies for the strains and injuries the horses and livestock seemed prone to in this wild country. Both the Cherokee were awake and watchful from their cage. It occurred to Hannah that McLarn would be a good man to consult regarding the mare, but she didn't see him anywhere. She looked upward at the loft and was just about to call McLarn's name.

"He's long gone," the Cherokee man said.

Hannah didn't say anything. She carefully picked up the wooden box, but she realized that her confusion must be apparent. The man's command of the English language was more than disconcerting, and once again, she hadn't expected him to speak. She certainly hadn't expected him to understand what she had been of a mind to do.

"Wait," he said when she turned to go.

She hesitated, then looked at him.

"When you leave for the fort, take a pistol with you."

"Pistol? I have no pistol—"

"Someone here must have one. Steal it if you have to. Keep it hidden."

"I have no need for—"

"Your journey is dangerous. More dangerous than you know. If you are taken, use it. Do you understand?"

"I cannot kill a man, sir," Hannah said, her eyes daring to meet his. She realized even as she said it that such a revelation was not something she should be telling someone her husband held prisoner. She knew, too, that he couldn't reach her through the slats, but she still took a step backward. She had seen him weeping—but she must not think him weak.

"The death shot is for you, mistress," he said bluntly.

Hannah stared at him. He was entirely serious, and if he meant to frighten her, he had remarkable success. She knew the stories of torture and murder—all the white settlers did—and she better than most, because her father had witnessed some of them firsthand.

"I cannot," she said, turning to go.

"Your husband has enemies," he said, moving along the stall with her.

"He is a British officer fighting against the French. Of course he does—"

"This is personal, mistress. The man he has wronged will take his revenge where he can. He will have no mercy. It's better to die at your own hand—quickly—"

He was staring at her so intently, and she kept backing away.

"I'm not the one you should fear, mistress," he said, but she refused to listen anymore and all but ran outside, carrying the box under her arm. She set it down on the ground hard and began to look through the jumbled contents for something that might give the mare ease. Her hands were trembling. Nothing in the box registered. She kept scrambling among the bottles and jars until she finally found a small clay pot of rendered fat and herbs. She fumbled to get the piece of waxed linen covering it untied and off. Then she began to rub some of the mixture into the swollen place on the mare's foreleg, too hard at first, making the animal shy.

It took a concentrated effort on her part to move more gently, and all the while she tried to convince herself that the Cherokee man was deliberately lying, perhaps trying to exact a kind of revenge of his own. But the reality, no matter what his motive might be, was that she believed him.

"Leave that!" Morgan said sharply behind her. "Hatcher, put that animal back into the stall and saddle the roan. He's docile enough for her. And you, Hannah, make yourself ready."

Hannah looked at him, knowing she should tell him what the Cherokee man had said.

But she didn't. It was likely that Morgan already knew he had made enemies in his campaign against the French and their allies, and that she might be considered a suitable target for revenge in his stead. Perhaps he really was trying to do what was best for her.

"Don't concern yourself about the mare," Morgan said. "I'll have one of the men see to her later. It's likely she'll be able to follow the wagon when we go."

She looked at him, surprised by the unexpected kindness. The mare meant a great deal to her, and she would never have thought he'd noticed. She gave the animal over to Hatcher and walked back to the house. She still felt shaken. She needed to gather whatever dried meat, fruit and bread she could find to take with her. She needed to—

The death shot is for you, mistress.

She stood in the kitchen, staring at nothing. Then, she abruptly went into the main house, moving quietly until she reached the back stairway. She stopped and listened for a moment. She couldn't hear anyone stirring overhead. As far as she could tell, all the Elways were still asleep. Certainly her departure would be no occasion for an early rising.

She climbed the stairs quickly, and she didn't stop until she had reached old Mr. Elway's door. She knew perfectly well what she was going to at least attempt to do. She entered the room as quietly as she could. One of the planks in the floor squeaked loudly when she tread upon it, and she froze in her tracks. But both the senior Mr. Elway and his servant continued to snore loudly in the semi-darkness. She knew precisely where to look— the table beside the old man's bed. She continued to move about carefully. If either of them awakened, there was no way she could explain what she was about.

The old man had showed her the pearl-handled and intricately engraved dueling pistols once. They had been a gift from some titled person in London, a duke or an earl, who had apparently once held the old man in high regard. It was obvious that the pistols were a source of great pride to him, and she felt a pang of guilt at what she was about to do. She had no doubt that they were valuable. Even so, her mind skittered away from her blatant thievery and went directly to whether or not she could make use of one of them in the manner the Cherokee advised.

How strange, she thought, that either choice—to do so or not to do so—would be a cowardly act.

The old man kept the pistols close at hand, because he was afraid of being murdered in his bed—not an unfounded concern in this young country. And, unless the manservant feared the old man might shoot him by mistake some dark night, she had no doubt that they were loaded.

Old Mr. Elway suddenly stirred, and she snatched the only pistol she could reach, nearly dropping it as she hurried to the door and closed it quietly after her.

Hannah didn't stop until she was downstairs again. Then she went directly across to the kitchens and into one of the pantries, knowing it was highly unlikely anyone would disturb her there. She lit a candle, pleased to note that her hands trembled only slightly now. Merely taking some kind of action, however foolish, left her less afraid. She knew far more about firearms than she cared to. Her father had left the family alone in the cabin much too often for her to be kept ignorant of such things. It was certain that her stepmother could never have functioned as the family defender.

She examined the pistol in the candlelight; it was loaded. Then she slid it through the slit in her skirt and into one of the large pockets dangling from the band around her waist. It was dangerous to carry a pistol in such a manner, but she had no choice. If she had the occasion to need it, she would need it quickly. And the incongruity of carrying a pistol in the same pocket with her Psalmody didn't escape her.

She returned to the kitchen to finish packing the provisions for the trip, taking the candle with her and for once not fretting about it. If she would no longer be living here, the household's supply of candles no longer mattered.

It suddenly occurred to her how unsure she felt that she would come back here again, and it had nothing to do with the danger of the journey. A sudden and acute sense of failure threatened to overwhelm her. She stood there, in Morgan's house, among his possessions, knowing that she would not be missed.

"Hannah!" Morgan called from outside, and she immediately responded, gathering up the sack of food she'd packed and what little courage she still possessed. She took her meager belongings and the cloak she would use both as a sleeping blanket and as protection against the rain.

When she came outside, Hatcher was bringing around the horses. It was nearly daylight, and it was drizzling. Yesterday's oppressive heat was long gone. A rooster crowed in the barn. She could hear a chorus of crows in tall pines on the other side of the half-plowed field.

Morgan stood impatiently, his hair and uniform jacket damp from the fine misting of rain.

"Morgan, I—"

"Hannah, please," he said. "You are wasting precious time."

She let it go. Clearly, as far as he was concerned, there was nothing to be said.

In the doorway of the barn, she could see the Cherokee man watching, hobbled, his hands tied firmly in front of him. He stood ready to follow Morgan's will even as she herself was.

She tied the sacks together by their drawstrings and put them over the saddle. Then she mounted the roan from the back step, ignoring Hatcher's outstretched hand as she did so, careful of the pistol dangling in her pocket.

She looked at Morgan, filled with regrets and unspoken pleas to be allowed to stay. She could feel her mouth trembling, and she bit down on her bottom lip. For a moment she thought he was going to say something after all, but the moment passed and he nodded curtly and turned away.

"God keep you, Morgan Elway," she murmured, and she urged the horse forward.

She rode past the barn. The Cherokee man stared at her gravely. This time she didn't look away. When she came even with where he stood, he said something. She gave no sign that she heard. But in spite of all she could do, when she reached the edge of the yard, she looked back. He was still watching, and he gave her the barest of nods.

Hatcher rode ahead of her, but only until they were out of Morgan's sight. It became obvious to Hannah then that the bondsman intended to stay entirely too close to her. She kept lagging behind until he finally took the hint. The last thing she wanted to have to endure was Hatcher's lecherous proximity. She knew that Fort Dobbs was some ten or twelve miles away—about three hours walking time, less on horseback. Not a terribly long journey, but long enough to make her uneasy.

At one point Hatcher deviated from the makeshift wagon road onto a lesser traveled path into the forest. When she didn't immediately follow him, he turned back.

"It's better this way, mistress," he said. "The French have been known to set an ambush in the thickets up ahead, the major said. It's better for us to avoid going that way."

She looked at him, but she still made no effort to head down the path.

"Truly, mistress. This way is safer."

Morgan had said Hatcher would know the better route, but she still wasn't reassured. He had always given her bold, if surreptitious, looks, the kind that would have disappeared in mock surprise if she'd ever challenged him, and he was looking at her that way now.

But then he abruptly glanced away, for once assuming the deference of a servant. "We are wasting time, mistress."

Time. Yes, she thought. That was true enough. She wanted to get to the fort as soon as possible so that she could be rid of him. After a moment, she pushed all her misgivings aside and finally urged her mount forward.

But the narrow path was hard going on horseback. The tree branches hung so low that she was constantly in danger of either being brushed off or having the horse bolt. Finally, she followed Hatcher's example and reined the animal and got off, leading the roan along, talking to him gently to keep him from shying at every waving, leafy branch. At times the path was so overgrown with tall saplings that she had to walk the horse well off the track and into the underbrush to get by. The smell of the forest—decaying leaves and wood— rose around her, intensified by the drizzling rain. She wondered how Hatcher could have any knowledge of a route that was so little used.

In no time at all, she completely lost her bearings, and with no sun visible, she had no idea where they were going. She had only the sensation that this direction was somehow opposite.

"Are you sure we're traveling as we should, Hatcher?" she asked at one point.

"Oh, aye, mistress. Just as we should."

She became winded from the exertion and weighed down by the pistol in her pocket, but she kept going, determined to keep up. She couldn't have said how long they'd been on the path or how far off the wagon road they'd come. Sometimes she completely lost sight of Hatcher, only to have him reappear when she least expected it.

"Do you need to rest, mistress?" he asked once.

"No. I want to keep going."

"If you need...privacy..."

"No," she said again. "I want to get to Fort Dobbs as soon as possible."

She glanced at him. He was smiling that sly and knowing smile she always found so offensive, and he had moved closer. He reached out as if to take a strand of her hair that had escaped out from under her cap. She jerked her head away.

The smile abruptly left his face. "You think you're better than me, *mistress?*"

It was all she could do not to cower. She stood firm, looking him directly in the eyes.

"You are too familiar, Hatcher, and you are very mistaken if you think I welcome it."

"What will you do, *mistress?* Tell the major?"

She made no attempt to answer. They both knew there was no point in her doing that. She tried to step by him, pulling hard on the horse's bridle to bring the roan forward and force Hatcher aside. It was an entirely useless maneuver. The path had all but disappeared. She had no idea which way to go, but she didn't stop. She was determined not to let him know that she was afraid of him, and she could only do that by conquering her fear of being lost in the dark gloom of the forest.

The rain was coming down harder now. She could hear it as it pelted the canopy of leaves overhead. The roan shied suddenly, nearly jerking free of her grasp. She dug her heels in, hanging on to the bridle for dear life. It was all she could do to keep him from bolting.

"Whoa—" Hannah kept saying. "Easy—"

"Hang on to that horse!" Hatcher yelled, trying to control his own mount.

The roan continued to toss its head, wild-eyed.

She couldn't see what might have startled him, and she had no chance to look. All she could do was keep talking and soothing and hoping that she wasn't about to tread on a snake or become a wildcat's prey. She didn't want to even consider that losing the horse might mean she'd have to ride double with Hatcher.

"Easy. Easy now—!"

The animal kept prancing, but she chanced a look over her shoulder. She didn't see Hatcher or his mount anywhere.

"Hatcher?" she called urgently. "Hatcher!"

She could still hear the pattering of raindrops overhead—and soft rustling off to her left, but this time she didn't dare look away from the problem at hand. She was not about to be left alone and on foot. After a moment, the animal finally began to settle down.

She stood there, panting from the exertion, then began to lead the roan back in the direction she'd come. She kept checking over her shoulder. She was still afraid, but it was a different kind of fear now, one inspired entirely by an instinct for survival. The roan had felt it. And now so did she.

She pulled harder on the bridle to bring the skittish animal along, and she didn't call out again. The path seemed even less visible than it had before. After a short distance, she stopped. The rain was beginning to seep through her clothes to her skin, and she shivered. She stared into the woods around her, trying to see something—anything—and all the while praying that she wouldn't.

The horse shied again, rearing suddenly and knocking her off her feet. She fell hard against a tree and into the wet leaves. She could hear the frightened roan crashing through the underbrush away from her.

When she stood up, Hatcher was there, and he was absolutely livid.

"Damn you!" he yelled. "You've lost my horse!"

"*Your* horse?"

"Aye! Mine!" He swore again.

Hannah moved away from him, alarmed by his anger. She didn't understand. How could he think such an expensive animal was his?

Hatcher reached out to grab her arm, but she eluded him, scrambling around a tree. He came closer. She kept backing away.

"It'll do you no good," he said. "The horse is mine. And you as well."

"Me!"

He laughed, clearly amused by her incredulity. "Don't tell me you didn't know?" he said. "No? Well, fancy that. And me here thinking you were ever so willing to leave the major for a better man—"

"What are you talking about!"

"I'm talking about the bargain I made with your husband, *mistress*."

"What kind of bargain?"

"Oh, a very satisfactory one, indeed. I get my freedom—and two horses."

"For what?"

"For taking you off his hands—" He suddenly made a face. "Now don't go looking at me like that. It wasn't *my* idea. The man doesn't want you—"

Hannah began to run, headlong into the trees. The briars tore at her clothes, branches slapped her in the face, because she had to keep one hand on the pistol. In only a moment, she could hear Hatcher coming after her. She dodged into a thicket, getting down on her hands and knees and scrambling to crawl through it to the other side. Hatcher was closer now, but apparently he hadn't seen her. He ran on by, cursing.

She waited for a moment, then dashed off in a different direction. Her only hope was to keep to the places where it was too tangled with undergrowth for him to go easily.

But Hatcher anticipated her maneuver and cut her off, running her down and catching her finally when she stumbled on the rough terrain.

"You keep this up and—you'll not be worth the trouble—to me. I'll sell you off at the first trading post we come to. The French—will pay a pretty price—"

"Be quiet!" she hissed at him. "Listen!"

"What? I don't hear anything—"

Neither did she, and that was the problem. They were not alone here. She knew that for certain. She kept looking wildly around.

"Don't you feel them?"

"You're addled in the brain, woman. No wonder the major wants to be rid of you."

Addled or not, she was not mistaken. She saw the first man over Hatcher's shoulder. He just... appeared, as if out of nowhere. Then another, and another, and two more.

Hatcher saw them now, and he began edging toward the horse, pulling her along with him.

"What are they? Are they Cherokee?" she whispered.

"How the devil do I know—?"

So far, there were only the five of them, but the war cry they sent up was so sudden and so loud that the remaining horse broke free of the tree where he'd been tethered. Panic-stricken, Hannah tried to run, but Hatcher held her to him.

"Let me go!" she cried.

"Quiet, damn you! I've no strouds, but by God, I've got *you!*"

She struggled harder. It was true. He had no cheap trade blankets, but if she could believe Morgan's Cherokee slave at all, Hatcher had something *much* better than that. He had Major Elway's wife.

And Hatcher was a fool if he thought he could bargain for his life with something that could be so easily taken. Their only chance—*her* only chance— was to try to escape into the thick undergrowth. She still had the pistol, and she had no time to wonder that Hatcher didn't feel it.

She brought her arms up and shoved him midchest with all her strength. Taking him completely by surprise she wrenched free of his grasp and began to run again, regardless of the consequences. She kept trying to get at the pistol as she ran. The ground was slippery from the wet leaves and rain. She could hear one of the horses running close to her. Her fingers finally closed around the pearl handle as she all but collided with the horse—and its rider—but she didn't stop.

"Hannah!" Morgan said sharply.

She whirled around. "Morgan—Morgan—"

She went to him, stumbling, collapsing heavily against the horse, her head resting on Morgan's knee, her hand still in her pocket. Hatcher had been wrong. Morgan didn't want to be rid of her. He had come to save her.

He didn't say anything, and after a moment she looked up at him. She might as well have been invisible.

"Morgan—how did you—know to come—?"

He didn't answer her. He spurred his horse on.

Chapter Four

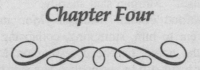

Five Killer stood hobbled in the rain, seemingly forgotten as Major Elway finally made his way to speak to the men gathered on his doorstep. Elway impatiently—painfully—shook off the hand of the bondswoman who attended him and who made the mistake of thinking he would actually sit down in the fancy chair yet another servant had carefully placed in the doorway. The exact location of the major's wound was not evident, only the result of it. He was pale from the loss of blood and obviously still shaken from his ordeal, lucky to be alive by any man's reckoning. Five Killer suspected that the major would believe it merely his due. He was a British officer, and the capacity the English had for arrogance was an amazing thing to behold.

At the moment, however, it seemed to Five Killer that Morgan Elway wanted the men here to think that great misfortune had befallen him. Morgan's woman had been taken, and Five Killer would have to give the man credit. He at least *looked* the distraught husband.

The word of Hannah Elway's abduction had spread quickly among the settlers up and down the frontier, but it was likely that these men had hurried here out of curiosity and concern for their families, rather than in deference to the British major's summons. There were a few familiar faces in the group, men Five Killer had actually had dealings with on occasion at the Rowan Court House settlement near the Trading Ford on the Yadkin River. But, if any of them recognized Morgan Elway's Cherokee slave, they gave no sign.

Five Killer shifted his weight to relieve the pain of the shackles, and the indentured man, the long-suffering bearer of Morgan's unused chair, looked at him nervously, obviously worried that what had happened to Hatcher and the woman on the road to the fort might happen to him as well. Who knew if Five Killer might somehow slip free of his bonds to do him harm? Who knew when Morgan might send *him* to his death by deciding that he, too, would make a better escort for a family member than the small company of soldiers so conspicuously on hand? The latter concern, at least, was not unfounded, given the number of Elways still about, any one of whom Morgan might find expendable.

Morgan Elway had been on the frontier long enough to have heard of the Cherokee law of vengeance. If he had deigned to pay attention, he might even know that there were those who had tried to run away from it by going to live with other tribes to the north and west. And, he would also know that such attempts were entirely useless.

A life for a life.

The law was unyielding and brutally severe, but it was necessary to keep the Cherokee world in balance. Sooner or later everything had to be set right again. There was no way to escape retribution. If the guilty party couldn't be found, then someone in his family would suffer instead.

Morgan had done murder against the clan of the Cherokee war chief, Maw, and Five Killer could see only one reason why the major would have seemingly put his own wife in harm's way. Morgan must have decided to give her over to someone who would be only too happy to deliver her to his sworn enemy. And Maw would not ask for ransom, as was sometimes done. Maw would satisfy Cherokee law and his need for revenge.

Whether the woman had comprehended the situation or not, Five Killer couldn't say. Out of respect for her father and in return for the water and the food she had brought him and the boy, he had tried to make her understand that if she was taken, a quick and easy death was the most she could hope for. As he watched her ride away yesterday morning, he knew that she had accepted at least the possibility that she was in danger. She recognized it, and yet she still went. He kept remembering the way she had looked at him. He had seen that look many times in the eyes of captives—men and women—when they finally understood the inevitability of their fate.

He drew a quiet breath, once again alarming the bondsman near him, and he immediately assumed what he hoped was a docile pose. There was another truth here, one he had no wish to ponder but one which dogged him every waking moment. Perhaps it was the real reason he'd tried to warn her. Perhaps he wouldn't have made the attempt at all if she had changed. But she hadn't. She looked the same—almost exactly the same—as she had when she was a young girl living in that cabin with the weeping white woman and her children. He knew that for certain because he had watched her many times, walking, laughing with the little boys.

He had seen with his own eyes her tender care of them—when they were not hers. He had wanted to save her then, because he needed someone—her—for his own motherless son. In spite of his grief—or perhaps because of it—he had seen her as the one person available to him who could teach his small boy what he needed to survive in the upside down, white-infested world the Cherokee suddenly found themselves in. His own knowledge was limited by the circumstances of his birth. He didn't understand their ways, even after living among them. He had naively thought of her as his son's only chance then. He *knew* she was his only chance now—whether she was dead or alive.

The bondsman was still anxious, still staring at Five Killer for some sign of mischief. Five Killer half-closed his eyes, briefly becoming the dumb animal these people had tried to make him. He had to hear what Morgan was going to say. He absolutely didn't want to be taken back to the barn. After a moment, the bondsman turned his attention back to Major Elway.

Five Killer was acutely aware now of the aroma of roasting meat coming from the Elway kitchens— a good faith gesture Morgan was making for the wives and children these men had hastily brought with them. His own stomach rumbled in hunger, but he had little hope of sharing in the bounty. Hannah Elway wasn't here anymore.

He opened his eyes. The major stood in the rain in all his glory, and when he finally spoke, he didn't hedge.

"You men know the situation. I need volunteers. Who will go?" he asked the group bluntly.

The men stared back at the major without answering, and Five Killer noted that not one of them shuffled awkwardly or looked at the ground. The British were losing their control in the colonies, and they didn't begin to know it.

"It's a job for the King's men," one man said finally. "Not us. You have soldiers here now. They can—"

"They have been recalled to the fort," Morgan said. "None of them can be spared. Even I—as I am—can't be spared. It is not my way to beg favors. But my duty...is such that...I..." He swayed on his feet, and the bondswoman put out a hand to steady him. Once again Morgan impatiently shook it off.

"I have my orders," he continued after a moment. "I cannot disobey them. The security of the frontier—*your* security—is too precarious. I ask you again. Who will go?''

''We are all family men, Major. We know nothing of the military tactics it would take to rescue your wife. The French and their murdering allies would be on us before we could get anywhere near her—even if we knew where to look. She could be taken in any direction—sold to the tribes up north. Or she could be dead by now.''

''Is it money you want?'' Morgan asked, and if he realized that such a question was an insult, it didn't show.

''Major, you can't pay enough for a man to risk his life for nothing. We can't abandon our own families.''

''Send them to the fort as *I* am doing!''

''And so we shall, if needs be, but we still cannot leave everything we've worked for to the French and their savages to plunder. I'm sorry for your trouble, Major. We all are—but we can't do what you ask.''

''Is that your answer then? Is there no one who will go?'' Morgan demanded.

''Morgan Elway,'' Five Killer called loudly, causing the chair-bearer to jump as if he would be blamed for the slave's suddenly finding his voice.

''Who spoke?'' Morgan asked, moving to the edge of the steps.

''I did,'' Five Killer said, ignoring the turning heads and the reaching for weapons.

The major stared at him. His slave's suddenly

casting off his mantle of silence did not suit him at all.

But the men gathered on his doorstep waited expectantly, and Morgan had no choice but to yield.

"Can you...tell us something?" Morgan asked finally.

"I can do better than that, Major."

"This is ridiculous," Morgan said impatiently. "I have no time for guessing games. You!" he yelled at the chair-bearer. "Take him to the cage."

"I am the only man here who can find her, Major!" Five Killer called, trying to hold the servant off with his bound hands.

Morgan laughed. "And you expect me to trust *you?*"

"If you want her back. You're right, Major. You have no time. Release me now if you—"

"I'm not a fool! I am the one here with something to lose—"

"Your wife might disagree," Five Killer said calmly.

"What guarantee do I have you could locate her—and return with her if you did?"

"None," Five Killer said. "Except for my word and the bargain we make now."

"What bargain?"

"I will go and find your wife. I will return her if she lives. If not, I will return alone. For that I want—"

"You *want?*"

Five Killer ignored the sarcasm. "For that I want

your word—here and now—in front of these witnesses—that you will give the boy—''

''What boy?''

''The boy you keep in a cage like an animal! He's done no wrong. He's had no part in your war against the French. I want his freedom and safe return to his people. That is my price. What do you say?''

''I say I'm not about to be out *two* slaves.''

''And what about your wife? Is *she* the only slave you're willing to part with—''

If Morgan had been able—or closer, Five Killer would have suffered for that remark. The man was barely able to control himself.

''I want the boy's freedom, Major,'' Five Killer continued. ''As long as you have him, you have the upper hand. I give you my word. You give me yours. That's how it's done here. I will return. Unless the ones who've taken your woman kill me, of course.''

There was a sprinkling of laughter among the men standing around. Morgan Elway had raised insolence to a fine art, but he clearly did not appreciate it in others, particularly in the ones he considered so…inferior.

''Your word means nothing here,'' Morgan said. ''You think I would take the word of a savage? Even an English-speaking one?''

''Will you take the word of a McLarn, Major Elway?''

Heads turned at the question. Colm McLarn sat

on horseback at the edge of the yard. Five Killer hadn't seen him arrive. Apparently, no one had.

"I'm waiting for an answer, sir," the old man persisted as Morgan's silence lengthened. Morgan suddenly decided to sit down after all.

"I...don't understand your inquiry, McLarn," he said after a moment.

"It's a simple enough question. Will you accept the word of a McLarn?"

"You cannot vouch for this savage—"

"Oh, aye, I can. But there's no need. My son, Robert McLarn, can vouch for himself, can you not, Rob?"

Five Killer said nothing. What did the old man think he was doing? There was a time when he would have given anything—*anything*—for so public an acknowledgement by his white sire. But it was too late now. He didn't call himself by his white name any longer. It had been years since he'd done so. He was *Hi-s-ki-ti-hi*—Five Killer—the name he had taken after he had avenged his young wife's murder. No one called him Robert McLarn anymore.

He had made his choice. When his mother couldn't bear her humiliation any longer and had chosen to return to her own people, he had put aside the only life he'd ever known, albeit merely on the fringes of the white society, and gone with her. In the bosom of his mother's clan he had found an acceptance he had never experienced among his father's kind. He was his mother's son and therefore

Cherokee. Unconditionally. Without question. He belonged.

Some of the men in the crowd were still looking around, as if they thought that Colm McLarn must surely mean someone else.

"This Cherokee slave is your natural son?" Morgan asked incredulously.

"He is," McLarn answered.

"How is it you have made no mention of it sooner? You said nothing when you were a guest in my house."

It was a good question, and Five Killer looked at his father to hear the answer.

"My son is his own man. He refused my help—for his own reasons. I am merely establishing for you that if he gives his word, it is as if I had given mine. You may rely on it."

Morgan said nothing. He sat there, gripping the arms of his chair. He had backed himself into a corner and he knew it—but his arrogance hadn't quite reached the point where he was willing to insult the influential Scotsman. Five Killer was certain now that the major had no wish to have his wife returned, that he only wanted it to look as if he did. Unfortunately, he had played his part too well. Five Killer had made a reasonable and acceptable offer, given the circumstances—regardless of the doubtful outcome. He was the only hope Morgan's woman had. There wasn't a man here who didn't know it.

"I'm willing to do for you what these men can't," Five Killer said. "It's her life, Major."

"No," someone said from the doorway of the house, an old man Five Killer had never seen before. "It's the boy's life."

"Father, what—?" Morgan began, but the old man held up his free hand for silence. Unlike his son, the old man had no compunction about being helped to get where he wanted to go. He held on tightly to the bondswoman's arm with his other hand.

"You—the McLarn bastard," Morgan's father said. "You can go. I accept your offer. Find Morgan's wife for him—or what's left of her. And while you're at it, find my damned dueling pistol—"

"Father, what are you talking about?"

"Your wife and my pistol!" the old man snapped.

"Father, for God's sake! You are not making any sense and this is not your concern!"

"I am still the head of this family!" the old man said. "In light of *your*...incapacity, I will exercise that prerogative. It's clear you are beyond making a decision, so I will make it for you. I accept your terms, Indian, but you, in turn, must accept mine."

"Go on," Five Killer said.

"It seems to me there is only one way to guarantee that you will do what you say. I will give you...from now through the winter until the spring to find Morgan's wife and return with her. I should think that would be adequate time. If you haven't come back here when the woods begin to bloom, then I will collect the bounty on the boy's scalp. It is my son's right, is it not? Captives can be either held in slavery or killed for the bounty.''

"And if the woman is dead?''

"For the boy's sake, I hope she is not," the old man said.

"I need a long rifle," Five Killer said, refusing to be intimidated by the old man's none too subtle ultimatum. "And powder and provisions. Strouds for a bribe.''

"Done," the old man said.

"You give your word? If I return with her, by the spring, then the boy has his freedom. No harm will come to him. He will be allowed to go home to his village.''

"If you take his place, yes.''

"Done," Five Killer said.

There were no other particulars Five Killer wanted to argue. There was nothing else to be said. He had to find Hannah alive and to do that, he had to get to her before the Green Corn Ceremony. There were only a few weeks left until the celebration would begin. It was a time for giving thanks for the new corn harvest and for starting life anew—for righting old wrongs. Her case would be heard before the tribal council then. Maw would demand blood for blood, and she would surely be offered up for her husband's sins. She would die slowly for them; Five Killer had no doubt about that. And if she died, then so would the boy.

He dared not consider that possibility, any more than he dared consider the possibility that there might be another way to get his son away from these people. He, too, had no time. Morgan would starve his slaves to keep them from having the strength to escape, but he would work them until they couldn't work anymore. Then, he'd turn in their scalps for the bounty. It was too late now for misgivings. Five Killer was trapped, and so was the major. Morgan had made a plea for help he likely hoped wouldn't be answered. He hadn't anticipated old man Elway's interference any more than Five Killer had.

Five Killer let his gaze rest briefly on Colm McLarn, who was waiting, as every man in the crowd was waiting, to hear the outcome. The rain fell harder, but no one made any attempt to find shelter.

"And what do you say, Major?" Five Killer asked. "Do you give *your* word? As a representative of the King?" He was not about to accept that Morgan's father could vouch for his son with the same certainty that the Scotsman could vouch for his.

Morgan stared at him, then stood, slowly, his face even more pale as he struggled for control. But he wasn't going to give in. Five Killer could feel the man's resistance as if it were a living thing.

"If I can end Maw's blood vengeance against you," Five Killer said. "What then?"

Morgan looked at him sharply, uncertain suddenly as to how much Five Killer knew. It still took him a long time to answer.

"Done," he said finally.

* * *

"What is happening?" the boy asked, the tremor in his voice belying his brave front. "Are they letting us go free? Five Killer, get me out—" He rattled the slats of the cage with both hands.

Five Killer continued to fasten his leather leggings. His hands were stiff from being bound so tightly. His arms strange-feeling, as if they might not move in the way he wanted. Both ankles were raw from being hobbled. It was good he was going now. In a short time, he would have been physically unable to do anything but pull Morgan's plow.

"Five Killer—!"

"I can't," he said with a calmness he didn't begin to feel.

"Please!"

"I can't!"

"Where are you going?"

"I have to find Morgan's woman."

"Where is she?"

"I don't know. But sooner or later Maw will have her."

"You will just leave me here?"

"I have to. It's the only way I can get you back to your mother's people. The major and his father have given their word—before witnesses. They will release you when I return with her. You have to stay here—for now. I don't want you to give them any excuse to break this agreement—"

"No!" The boy hit the slats with both fists. "We can escape!"

"How! They keep us chained—"

"*You* are not chained!" The boy was young and

headstrong, certain of his own invincibility as only a boy yet standing on the brink of manhood could be. He wouldn't have been with Five Killer in the first place, wouldn't have been captured, if that were not the case.

"I've given my word," Five Killer said. "For now, you will yield."

"I will not yield! I will escape if I can!"

"You are a boy and you will do as I say! You will yield! And if a chance for escape comes and it seems easy, you will pass it by. They will want you to take it so they can kill you and no one will be able to say they broke their promise. Stay as you are. It's only until I bring back the woman."

"Maw won't let you have her. Don't leave me here!"

"I have no choice. I have made a bargain."

The boy looked at him. He had his mother's eyes, and it was as if *she* was the one who accused him of abandonment.

"You'll never get her away from Maw alive," the boy said. "Never."

"Your mother's people will speak for me," Five Killer said. "If Morgan's woman is alive, I *will* bring her back—one way or the other."

"Maw will get his revenge—"

"Then let him take it on the one who deserves it. He knows where to find Morgan if he wants his blood."

"Five Killer—" The boy abruptly stopped, and Five Killer looked around. McLarn stood in the doorway of the barn, his way barred by the soldiers who were in attendance to make sure that Five Killer didn't try to set the boy free now and make an escape.

"A word with you, Robbie," McLarn said.

"I have no time," Five Killer answered. He had to work hard to keep his indifference. He hadn't been called "Robbie" since he was twelve years old, and he was taken by surprise at the sudden longing it caused in him.

"Make the time. There is something I want to say to you."

"What is it?"

"I can't buy the boy's freedom. I haven't the coin, even if Morgan would agree."

"I haven't asked you to."

"I would have done it without being asked," the old man said. "If I'd known," he added significantly.

Five Killer didn't say anything, and the silence between them lengthened.

"Were you not going to tell me about him?" the old man continued. "The other day—when I spoke to you. All those years since I last saw your face and you said nothing—"

"There was no need," Five Killer said. "Did you not believe your own words out there, McLarn? You told them I mean what I say. But you don't believe me when I tell *you* I want nothing—*nothing*—from you."

"That boy is my blood!"

"And he's not going to suffer for it the way I—" Five Killer abruptly stopped.

"Where is his mother?" McLarn asked.

"Dead. British soldiers murdered her."

"I'm sorry."

"There is no need for *you* to be sorry. They didn't live to brag about it. You remember how they used to do that, McLarn? Sit around the campfire and talk about what they did to savages? Especially the women."

"I should have kept you away from that," the old man said, and Five Killer gave a derisive laugh.

"You're a fool, McLarn—"

"I loved your mother! I loved you both!"

"Ah! In that case, who has cause for complaint? Not me. Not *her.*"

"Are you up to this journey?" McLarn asked, ignoring the sarcasm.

But it didn't matter if Five Killer was "up" to it or not, and they both knew it. He had to go. His son's life depended on it.

"Look at him, old man. How long do you think he will last in there?"

"I *will* do the best I can to see that my grandson is not mistreated," McLarn said. "What is he called? He's very much like you, you know."

"No, McLarn. He isn't. He never lived as a bastard half-breed in a white settlement."

"Your mother is...well?" the old man asked, ignoring that remark, as well.

"I don't know," Five Killer said. It was the truth, but it sounded like a lie.

"I *am* sorry, Rob—sorry that everything has

come to this. I never meant it to be so. The trouble between your mother and me—''

''Don't!'' Five Killer said. ''Whatever it was, it's no concern of mine. Not then and not now. It's between the two of you. I don't want to hear it.''

''I have...regrets, if that means anything—''

''Not much, no.''

''I want you to tell her that.''

''*You* tell her that, McLarn,'' Five Killer said. ''But you'd better know this. My mother believed you. She believed every lie you ever told her. She waited for you a long time. She doesn't wait anymore.''

The two men stared at each other. The old man finally sighed.

''I will do what I can for the boy,'' he said again.

''Five Killer—'' the boy said from the cage.

''What is your name, boy?'' McLarn interrupted, asking the question in his once proficient Cherokee.

The boy glanced at Five Killer, but didn't answer.

''I...call him *Do-sa*,'' Five Killer said after a moment, and McLarn laughed.

''Mosquito! Little—but still able to draw blood and plague his enemy. It's a good name.''

''For now,'' the boy said. ''I'll be *Tlv-da-tsi'*—when I am a warrior.''

The old man nodded. ''Panther. A good name, as well.'' He looked at Five Killer.

''I wish—''

Whatever he had been about to say, he obviously changed his mind. "God keep you safe, Rob," he said quietly. "Hannah Albrecht is a good lass. I pray she still lives, but for *his* sake, not hers."

Chapter Five

It's raining. Still? Or again?

Hannah didn't know, didn't care. Her mind was too indifferent to consider anything so insignificant as the weather. She simply stood where she'd been left, the rawhide tether around her neck tied to a wooden post.

Her mouth felt...dry. Her mind poked tentatively around the sensation, and after a time, she tilted her face upward, eyes closed, letting the rain beat down on her and trickle over her lips. The movement caused a sharp pain in the back of her head.

Why is that? she wondered.

Yet another question. This time she tried to search for an answer, but none came.

It doesn't matter, she thought.

There was a another burst of pain, completely unexpected, against the side of her jaw. She staggered under the impact of it. Her eyes flew open in time to see yet another rock-thrower disappear into the nearest log shelter.

A second rock struck her behind the ear. Her knees buckled.

It doesn't matter, she thought as she pitched forward into the mud.

"Lv-la," someone said urgently.

Hannah made no effort to move.

"Lv-la! Come!"

She tried to raise up, not because she wanted to, but because it was the only way she could get the pulling on her arms to stop. She could feel hands on her, rough hands searching among her clothes for what she didn't know—or care.

There was an argument of some kind. Angry voices and pulling on her arms, as if she had been claimed by two opposing forces, neither of which were about to concede. The tether rubbed hard against her neck, but it took too much effort to do anything about it.

Finally, one of them won and the tug-of-war abruptly ended. Finally, she was left in peace.

"Hannah," a third voice said.

She strained briefly toward the sound of her name, then let it go. She had no interest in anything save oblivion.

"Hannah!" the voice insisted.

But there were other voices now, besides this intrusive man's voice, and she was spared having to answer. She could not hide her body from these people, but she would hide her mind. She searched frantically for some thought to latch on to and finally found it.

The song. McLarn's song.

She began to hum, letting the words drift through her mind, the sentiment as foreign to her as this place.

...Near me, near me...Lassie, lie near me...

Five Killer put down his pack and squatted down so that he could see Hannah more closely. There was nothing he could do for her—not now, at any rate, when he'd only just entered the village. He had spotted her immediately—after days of traveling through the territory commanded by the Lower Cherokee. He had visited settlement after settlement. It seemed that everyone knew that Maw had his captive, but no one knew where he would take her.

"How long has she been like this?" he asked an old woman nearby.

Hannah was thin and unkempt. But it wasn't just that alone that alarmed him. It was the emptiness in her eyes. He moved directly into her line of vision without her ever registering his presence. Wherever she was, wherever her mind had taken her, it was *not* here.

"Is she sick?" he asked. He reached out to touch Hannah's forehead. Her skin felt cool. She made no attempt to shy away from his hand.

"Her mind has run away," the old woman said. "But her body is well."

"For now," Five Killer said, and the old woman made a soft noise of agreement. Hannah Elway was willing herself not to live, and at the rate she was going, she would deprive Maw of his revenge well ahead of the Green Corn Ceremony.

Five Killer had seen the cornfields on his way into the village and the platforms built for the women whose job it was to watch over the crop and keep it safe. The corn was lush and green, nearly ready for harvest. It had been a good growing year. The people would want this ceremony to be something particularly special.

He stood and looked around him. He could smell the smoke from the cooking fires and from the logs being burned and hollowed out to make canoes. There was a soft chatter of women's voices, old women who sat in the dappled shade of a brush arbor and made their baskets and clay pots, young women who tittered at the unexpected arrival of a stranger and who were scolded sharply for it.

He expected a certain hospitality—eventually— provided he didn't pay too much attention to the captive. But first, he had to speak to the men in authority. He would ask to stay until the Green Corn Ceremony—when he would say why he had come and what he could offer. His mother's people had a very efficient way of managing life's ups and downs. There were two chiefs, one for war and one for peace. He would have to approach them both. Unfortunately, there was a good chance that the war chief here was Maw.

The people of the village were beginning to gather around. Five Killer didn't see many men among them. He knew that they might be away hunting game, but it was more likely that they were waiting to see what his presence indicated, whether or not he was scouting for an enemy who wouldn't be far behind.

He moved away from Hannah and more into the open. He had his long rifle, and he didn't want to seem a threat to the men who remained. He wouldn't be a threat to the ones he couldn't see. He knew that a well-placed arrow from behind a tree could take him down before he could raise his weapon, but he didn't want to appear afraid of them. He wasn't known here.

He had identified himself as Wolf Clan to the first person he'd come to, the elderly woman who had stopped two younger women from fighting over what was left of Hannah's clothes. The old woman watched him closely now. She was surely a person of authority in her own right, perhaps a "beloved" woman, one whose wisdom far exceeded what was expected of any member of the tribe. Such women were so esteemed that they were allowed to say what would be done with captives, whether they would be killed or adopted into the tribe. The old woman might have intervened to keep Hannah from being mistreated, but clearly she had as yet made no move to take her in.

Five Killer waited, giving them as much time to measure his intent as they wanted. He made no attempt to speak to anyone. They would reach a decision about him without his participation. The children, at least, had made up their minds. Several little boys approached him cautiously, but it was a little girl who simply walked up to him and took him by the hand.

She began to lead him around the compound, unmindful of the amusement her gesture caused some of the onlookers.

"Lv-la!" she said when he didn't walk fast enough. He smiled and picked up the pace—and her—much to her delight. The game became much better now. He kept following her directions to go here or turn there, making her squeal when he went the wrong way.

Five Killer was still laughing when a man—an angry man—rushed up and snatched the child off his shoulder. The man handed the child over to the nearest woman then struck Five Killer hard in the face with his fist. Five Killer staggered from the blow, but he didn't go down and he didn't retaliate. He stood braced and waiting, on guard and angered by the insult when he clearly meant no harm.

The man made a few more threatening gestures. Someone else threw a rock. But the suddenly hostile atmosphere was just as suddenly tempered by the arrival of yet another man, one who had the help of a young woman to make his way.

"No," the old woman whispered when Five Killer was about to step forward. "Stay here. I will speak."

Five Killer looked at her. If she was one of the "beloved" women, she would carry much more influence than he did. The only problem was that he had no idea what she would say. He hadn't explained who he was or his purpose for being here.

He was not in the least inclined to leave the fate of his son in the hands of this stranger, beloved or not.

"I have business with the chiefs—"

"You have business standing just where you are," she interrupted.

"I must—"

"You will stand," she said.

The old woman waited for further protest from him, and when there was none, she left him to approach the chief. If Five Killer had had any doubt as to her elevated status among the people here, the chief's demeanor soon ended it. The old chief's immediate deference indicated that she was not just a "beloved" woman. She was also a "war" woman, one who had at some point literally taken up weapons to defend the people, and one who could not be more revered.

The old woman looked at Five Killer once—to make sure he'd stayed where she left him, no doubt, then she began to speak earnestly to the chief in a voice Five Killer could not hear without defying her and coming closer. He listened hard, but he was only able to catch a word now and then. The little girl he'd carried on his shoulder earlier stood well back from him now, as if he had already been declared an enemy. His jaw still throbbed from the blow her relative had given him.

From time to time the old woman gestured in Five Killer's direction. He waited. He was willing to see where this was going, for the moment anyway. A shrill cry behind him told him that someone was plaguing Hannah again. He couldn't see the angry man who had struck him earlier, and it was all he could do not to turn around. He could feel the others watching—waiting—for his reaction. He kept his eyes on the old woman and the conversation she was having with the chief, and he kept his mind on the memory of his son's face looking through the slats of the cage in Morgan Elway's barn.

Finally, the talk ended, and the crowd's animosity had returned. People began to turn and stare at him. The murmuring among them became louder and louder. He could see the little girl's face. She was terrified.

The old woman came to him quickly.

"Come," she said.

"What's happened?" he asked.

"They are afraid," she said. "No one says no to Maw."

"Except you."

"Me," she agreed. "And maybe you. He is not here now. Chief Utsala is old, but he still has the power to give me this white woman. Now you will take her and follow me—and she is nothing to you. Remember that when you lift her up."

He looked at the old woman sharply, and he had to work hard not to make some kind of denial. He had thought that he had only shown the degree of interest in a captive that would be considered natural. Obviously he was wrong.

The old woman held out her hand for his pack and his long rifle.

"Brave men have no need of weapons," she said, and after a moment he gave it to her.

But the truth was he wasn't brave at all. He was desperate. And he suspected that this old woman knew it.

Hannah was still lying on the ground. Five Killer had once thought her long hair was the warm golden color of honey. Now, she was so filthy and mud-caked, he could see no color at all. He could see nothing of the young girl who had lived in the cabin with the weeping woman and who became Morgan Elway's wife.

People were crowding around him, trying to see what was happening when it was likely they knew more about the situation than he did. He knelt down and cut the tether loose from the post, then pulled Hannah none too gently to her feet and slung her over his shoulder. She struggled briefly, then went limp. Something fell from among her clothes—a small book. One of the women rushed forward to get it, and he stepped on it with his foot. After a moment, the woman retreated, and Five Killer struggled under Hannah's weight to retrieve it. He put the small leather-bound book inside his shirt.

"Come," the old woman said, and he began to follow her across the compound and down a narrow path into the trees, side-stepping no one, making them part for him as he went. He carried Hannah past the women making baskets and pots and past the men burning out the log for a canoe. All of them stared. A few of the children began to tag along after him, but they were quickly called back.

"Where are we going?" he asked the old woman after a time.

She didn't answer him. She picked up the pace, in spite of carrying his pack and long rifle. The path began to wind uphill. Hannah weighed heavily on his shoulder, and even though they were traveling upward, it seemed he could hear the sound of the river better here.

They kept going until they reached a small clearing with several log dwellings about. People stopped whatever they were doing to stare. The old woman motioned for him to take Hannah inside the closest one. He did so, carefully stepping down as he went through the low doorway, because the actual floor was lower than ground level in order to make the dwelling warmer in winter and cooler in summer.

He placed Hannah on a dirt ledge that had been carved out against the far wall. The ledge was covered with a bear skin and had been padded underneath with grasses and leaves. Hannah made no sound when he lay her down. Her eyes were open, but she still didn't see.

"Hannah?" he said, and for a brief moment her eyes flickered.

"Hannah!" he said loudly, taking her by the shoulders and shaking her hard.

"No," she protested. She tried to turn her face away. He wouldn't let her.

"Hannah!"

"Leave me be..." she whimpered.

What was it McLarn always said?

Be careful what you wish for. Yes. That was it. He would give Hannah Albrecht her wish. He would leave her alone.

But not here.

He picked her up again, and he carried her out of the shelter, ignoring the shrill protests from the old woman. He stood for a moment to get his bearings, then began making his way toward the sound of the river. There was another path off to his left, one leading downward, and he followed it. The sound of rushing water grew louder. Startled birds flew upward as he strode along. Hannah struggled from time to time, but he paid no attention to it.

Eventually, he came to the river's edge, and he walked out onto a large flat rock. The water formed a pool here, and he stepped into it, carrying Hannah well away from the bank. He didn't say anything. He didn't hesitate. He dumped her into the water. She cried out from the shock of it, and he gave her no time to do anything else. He immediately pushed her head under and held her there. She clawed at his hands and fought to get to her feet. He brought her up just long enough for her to draw another breath, then plunged her under the surface again, and then again, holding her down as she thrashed about. Finally, he brought her up. She was gasping for air, clinging to him. He could feel her breasts and her belly pressed hard against him. She was trembling, and she wouldn't let go.

He abruptly pushed her away from him, and he left her there, shaking, huddled waist deep in the river. But then, just as abruptly, he waded back to her.

"You see?" he said, grabbing her roughly by the shoulders to make her look at him, his face close to hers. "You want to live."

Chapter Six

Hannah lay face down on the flat rock, the rough surface hot and gritty against her forehead. She was shivering, in spite of the summer heat and the sun beating down on her back. Her teeth chattered. She felt hot *and* cold, the way she had once when she was a little girl and dangerously ill.

She had been safely numb for so long, and now her body and her mind were being assaulted by a myriad of sensation and sounds. She could smell the woods and the river. She could hear the birds and insects and children's voices and splashing somewhere off to her left—things that sounded so incredibly normal. Her body ached all over. She was hungry. She was afraid.

And she was angry.

She had no idea how long she had been lying on the rock. Someone came very close to her once. She had the vague notion that it was *him*, come to finish her off, but ultimately whoever it was left her undisturbed. She wanted to cry—her throat ached with unshed tears—but she couldn't give in to it. If she did, she might never stop.

You want to live.

Yes. She obviously did. If he had been civilized, if he had tried to reason with her, he would never have succeeded. But this man hadn't wasted time with words. He had simply *shown* her how much living still meant to her, regardless of her circumstances, regardless of what may come. And he'd left her to decide.

Crawl to the bank and live.

Wade out into the current and die.

She hated him for bringing her back into the real world so abruptly. She had been in a dark safe place, and he had forced her into the sunlight. She hated him for presuming to know what she herself didn't. And she hated him for being right in that presumption.

Hannah finally tried to get up. The effort caused her to cry out. After several attempts, she managed to get to her knees. Both were scraped raw, and she couldn't keep from weeping now. Tears rolled down her face. She had no idea what she should do or where she should go. And she *hurt* so. Her arms and legs were covered with bruises and briar scratches she didn't even remember getting. Her wrists were raw from being bound. Her head ached. Her neck burned under the tether she still wore. She looked down. Her clothes were in tatters, her breasts all but visible through what was left of her shift. Crazily, her first thought was how very much Morgan would disapprove.

Morgan.

She didn't want to think about Morgan. Or Hatcher.

"Lv-la," someone said. An old woman stood there with a blanket over her arm—a stroud like those the traders used as money. She kept motioning for Hannah to come with her.

Hannah got slowly to her feet and let herself be wrapped into it. It was brown. And new.

The old woman led her away from the river and into the woods, pulling her by the wrist when the path became too steep. The pain under the old woman's grasp was excruciating. Still crying, Hannah used all the strength she had to keep up.

At last, they reached several log dwellings. Hannah looked at them, trying to remember if she'd been here before. She must have, but she wasn't quite sure. She didn't remember anything but the shock of the water and the Cherokee slave trying to drown her. The questions were beginning to form. What was he doing here? How did he get free? And where was he now?

The old woman took Hannah inside one of the dwellings and immediately began to strip off her tattered wet clothes. Hannah tried to resist, but it was no use. The old woman scolded her sharply, and she was surprisingly strong. Hannah was no match for her. She was only delaying the inevitable.

Hannah looked around at a sound. The Cherokee man stepped down into the log hut. If he was startled by encountering a half-naked woman, it didn't show. Hannah tried to cover herself, then gave up.

The old woman was still poking and pulling at her, but Hannah had done enough cowering. She stood there, angry still.

Let him look.

He did just that. Then he came close to her and drew his knife from his belt. She tried to back away, but he caught her by the tether and deftly cut it from around her neck and let it fall. He let his eyes sweep over her again, then turned and picked up a bundle of some kind in the corner. On his way out with it, he said something to the old woman. Both of them laughed.

The old woman wrapped Hannah in the rough blanket again. Hannah reached up tentatively to touch the raw place on her neck. Her fingers came away sticky with blood. Her knees were beginning to tremble. She had just enough strength left to be indignant.

"What did he say?" Hannah asked, trying not to sway on her feet.

The old woman didn't answer her. She merely chuckled to herself.

"What did he say?" Hannah asked again, not knowing if the woman spoke any English or not. If she did, Hannah had no time to hear an answer. She just made it to the bearskin before her legs buckled under her. She sat down heavily, teetering for a moment before she toppled over on her side.

She lay there, breathless, her head spinning. The old woman came and peered at her closely, then chuckled again.

How fortunate you are to have me to liven your

day, Hannah thought. She felt less giddy after a moment, but she made no attempt to sit up again. The old woman kept staring at her, still amused. Hannah closed her eyes.

"He said you were too skinny and ugly for people to look at," the old woman said finally, and Hannah's eyes flew open. "He said he would go try to trade for something to hide you in."

Hannah tried to expand the anger she already felt and couldn't. She let herself smile, then laugh softly, in spite of her considerable misery. It was the truth. She wasn't fit to be seen—even here. She closed her eyes again. Some insect chewed noisily inside the log next to her head.

She must have slept for a time—it was barely daylight when she opened her eyes again. The blanket she still had around her was hot and uncomfortable, but she had little choice but to wear it. She sat up. Her head pounded from the exertion. She needed desperately to answer the call of nature, and with some effort she got up from the bearskin and stepped outside.

The old woman was squatted down, feeding wood chips to a cook fire. She glanced in Hannah's direction, but said nothing—and she could have— in English—Hannah suddenly remembered.

Hannah moved carefully away from the dwelling into the woods, trying not to trip over the blanket or upset the old woman. The old woman didn't protest, so Hannah kept going until she was far enough away for some privacy. When she returned, the old woman was filling a gourd with whatever she had cooking in a small iron pot like the ones Hannah used to see when she went to the trading post with her father.

Hannah sat down on the ground facing the fire where she could smell the aroma of the food. Her stomach growled with hunger. She licked her lips and watched intently as the old woman slowly sipped from her gourd, but she didn't dare try to take anything for herself. She waited. And suffered.

Three more women and several children came around to partake of the meal, filling gourds, wooden bowls, and small clay pots that let the liquid drip through onto the ground. A little boy passed close to her with his portion. It was all Hannah could do not to snatch it away from him and run with it. She was so *hungry*—too hungry to realize anyone else was close to her until she was prodded on the shoulder. She jumped in alarm. The Cherokee man was there, holding out a small wooden bowl to her.

"Eat," he said.

She looked up at him, ashamed to have been caught planning to steal food from a child.

"Are you going to try to drown me again if I don't?" she asked, in spite of the fact that she was literally starving, and he knew it.

"If I wanted you drowned—drowned you would be," he said. "Suit yourself," he added when still she didn't take the bowl.

She reached out and grabbed his wrist to keep him, snatching the bowl out of his hand and drink-

ing from it, greedily. She had no idea what it was—
something with corn. It didn't matter. It was edible.

"No," he said, pulling it away from her mouth.
"Slowly—or it won't stay down."

She tried to do what he said—and failed. He took
the bowl away from her and held it himself, allow-
ing her to have only small sips at a time.

"Enough," he said, when she would have taken
more. Much more.

Hannah tried to hold on to his wrist again, but
when her eyes met his, she reluctantly let go. She
was so hungry still. It was all she could do not to
beg. She had no dignity left. She licked her fingers
to get at whatever had spilled over her hands in the
struggle. She could feel the women staring at her.
One of the children began to cry.

The Cherokee man went away, but he came back
almost immediately.

"Here," he said, throwing a worn and faded,
blue-striped skirt and a man's homespun shirt at
her.

She looked down at them, then at him. She immediately recognized the shirt. It was his.

"I don't—"

"You know the saying white people have, Mistress Elway," he interrupted. "The one about beggars and choosers?"

She looked at him for a moment, then picked up
the clothes and carried them into the log dwelling.
She sat down on the bearskin for a time, staring at
her new attire. She wondered what the old woman
had done with her shift—shredded though it may

have been—and her corsets. She didn't feel decent without them. She thought suddenly of the other Elway wives, of the day they had arrived from England. Hannah had been so taken by their dresses of finely embroidered brocade. How long ago that seemed now.

The striped skirt was much too big for her. After considerable effort, she was finally able to tear a strip off the bottom to tie around her waist to keep it from falling down. She tried not to think who might have worn it last.

She put on his shirt. Neither garment did anything to enhance her appearance, but at least she could move more freely. She found herself folding the blanket and placing it carefully on the bearskin—as if she were a visiting relative who didn't want to make her stay troublesome to her hostess.

She drew a quiet breath. She was no visitor. She knew exactly what she was. There was no way she could hide from the truth anymore. She was a captive, and she had three possible fates. She could be adopted into the tribe. She could be sold to the French allies. Or she could be killed. She knew from her father that Cherokee captives were often well treated—until the time came for them to die. She didn't believe for a moment that she would be rescued or that she could escape. She didn't know where she was, or which way to go in the dense forest. She couldn't follow the river—the terrain was too rough. Unless she could follow the *sound,* she suddenly thought.

She looked around sharply. The Cherokee man stood just inside the doorway.

"Are you sick?" he asked, and, incredibly, she found the question amusing.

"I'm not sick," she said, trying not to smile. "I'm dead."

Her attempt at gallows humor escaped him entirely, and he immediately turned to go.

"*You* told me what I could expect," she said.

"Yes," he answered with his back still to her. His bare back, because she had his shirt. She could see numerous scars in various stages of healing, scars that must have come from a whipping. She wondered who had done it. Morgan? No. Morgan would have ordered someone else to do it. Hatcher.

"I...assume there is no reason to think the situation might have changed," she said.

"No."

"No," she repeated. "First, you tell me to take my own life—and then you force me to see that I can't do it. Why is that?"

He didn't answer her. There was a sudden commotion outside—agitated voices speaking all at once.

"Stay here," he said. "I mean it."

She stood there, annoyed because she hadn't intended to follow him. He went outside, and the commotion grew louder. He returned almost immediately.

"Let's go," he said, taking Hannah roughly by the arm.

"What—?"

"I can't save you from this."

He shoved her toward the door. A ring of women stood outside waiting, and they sent up a chorus of shouts the second Hannah appeared. They kept yelling and shaking their fists at her. Someone threw a rock. It glanced off her shoulder. The Cherokee man pushed his way through the crowd, dragging Hannah along with him. Hands pulled at her clothes and hair. She kept trying to push them away.

"Run," he said. "That way. As hard and fast as you can. Don't stop."

"What—"

"Do it!"

He gave her another shove. "Go on!" he yelled at her, and she turned to run.

But Hannah didn't get far. Someone grabbed her by her hair and pulled her backward until she fell hard onto the ground. The closest woman kicked her. Hannah tried to roll away, but here was nothing she could do except cower. She tried to fight back, to protect her sides and belly from the rain of blows.

Suddenly, it all stopped. Hannah struggled to her feet, looking around wildly. She could no longer see the Cherokee man. She began to back away, and then to run. She crashed headlong into the underbrush. A long, high-pitched human wail rose behind her. The women were coming after her. She tried to run faster, but there were too many obstacles in her path—fallen logs, rocks, dense thickets. No matter how hard she tried, she couldn't seem to get anywhere. It was like being caught in a child-hood nightmare, only this time the chase was real.

Hannah finally stumbled on a root and fell heavily to her knees. The pain was excruciating. Panicked now, she could hear the women not far behind, and she looked wildly around her. If she couldn't run anymore, then she would have to hide. Ahead of her, the ground sloped upward to a ridge of pine trees, and she struggled to get up the incline. The pine branches grew low to the ground, and when she crawled into them, she found that the trees were not on a ridge at all, but on the rim of a depression in the earth. She was lying in a shallow hole on a thick carpet of pine needles. She reached up and stopped the branches over her head from swaying.

After a moment, Hannah heard a rustling off to her left, then voices. She couldn't see anything. Someone passed by, very close, beating the under-brush with a stick. It sounded as if the women were all around her, and it was soon apparent that where mere pine branches would not have hidden her, the depression in the ground did.

She lay there, every muscle in her body tense in her effort to stay perfectly still. But her fear gave way to complete exhaustion. Her body began to tremble with fatigue, tears streamed down her face. She reached up to wipe her cheek with the back of her hand, disturbing a dead branch in the process. The sound was muffled, indistinct, but it was enough.

They were coming back.

Oh, God! Hannah thought. She closed her eyes. She could literally feel how close they were to her hiding place. She could smell them—a sweaty, leather smell. She didn't dare move. Someone poked among the pine branches with a long stick, but it passed over her head without making contact.

None of the women were leaving. Hannah could hear them tramping back and forth, looking, talking. Some of them were even laughing.

What kind of game is this? Hannah thought wildly, but she knew. It was a deadly one. There was no other kind here.

The sun went down. Still, the women stayed, until finally, finally they began to disperse.

Hannah let herself draw a long, slow breath, but she didn't dare move yet. The tears were coming in earnest now, and she made no attempt to wipe them away. She tried to think what to do, but she couldn't get past the physical pain.

And the fear.

She kept thinking of all those long, sleepless nights she and her stepmother had stayed alone in the cabin, completely at the mercy of whatever predatory animal or human passed their way. She had been afraid then, mindlessly so—she had thought. But that fear was nothing compared to now. Now she truly had nothing and no one to call upon, and no one in the settlement or beyond would know what had happened to her, save Morgan and perhaps the Cherokee man—neither of whom would be inclined to carry the tale back to civilization.

The saddest part, she supposed, was that no one would really care. Whatever regrets her father might harbor at the loss of his only daughter would be quickly assuaged by his devotion to his calling and by the fact that he had his sons. She would simply disappear as if she had never been.

The moon had risen. She could just see it through the tree branches above her head. The sounds of the night creatures—insect and animal—swirled around her. She had once found the wilderness night sounds pleasantly soothing after a hard day's work. Now it only lent credence to her feeling of abandonment and despair.

She closed her eyes and tried not to weep. Crying never helped. She had lived with her stepmother far too long not to have learned that. But the realization that she would never see the little boys again was nearly more than she could bear. They were the only ones she would truly miss.

You want to live.

Yes. She did.

I have to get away from here. Before they come back and find me—

Hannah tried to sit up; her head swam. She fell back on the ground. After a moment, she struggled to crawl to the edge of the rim. She had to get away. She had to put some distance between herself and the village—and then she would worry about what to do next.

She stayed crouched under the pine limbs for a long time, listening intently, trying to sense as she used to when she lived in the cabin if someone was near. But if there was another person nearby, she couldn't tell. She came slowly out of hiding, taking the time to get her bearings. She couldn't hear the river now. Her only landmark was her hiding place, and she was almost certain which direction would take her away from the village.

Almost.

Once she stepped clear of the pine trees, she didn't hesitate, but she couldn't run. She couldn't see where she was going well enough for that, and the last thing she needed was to fall in the dark. But it was hard going just to walk the steep terrain. She got a stitch in her side almost immediately, and she bent double to ease it. When the pain receded, she plunged on, dodging among the trees.

She entered a clearing. The moon went behind a cloud. She had to stop. When her eyes had adjusted somewhat, she moved ahead.

She stopped again, abruptly, and for what reason, she could not have said. She stood hidden in the darkness, listening intently.

"Hannah."

She made a soft "oh" sound. The voice came from her left. She tried to see where it had come from.

"Don't move," he said. "You'll fall."

Fall?

Even as he said it, she could feel that the ground underneath her feet was not stable.

"Hold out your hand," he said, his calm voice belying the danger she must surely be in.

She didn't hesitate. They both understood her revised position regarding her survival. She extended her hand. He grasped it immediately and pulled hard, jerking her off her feet. She stumbled against him. She could hear the dirt behind her crumbling away, and she could sense now the great open space she'd had no inkling was there just moments before. Belated fear swept over her, and once again she found herself clinging to him for dear life. *Her* dear life. He suffered it briefly, then pulled away.

"Try to keep up," he said.

After a moment's hesitation, Hannah followed after him—or tried to. He made no exception for her whatsoever. She could keep up, or she could stay here and face whatever might be in store for her at the hands of the women. She kept losing him in the dark. She had no idea where they were going—except upward. And she was mystified that she should be struggling so hard to stay in his wake. He was certainly not her savior. It was he who had given her up to the women in the first place.

Finally, he stopped, and she stood waiting, swaying with exhaustion. He said nothing to her, offered no explanations. She didn't understand any of it. Did he want her dead or alive?

They were near what seemed to be a wall of exposed rock. She watched him warily. She had no idea what he intended, and the conundrum was simply too involved for her to unravel. She didn't really want to know the answer. She sank to her knees. Once again, all she wanted was oblivion, but he had no intention of letting her have it.

"Get up," he said, pushing her with his foot.

She struggled to get to her feet, too slowly apparently, because he reached down and pulled her up. It was all she could do not to cry out.

"Over there."

She had no choice but to go in the direction he pushed her. There seemed to be a space in the rock—a cave of some kind under an outcropping, one side of the wide opening a smooth arc, the other jagged and irregular. The moon disappeared, and she stood there in total darkness.

"Go," he said.

She moved blindly under the overhanging stone, hands outstretched.

"Stay here out of sight—no matter what you hear."

"What's happening?"

He made no attempt to explain anything to her. He just gave her another push.

He stayed gone a long time. She was afraid to move around for fear of being heard or encountering some creature that might have laid claim to the place first. Indeed, something scurried by her in the dark.

She waited, daring to move closer to the opening so that she could try to see where he had gone and what he was about. Once, she thought she heard voices, but the sound was too muted for her to be sure. She had no reason in the world to do what this man said, and yet here she stood, exactly where he left her. She should run again, she kept thinking, and she knew full well that the next time there might not be anyone to keep her from falling off a cliff.

Hannah moved farther out. Her toe dislodged a stone. She bent down and felt for it. It was a good size for her hand, and she picked it up. It wasn't much of a weapon, but it would have to do. She held on to it tightly, but she had no opportunity to use it.

He was there suddenly, so close, she could feel the heat of his body, smell his heady masculine smell.

"It's me," he said. "Sit down. I'm not going to hurt you."

She backed away from him as far as she could get, still clutching the stone and made no attempt to sit. She didn't trust his remark for an instant. Morgan had said the same thing on her wedding night—and he was supposedly civilized.

"I'm not going to hurt you," the Cherokee man said again.

"I don't believe you," she answered, and she cursed the fact that she couldn't keep her voice from trembling.

"Suit yourself."

Hannah could hear more than see him moving around in the cramped space. She shivered, not because she was cold, but because she was afraid. Of being in the dark. Of being found. Of him.

Her eyes eventually adjusted to the darkness. She could just see him sitting across from her. She finally sat down on the ground and pulled her legs up under her to make herself as small as possible.

"It's going to rain," he said after a long time, and she nearly laughed. She was terrified and yet the remark was so like something a visiting gentleman might say while sitting in the Elways' best parlor.

"What—?" Hannah began, then immediately stopped. She had actually been about to try to engage him in conversation. She wasn't in a parlor, best or otherwise. She was on the run from these people—savages—who wanted to kill her.

She could feel him staring at her in the semi-darkness. Waiting. She abruptly moved closer to the entrance. She didn't want to be cornered in this place. The wind had picked up, and there was now no moon. It was indeed going to rain. She could feel it, smell it in the air. She was so...thirsty suddenly. She kept swallowing. It didn't help.

"What is your name?" she asked in an effort to take her mind off her parched throat.

"Robert McLarn," he said.

"What?" Hannah asked, startled.

"You heard me. Or did you mean my Cherokee name—Hi-s-ki-ti-hi. It means Five Killer. Not four. Not six. Five. You see I only killed five. The Cherokee say what they mean."

Hannah understood the heavy-handed subtleties of the remark perfectly, and the unspoken rest of it.

Unlike your *people.*

But now that the conversation had begun, she refused to be deterred.

"You are called after Colm McLarn then?" she asked tentatively.

"Called after? I don't know 'called after.' It's my English name. *He* gave it to me, if that's what you mean, I hate it."

"Why did...?" Hannah let the question trail away.

"Why, what?" he asked, and his tone of voice changed now, hard. She realized immediately that he thought she had been about to ask about his relationship to McLarn. The truth was, she didn't have to ask. The minute he said the name she remembered the day McLarn had gone to speak to him, and she now recognized that he had the Scotsman's look about him, a look disguised by his savage appearance and his lean physical build, but there, nonetheless. Actually, she had been about to ask why—if he hated the name—did he mention it?

"Why...did you kill these five...people?" she asked instead.

"People? They were not 'people.' They were British soldiers like your husband. And I killed them because they murdered my wife for no reason but that she was handy and not white."

Hannah didn't know what to say. She was full of questions, but she could sense the hostility in him, and she decided that he wanted her to make some token comment regarding his startling revelations that he could throw it back into her face— or worse. So she said nothing. A flash of lightning lit up the night sky, and the thunder rolled overhead. The rain came in a sudden downpour. She was close enough to the entrance to get wet, but she didn't move. She was too tired to move. She sat there, hugging her knees. After a moment, she rested her head on her arms and closed her eyes. She could hear him stir, and she immediately lifted her head.

"Did the boy escape with you?" she asked abruptly.

"No."

"I'm sorry," she said, and she meant it.

"A good wife doesn't favor the loss of her husband's property, Mistress Elway. A good wife doesn't wish her husband...ill."

Hannah looked at him.

He knows, she thought. This man—this Five Killer—knew what she had done. And she was no different from him. In their anger, they had both done murder.

"No matter, mistress. You are not yet a widow."

"Morgan is alive?"

"When last I saw him."

She realized that she had been holding her breath, and she slowly let it out. Morgan was alive.

"You are sure?"

"Very sure, mistress."

"Is he...hurt badly?"

"He was able to stand, to talk."

"And Hatcher?"

"I know nothing of Hatcher."

"Is that how you escaped?" she asked. "Hatcher wasn't there—and Morgan couldn't—"

"Be quiet," he said. "Sleep. You will need it."

"What are you going to do with me?"

"Sleep," he said again, instead of answering her.

Hannah stared at him in the darkness. Whatever was in store for her, it was no mystery to him. Of that she was certain.

She became acutely aware of the rain suddenly, and she moved toward the entrance. He was on her in an instant, toppling her and pinning her to the ground. The stone she had been clinging to desperately rolled from her hand.

"Let me go! Please!" Hannah cried, trying not to weep because he was hurting her. "The rain— it's nearly stopped. I'm so thirsty—"

His body lay heavy upon hers, one knee between her thighs. His breath came warm against her face. She was looking into his eyes.

He abruptly moved off her.

She scrambled away from him and outside, sitting on the ground and cupping her hands to try to collect enough falling rain to swallow. But she was so thirsty. She hadn't the patience to wait. She licked her fingers and her palms, and she was crying openly now.

Five Killer was suddenly there.

"Here," he said, holding a small animal skin bag out to her. She didn't know what to do with it— how it fastened. He opened it and held it to her lips. She tipped back her head and drank greedily. Once again, he stopped her when he thought she had had enough.

The rain beat down on her. Her hands still rested on the water bag, her fingers touching his.

"Thank you, Robert," she whispered when he was about to take the water away, because it was to that part of him—to Colm McLarn's son—she wished to speak.

He seemed to soften for a moment, only a moment, and then he moved away.

Chapter Seven

"She has much to answer for," the old woman said.

Five Killer chose not to comment on the observation. He continued to watch Hannah as she struggled to understand what was expected of her. He could go explain it to her and briefly put an end to the current tirade from yet another woman trying to put her to work, but it wasn't his place to interfere. To do so would only make matters worse. *He* could see that Hannah was not lazy or unwilling—she simply didn't know how to do what the woman wanted done. Mistress Elway had no skills that were of any use here. She knew nothing of the intricate task of basket weaving. Clearly she had never made clay pottery. And to make matters worse, she wasn't physically strong enough to carry the heavy loads of wood and water that needed carrying. She tried—but not without falling or spilling or dropping.

He abruptly looked away, because she was about

to be beaten again for her clumsiness, and he realized that his interest in Hannah Elway had not gone unnoticed.

"She has much to answer for," the old woman said again.

He shooed a fly away from his face. "*She* has done nothing," he said, and the old woman chuckled softly.

"You would do well to point that out when she is judged at the Green Corn Ceremony."

He frowned. He had said nothing about speaking on Hannah's behalf—which, of course, was what he would have to do. It was the only thing he could do if he intended to take her back to her husband. The tribal council was swayed by persuasion and logic, not coercion, and Maw's case was a strong one. His entire family had been murdered when Morgan Elway and his soldiers raided the village. Maw's wife, two sons, his mother. It would take great eloquence on Five Killer's part to somehow influence the tribal council to spare Hannah Elway.

And to give her to him.

It suddenly occurred to him that Maw might ask for her himself, that he might not want her burned. Thus far he had stayed away from the village— when he could be here rallying the people to his side. If he took Hannah as wife, he would have months, perhaps years of revenge before she died of ill-treatment.

Five Killer couldn't let either possibility happen. The sudden mental picture of his only child caged like an animal in Morgan Elway's barn was akin to a physical pain to him. He had no expectations for any help from Colm McLarn.

No expectations.

Hannah Elway apparently knew the feeling well. Five Killer had seen it in her eyes when she realized that he was taking her back to the village. He saw it now, whenever he could make himself meet her sad gaze. She had been betrayed by her own husband, and she clearly expected no less from her husband's former slave—Colm McLarn's by-blow or not.

"You have a short memory, Five Killer," the old woman said cryptically. But she didn't wait for him to inquire as to what she meant. She walked off in Hannah's direction to add her own voice to the melee.

"Lv-la."

Hannah covered her face, expecting yet another blow. But the old woman stood with her hand outstretched, motioning for Hannah to come with her, much as she had that day at the river.

Hannah stepped forward, expecting at least some protest from the other women, but none came. She followed in the old woman's wake, and she didn't dare look back. If she had taken that liberty, it wouldn't have been to see the reaction of the women who had been harassing her. It would have been to see if her departure had caught the notice of Robert McLarn.

If she'd been asked, she would have been hard-pressed to say why, just as she was hard-pressed to understand why she sometimes needed to think of him in terms of his English name. She understood perfectly that he was *not* white. He was Cherokee. He had chosen it; it was obvious that he lived it, or he would have used his sire's name to get himself free of Morgan's enslavement. His situation—he, himself—were just another mystery she couldn't begin to fathom.

The old woman took a different path away from the village, one Hannah hadn't been on before. It wound through the shady coolness of the woods and eventually into the bright sunshine of a clearing with a large cornfield. She could see beans growing in amongst the cornstalks, and gourds and sunflowers and squash. There were high wooden platforms built at intervals around the perimeter of the field, and the old woman began to climb the nearest one. She managed the ladder rungs with remarkable ease for someone her age. Hannah followed, and with nowhere near the agility. Her many bruises and scratches, and the half healed scrapes on her knees made the climb nothing short of an ordeal.

Hannah was out of breath when she finally reached the top. There was a roof of sorts, one made of cut pine branches to provide some shade. The old woman motioned for her to sit down, and Hannah did so gratefully. She could see over a good portion of the cornfield from her vantage point. The corn looked to be nearly ripe and ready for harvest, and she tried not to think about how hungry she was. It was rare that she was ever *not* hungry. What she would give for boiled fresh corn in butter?

She turned her attention to the other platforms—five in all. Each of them seemed to be occupied by an old woman who had other younger women or several children with her. But if there was a point to Hannah's having been brought here, clearly she was going to have to wait to find out what it was.

Hannah waited, tense and wary, knowing that sooner or later she would somehow offend or fail to comply and precipitate yet another rash of scoldings and punishments. She was happy to be here instead of on the receiving end of a hickory stick, but she, by no means, dared to relax her guard. The days since Five Killer had brought her back to the village had been filled with nothing but insults and castigation for her perceived sins. She worked almost constantly, daybreak to sundown and beyond. Her situation in that respect was hardly different from what it had been in her father's house and later in Morgan's. The Cherokee village, for her, was just one more place of backbreaking work.

Hannah saw Five Killer often—from a distance—sometimes showing the young boys his prowess with a bow and arrow or a blow gun, and sometimes teasing the young girls, who giggled and blushed as any young maidens in the presence of an intriguing male might do. He had a new shirt now, a gift from one of the younger women who had made it with her own hands. Hannah had often seen her working on it, and she had been nearby when the young woman finally presented it to him. Hannah had watched it all with something very akin to jealousy. Regardless of his English name, Hannah had thought him incapable of appreciating such a *civilized* gesture. But clearly that was not the case. The shirt had pleased him. The young woman had pleased him. And he showed it.

Five Killer never came near Hannah except at meal times. Apparently he was welcome at the old woman's fire. Twice, he had actually slept in the log shelter with them, falling asleep in a corner long before Hannah was allowed that luxury and then leaving before she awoke before dawn. He never spoke to her, never seemed to take notice of her at all. He conversed with the old woman, however, at great length. Once or twice, he even laughed at some remark the old woman made.

Hannah didn't understand him—or anything else in this place, and all she knew to do was to try and endure. She still toyed with the idea of escape. She had every reason to expect that she would not survive here, and perhaps there would come a time when she wouldn't be watched so closely. She remembered her father's stated way of traveling in the wilderness when he ministered to his many congregations. He searched out the Indian footpaths that usually followed a stream, he said, because they let a traveler pass more easily.

A traveler. Not an escapee. Time would be the deciding factor for her. She would have to have a good head start if she was to succeed. She would watch and she would wait, and if—when—an opportunity came, she would take it.

She reached up to touch the small spot between her eyes that ached. Sometimes planning her escape was a comfort to her. Sometimes—like now—it only filled her with hopelessness. She gave a quiet sigh and closed her eyes, letting herself become aware of the sounds around her. Cornstalks squeaking in the heat and the faint breeze. A flock of crows. The repetitive "work" chant of an old woman on one of the platforms close by.

And...

Hannah turned her head sharply to her right. She could see them easily—a young man and woman lying in each other's arms in the tall grass near the edge of the cornfield. She recognized the woman immediately. It was the same one who had made Five Killer's shirt. But the young man was a stranger to Hannah, and she had to work hard not to acknowledge the relief she felt that that was the case. Hannah watched the two of them unashamedly. The young man touched the woman so gently, so lovingly, caressing her breasts, her thighs until her body rose under his hands.

Hannah could hear them murmuring to each other, then laughing together.

Is this how it's supposed to be?

Then the young man's body covered the woman's, and she cried out in pleasure as his body entered hers.

Hannah abruptly looked away, feeling none of the things propriety demanded that she feel. She wasn't incensed. She wasn't offended. The only names she could give to the intense emotions that washed over her were regret and sorrow at knowing that she had never experienced this kind of joy and never would. And if there was any indecency here, it was on her part for spying.

There had never been that kind of gentleness from Morgan, and Hannah would never forget the way he had looked at her the last time she saw him—the day she had been captured. No. The day she'd been given away to pacify his enemies. But if she hadn't known before that she meant absolutely nothing to him, that look alone would have been enough to convince her.

She turned away from the young couple and once again stared out over the cornfield.

"That is not what you are up here to see," the old woman said quietly, and Hannah could feel her cheeks flush. "You are here to keep the animals from destroying the crop. You are here to watch for the Shawnee—or your white husband and his soldiers. You think this will be easy? Yes—if our enemies don't come. If they do—we are the ones they look for and murder first, so that there is no one to give the alarm."

"Is that—" Hannah began, then stopped. She had been about to ask if that was what had happened to Five Killer's wife. Had *she* been watching from a platform, away from the village, when the British soldiers came?

"In the mornings you must give thanks," the old woman went on. "You must go down to the river and you must step into the water and wash yourself. The rivers and the streams are the lifeblood of our mother, the earth. Every day, before you do anything else, you must go there and thank her that *you*

live. We are the principle people. It will go easier
for you if the others think you are trying to learn
the true way.''

Hannah glanced at her, but said nothing.

''You think Five Killer put you in the river to
hurt you that day. No. He put you there to save
you.''

Hannah didn't believe for a minute that Robert
McLarn—Five Killer—had any intention of saving
her—then—or ever. If he had, he would not have
brought her back to the village.

''Look there,'' the old woman said, pointing to
a log hut Hannah could just see through the trees.
''If your monthly bleeding comes, you will go there
and stay until it's over. You will stay apart from us
and you will eat only what is brought to you. Do
you understand?''

Hannah didn't answer her. Her mind was completely occupied with but one word the old woman
had spoken.

If.

I am not with child, Hannah thought. She might
as well have spoken the words aloud.

''When you ran from the village, Five Killer
found you and kept you all the night,'' the old
woman said, as if she thought Hannah was so va-
cant-headed that she had forgotten the incident.
''Who knows if his seed won't take root and
grow—?''

''I am not with child,'' Hannah interrupted.

''The spells are strong,'' the old woman said.

''What spells?''

"*My* spells," the old woman said. "I am Red Paint. My clan is the medicine clan. I know the spells to be done. For sickness. For the hunt or for war or for a safe journey. And for love. Spider was called—to spin the web that will bind your soul to his. I see your longing for him—"

There was a sudden noise in the cornfield—children chasing a deer in this direction—with a number of the young men with bows and arrows in pursuit as well.

"Go," the old woman said, pointing in their direction. "Help them."

Hannah hesitated, then scrambled down the ladder. The deer was almost upon her when she reached the ground, and she whirled around and waved both arms, yelling loudly.

The animal veered sharply to the left, crashing in among the corn stalks instead of away. The warriors had taken the lead in the chase, and the children ran after them, shrieking. Hannah followed, running back and forth, trying to keep the terrified animal from trampling any more of the cornstalks than it already had. Finally, it reached the edge of the cornfield and bounded into the woods.

Hannah bent over slightly to catch her breath, and she straightened to find the children gathered around her. Not too close, but closer than any had come before. One of the little boys inched forward and tentatively held out a handful of blackberries. Hannah hesitated, as wary as he was. Finally, she extended her hand. He carefully tipped the blackberries into her palm and immediately ran away, stopping once to look back at her—as if he knew he had done a very brave thing in approaching the captive, and he wanted to see if she appreciated that fact.

And if she didn't, then perhaps their audience did. Five Killer stood in the tall grass watching for a moment, then followed the boy.

Hannah stared after them, until, overcome by the hunger she had to work so hard to keep at bay, she wolfed down the blackberries without even tasting them. She walked back to the platform, and it took a great deal of concentration on her part not to look over her shoulder to see if Five Killer had perhaps returned.

I see your longing for him.

Of course, she didn't long for him. Hannah found the idea ridiculous. It was simply that he spoke English. And he was the son of Colm McLarn—a man who had always been kind to her.

And he had such sad eyes....

The old woman was coming down the platform ladder. When she reached the last rung, she rested her hand on Hannah's shoulder to get to the ground.

"Lv-la," she said, leading the way in the direction Five Killer had gone. Hannah followed, and when they reached the next platform, the old woman stopped and called up to someone. A tightly woven, handleless basket promptly dropped over the side and fell at the old woman's feet. The old woman made no attempt to pick it up. She walked on, as brisk a walker as she was a climber of ladders. Hannah gave a quiet sigh. It was either her

responsibility to bring the basket or it wasn't, and whatever she chose to do would likely be wrong.

Hannah picked up the basket. The old woman took a second unfamiliar path through the woods, until they came to yet another clearing—a kind of meadow crisscrossed with thicket after thicket of ripe blackberries. Women, young and old, and an absolute herd of rambunctious children were hard at work gathering the fruit. The atmosphere was festive, almost party-like.

A number of the young men stood about in an all-male group, but it was obvious that they considered berry-picking beneath them. It was the berry-pickers themselves that were of interest, and that interest translated into boisterous laughter and pushing and shoving each other in the hopes that one of the young women would notice. But the more bravado the young men showed, the more their quarry ignored them.

Hannah began to fill the basket she was carrying. It took great concentration on her part not to look for Five Killer. He wasn't among the young men bent on showing their prowess. She kept picking, trying to be careful of the thorns and the snakes and the wasp nests she knew to be hidden in blackberry thickets. Such delicious fruit was not taken without a price. Now and again, she managed to eat a few of the berries without consequence.

The sun beat down upon the top of her head. No one she knew would go out in the sun like this bareheaded—or anywhere else for that matter. Until her captivity she had never been without a mob cap covering her hair—even when she slept. When her basket was finally full, she carried it to the old woman, who nodded her head approvingly and poured the contents into a bigger communal basket and sent Hannah back to the thickets again.

The young men had started a game that involved a great struggle to keep each other from hitting a leather ball along the ground with a stick. Hannah watched out of the corner of her eye, still looking for Five Killer. She didn't see him. She tried to concentrate on other things. On the fact that she was still alive. On the beautiful summer day. On the murmur of conversation around her, that was somehow pleasant, even if she didn't understand the words.

Women here talked to each other as they worked. There hadn't been much of that in her experience. Her stepmother was always too sad to talk. In Morgan's house, Hannah's social station had been too far below the Elways' and too far above the indentured servants' to inspire spontaneous conversation.

Hannah looked sharply around. The game had migrated in her direction, and she was suddenly surrounded. The players, completely unmindful of her or her berries, pushed and shoved her to get to the rolling ball at her feet. She fell forward into the thicket. Briars tore at her face and arms. The basket flew out of her hands, and the berries spilled all over the ground. Hannah righted herself. She was furious, not at the pain inflicted upon her once again, but at the indifference that had rendered all her hard work to naught. She gave no thought to her situation or to anything else. She snatched up the basket and hit the nearest offender with it as hard as she could. He gave a yelp of surprise.

"Look what you did!" Hannah cried, hitting him again, much to the amusement of his peers.

But he was not about to be chastised by the likes of her. He lunged at her, raising the long game stick he carried, and he would have struck her with all his might, if one of the players hadn't stayed his hand.

Five Killer.

"Go back to the women," he said to Hannah, struggling to restrain the warrior who still intended to do her harm. "Now!"

Hannah dropped the basket and did as he said, running the entire distance to the women, who stood watching, both with interest and alarm. Hannah went, but she didn't expect to find refuge. She expected more of the same, and she was very afraid. She—a worthless captive—had struck one of the "principle people." Not once, but twice. She had behaved in a way that could cost her her life, and she knew it. But when she had lost her temper and swung the basket, the only thing in her mind had been the careless behavior of yet another inconsiderate male, the kind she had been surrounded by all her life.

Hannah stopped just short of the old woman who now seemed to have charge of her. But the old woman paid no attention to Hannah whatsoever. She—all of them—were staring at Five Killer and the young man who refused to be mollified. The situation had escalated, and it was clearly past arbitrating. Hannah had overstepped the boundary, and so had Five Killer by his interference. The warrior Hannah had humiliated would not be denied.

The two men circled each other, knives drawn, the rest of the young men giving them plenty of room.

It was so strangely silent. No one cheered. No one egged the two fighters on. The only sounds were the grunts and the labored breathing that came from two men trying to kill each other.

Hannah stood there, her hands clasped tightly against her breasts, as if she could somehow keep the fear out. She hadn't meant for this to happen. More warriors were coming into the meadow—a party of five or six. The old woman next to Hannah made a soft sound.

"Who is it?" Hannah asked.

"That is Maw," the old woman said. "The man who wants to burn you for his dead family."

Hannah watched as he moved across the meadow. He paid no attention to the two men fighting. He was coming straight toward her. Panicked now, she would have bolted if the old woman hadn't caught her arm.

"Where can you go?" she asked Hannah quietly. "Be strong. Show him you are brave—a war woman. Show him you are not like your white husband."

Hannah glanced at her. She was not brave. She could feel her body trembling. The old woman's leathery hand tightened briefly, then let go.

Hannah drew a wavering breath and stood her ground, her mouth gone dry and her heart pounding.

Maw stopped just in front of her, his eyes riveted on her face. He was slightly taller than she, his tense body muscular and scarred and ready to snap with pent-up rage. He had completely shaved his head. Hannah's eyes went briefly to the scalps hanging from his belt, some blond, some red. The series of slashes on his forearms looked oddly familiar to her. Her stepmother had similar injuries— ones that had been self-inflicted when her melancholy overwhelmed her.

Hannah had never seen anyone so fierce. She had literally felt the hatred of the people here, but it was nothing compared to what she saw in the eyes of this man. There would be no reasoning with him, no explaining. Nothing. The old woman was right. Where could she run?

Hannah waited. *She* had done nothing to Maw, and she could not behave as if she were guilty. There was no room for guilt when she was so filled with terror.

He continued to stare at her, then he walked around her. Slowly. Somehow she knew that she dared not look at him, and she fixed her gaze straight ahead. When he came behind her, the skin on the back of her neck prickled. She was too terrified to move. He abruptly stepped forward and grabbed her by the hair. Her knees buckled, and he jerked her upward, dragging her along with him to where Five Killer and the young warrior she had offended stood. The two were no longer fighting. They were waiting, as she was waiting, for her death.

Maw held her fast, dragging her along, never quite giving her time to get her feet under her. When they reached Five Killer, Maw sent her sprawling into the dirt.

She managed to get to her knees, and when she lifted her head, she looked directly into Five Killer's eyes. She saw nothing of Morgan's cold indifference there.

"Robert—" she whispered, barely realizing she had spoken.

He took a step toward her.

Too late, she thought. *Too late.*

Hannah could see that the old woman had come nearer, but not near enough to intervene—even if she'd been so inclined.

Maw abruptly reached down and grabbed Hannah by the hair again, jerking her head back and then pulling her to her feet. She bit down hard on her lip to keep from crying out.

"What punishment?" Maw said to Five Killer in English.

Hannah understood the reason for the question. Maw was asking him to name consequences of her insolence. There was no doubt that she was guilty. Maw himself must have seen the incident with the basket. Clearly he wanted Five Killer to establish where his loyalty lay here and now.

The warrior Hannah had injured cried out something in Cherokee. Hannah had heard the words before many times, and even without knowing the language she understood their meaning.

Kill her!

"What do you say?" Maw asked Five Killer, ignoring the young warrior's outburst.

Five Killer remained silent, and Hannah was certain now that his fate was at stake as much as hers.

"Are you *white* or are you Cherokee?" Maw cried, thrusting Hannah forward. "What do you say!"

"I say an eye for an eye," Five Killer answered. And he didn't hesitate. He stepped forward and struck Hannah hard. She crumpled under the blow.

He stepped over her and walked away.

Chapter Eight

Hannah sat huddled as far away from the old woman and the rest of the women as she dared. The sun was going down, and the women worked at their cook fires. The aroma of the evening meal filled the air—boiling hominy and roasting meat. She could hear a whippoorwill somewhere nearby, feel the coolness of the coming night against her skin. Her hands trembled, not so much from fear now as from the emotional exhaustion that followed it. Her jaw ached where Five Killer had struck her. She could barely stand to touch it.

What's one more bruise? she thought miserably.

Someone knelt down beside her, but she didn't look up. She kept her face hidden, and her mind raced back and forth like that frightened deer in the cornfield, trying to find some way out, some way of understanding these people.

No.

Not "these people." Him. Five Killer. *He* was the one she wanted to understand. Incredibly, she didn't feel as if she were merely a victim. It was so much more than that. She felt…shamed—and stupid. She had looked into Five Killer's eyes and she had seen something that had never been in Morgan's.

Concern for her. Compassion.

Or so she thought. She had blindly trusted her assessment of his supposed feelings, and she had been completely wrong. It seemed that she had to keep learning the same lesson over and over. She had to stop judging men by anything other than their deeds. Not their words. Not what she *thought* she saw in their eyes. Only their actions.

"Hannah," Five Killer said, and she shrank away from him, expecting another blow or another humiliation. "I've…brought you something."

When she still didn't acknowledge him, he reached out and took her hand, placing something into it. A book. *Her* book. The Psalmody she had put into her pocket the day she left Morgan's house. She clutched it to her. The shell and rawhide necklace she used as a marker was still in it.

"Read," he said, and she finally looked at him.

"It's too dark," she said, her voice husky and strange-sounding.

He immediately went to the fire and dug out a pine knot, raking it carefully onto a shorter piece of wood that was flat on one side and carrying it to her. The flame wavered back and forth, but continued to burn.

He motioned with his hand for her to open the book.

"The Third Psalm—read the verse, number six," he said.

Hannah looked at him doubtfully.

"Please," he said. He sounded so earnest that she nearly laughed. How civilized he seemed.

But she wouldn't be fooled again. She had her aching jaw to remind her of his true nature. After a moment, she opened the Psalmody. She found the verse he wanted and squinted to make it out in the dim light.

"Read it out loud," he said.

"Why?"

"Read it!"

Hannah took a quiet breath and began to read.

"I will not be afraid of ten thousands of people, that have set themselves against me round about..."

"It is what *your* father believes, is it not? And perhaps mine."

She looked away.

"Is it not?" he asked again.

"Don't!" Hannah said. "Don't you dare try to give me hope."

"Hope is all you have, Hannah Albrecht," he said quietly. "Are you afraid of dying?"

"Aren't you?" she countered.

"I am afraid of not dying well."

"You mean not being able to stand being tortured to death—burned alive—without making a sound?" she said.

"Yes," he said simply.

"My father says—" She abruptly stopped. He

was a savage. He wouldn't understand the logic of Jacob Albrecht's clerical mind.

"Go on," Five Killer said after a moment. "Your father says what?"

Hannah looked at him. "My father says that your custom of silence under torture is what perpetuates it. It helps you to fool yourselves."

"Fool ourselves?"

"Yes. If the people—the victims—you murder so savagely make no sound, then how very much easier it is for you to convince yourselves that the hideous thing you have done is not all that bad. He says if your victims cried out their suffering so loudly that even their dead ancestors could hear them—such tortures would soon end."

Hannah glanced at him. He had a slight frown, but he had been listening.

"There is no Cherokee word for guilt," he said. "Did you know that? And none for heaven or hell or for the devil. So how can we fear the loss of what you call heaven and being punished by the devil in the place you call hell? Without that fear, without the guilt, we cannot see the wrong in blood revenge—even if the victim cries out."

"But when you die, where do you think your soul goes?"

"West," he said. "To a dark place. To die in sin—for us—is to die unmourned. You see?"

Hannah didn't see at all. She closed the Psalmody and sat clutching it tightly. He reached out to finger the necklace that dangled from it.

"I will think about what your father said. But the

worst tortures I have seen were done by white men. We—the Cherokee—don't understand *their* ways.''

Your way, too, Hannah wanted to say. It took everything she had not to.

''White men don't care enough to take vengeance on the person responsible for what they believe is an injury to them,'' he went on. ''No. They go anywhere and find anybody. It doesn't matter to them. Blood is blood, even if it comes from those who trusted them, who aren't even of the same tribe. So tell me. Who is the savage then?''

With that, he walked away.

Hannah didn't see him again until the next evening, and then only from a distance. She caught him looking at her, but he made no attempt to come nearer. She wanted to think that she had misjudged him, that somehow—by hitting her—he had only been trying to save her again.

No, she admonished herself. *He is a savage—like Maw.*

Maw watched her as well. She could feel his eyes on her constantly, even when she was keeping vigil with the old woman on one of the platforms at the cornfield.

Hannah began to accompany the old woman to the river each morning to bathe and to give thanks, her long established modesty vanished somehow. She was no longer Hannah Albrecht Elway, who heretofore would have considered herself naked if she'd been seen in her shift. She was…someone else, someone whose identity was still evolving and who no longer cared about much of anything, not even her privacy.

But she needn't have concerned herself about that. There were only other women about. Apparently, even Maw himself was not allowed to spy on her here, and after the initial shock, Hannah found dunking herself in the river to be less an ordeal and more a refreshing way to begin her labors. The water was always cold, but she warmed quickly afterward. She couldn't deny that she felt better for the experience, pagan ritual or not. One morning, she even took the time to wash the shirt Five Killer had given her and to braid her unruly hair. Hannah looked up to find the old woman nearby, and she braced herself for yet another scolding for delaying whatever work had been planned for her.

But the old woman sat down on the rock beside her, closing her eyes and clearly enjoying the warmth of the sun. She said nothing. Hannah appreciated that particular aspect of Cherokee behavior. From what she had observed, there was never any pressure to converse unless one had something specific to say, and oddly enough, it was Hannah who wanted to talk today.

Hannah continued to sit, however, letting the sun dry her hair and Five Killer's shirt and listening to the rhythmic sound of the women already at work pounding and grinding the corn. The Cherokee grew two kinds of corn—one to be pounded for hominy, one to be ground for flour. Hannah realized suddenly that she seemed to be gathering tidbits of information about life here among these people, whether she wanted to or not. She had some information certainly—but she didn't necessarily understand it.

"My name is Hannah," she said abruptly and the old woman looked at her. "What is your name, please? In English. The Cherokee language...there are so many syllables—sounds—for things...the words are hard for me...to remember..." she finished lamely, certain by the old woman's expression that she had once again committed some terrible breech of Cherokee decorum.

The river flowed lazily by them. The birds twittered in the treetops.

"Wa-le-li," the old woman said finally. "Humming-bird," she added pointedly, in case Hannah wanted to compare the number of sounds in each language.

Hannah couldn't keep from smiling, both at the old woman's subtle wit and at the name itself. It was a perfect name for her. The old woman flitted from one place to the next all day long—but always with great purpose.

"Speak the rest of it," the old woman said after a moment.

Hannah glanced at her. "I...don't understand."

"White people always come from a long way off when they talk. It takes too long to get to what is in their heart. You speak now. Ask what you want to know."

Hannah was taken aback by the old woman's astuteness, and she couldn't deny that she had indeed started "a long way off" or that she, too, was flitting with a purpose.

"I...want to know about the spider," she said bluntly.

Wa-le-li looked at her.

"You said our...souls were bound together—Five Killer's and mine," Hannah said.

"He doesn't remember," the old woman said. "His sorrow was too great."

"What doesn't he remember?"

"I lived in his mother's village then. I worked the spell for him to have you."

"Me?"

"Long time ago," the old woman said, dismissing the subject with a wave of her hand.

"But I never saw him until just a few weeks before I was...captured..."

"Captured" was not the word for the way she had arrived here. "Betrayed" was the word, but she didn't want to say it.

The old woman smiled. "He saw you. He wanted you. And so he came to me to make sure it happened. I put your soul into the center of his soul. And Black Spider bound you together—you doubt this?"

"Yes," Hannah said simply.

"The love spells take their own time," the old woman said. "Sometimes they don't work until both are old. But work they do."

They sat for a time in silence while Hannah thought about the old woman's revelation.

"What did you mean?" Hannah asked abruptly. "When you said his sorrow was too great?"

"The British murdered his wife."

"Yes," Hannah said. He himself had told her that.

"His son had no mother. He was afraid to take another Cherokee wife. He wanted a white woman to take care of his child—so she could teach him how the white people think and his boy could understand their ways and be safe from them. Hi-s-ki-ti-hi thought *he* understood them, but he did not."

"Didn't he?"

"He had the love spell done and he thought he could ask your father for you. He thought your father would be glad that he had taken care of you—and the weeping woman and her children—when you were hungry and you had no food. He thought your father would let you go. But he gave you to the Red Coat, Elway, instead." The old woman stopped and took a quiet breath. "Hi-s-ki-ti-hi doesn't remember that I worked the charm for him. Maybe he doesn't remember wanting you, either."

Hannah looked out across the water, far from satisfied by the additional information she'd gleaned. Sibyl's little tale of Hannah Albrecht's Cherokee suitor must have been true—but if it was, Five Killer—Robert McLarn—had certainly never given Hannah any indication that he was the one who had taken her watercolor sketches. And even if he didn't recognize her now, wouldn't he have recognized the necklace in the Psalmody? She had seen many necklaces since she'd been in the village—but none other like it.

She sighed. All of this was simply more parts of a riddle she didn't—couldn't—understand. She understood the concept of blood revenge, however. She had even tried to carry it out.

Hannah shivered suddenly, remembering the look in Morgan's eyes when she raised his father's dueling pistol. Never had he considered the possibility that she might be privy to his plan for her or that she might have a weapon. He certainly never considered that she would have the audacity to use it. Was it true what Five Killer had said? Did Morgan still live or had she done murder?

The old woman got to her feet. "We have work to do," she said. "It will soon be time."

Hannah didn't ask time for what? She had far too much to think about. She realized as she followed the old woman into the village "square" that something was happening. There was a flurry of cleaning everywhere she looked. Even the ground was being swept clean. Five Killer and a number of the men were building new brush arbors and repairing the step-like benches in the council house. Every now and then there was the sound of breaking pottery as a woman threw a pot or bowl outside of whatever dwelling she was in and it broke on the ground. Several of the women looked up as Hannah passed by, and they all had the same expression, the veiled kind one wore to keep an outsider from knowing too much.

People kept staring at her, especially the children—when she should have been a familiar figure among them by now. One of the little boys ran up to her, yelping loudly as he tugged her skirt and then ran away again.

And Maw. Hannah's heart sank when he emerged from the council house. He was carrying something—a small basket. He stopped in front of her and held it out to her. It was filled with blackberries.

Hannah stood there, not knowing what to do. She could see more and more people gathering around now, the young woman who had made Five Killer's shirt and her lover. Five Killer himself. Hannah looked at all their faces, and they told her absolutely nothing. The only thing she knew for certain was that nothing had changed. Maw's hatred was as strong as ever. There was no mistaking it.

"Wa-le-li," Hannah said finally, keeping her eyes downcast and her voice quiet. "What am I to do?"

She glanced at the old woman, who looked back with approval. Apparently, it was not so terrible a thing if one asked for help in mastering one's ignorance.

The old woman began to speak to Maw in Cherokee, her voice soft but filled with authority. Hannah couldn't tell at all if he was listening.

"Take the basket," the old woman said to Hannah.

Hannah did so, her hands visibly trembling in spite of all she could do. She dared to look up into Maw's eyes, then immediately looked down again.

"Maw gives you these to show you he has no wish to harm you," the old woman said.

A lie, Hannah thought, trying to fight down her growing panic.

"He has no wish to harm you, but the blood of his family cries out to be avenged," Wa-le-li said.

Hannah was about to say something—anything—but Five Killer had moved directly into her line of vision and had taken up his long rifle. She glanced at him. Everything about him seemed to be saying the same thing.

No!

And she heeded it, in spite of her previous experience. She continued to stand there, clutching the basket of blackberries, her eyes downcast. Maw came so close she could feel his breath on the side of her face. But he said nothing, did nothing. Finally, he moved away.

"Lv-la," the old woman said, and Hannah followed her out of the square directly past where Five Killer stood. Her knees were trembling.

For a moment Hannah thought briefly that Five Killer was going to say something, but he didn't.

"Hannah," he called when she had gone well past him.

She stopped and looked at him.

"Well done," he said, coming close to her.

"I didn't do anything."

"If you'd spoken—said anything at all—Maw would have used it as proof that you are not worthy to come before the tribal council. He is afraid Wa-le-li will ask the council to adopt you into the tribe and he might not get what he wants—''

She moved to get by him. She had to think, to make some kind of plan. She already knew what Maw *wanted*.

He stepped into her path.

''If you try to escape, you *will* be caught,'' he said. ''Make no mistake about that. And you will lose your chance.''

''What chance!''

''The chance that the council can be persuaded to spare you,'' he said. ''It's the only way Maw will let go.''

Hannah shook her head, her mind refusing to even consider that possibility. The case he had made for her suicide in Morgan's barn had more than convinced her, even before she'd been taken. Escape was the only way, and she suspected that Five Killer knew it.

Again, she moved to get by him, and he caught her arm. She didn't try to pull free. She stood there, still holding her basket, looking straight ahead.

But she was by no means unaffected. She realized suddenly how alone she was, how alone she had always been. Not since she was a small child had anyone touched her except in anger or on the occasion of her wedding night—drunken lust. And there was no one's touch she would have welcomed—until now.

Until his.

Just the feel of Robert McLarn's warm hand on

her arm made her want to weep. She looked up at him.

How can this be? she thought.

I put your soul into the center of his soul.

No, Hannah thought wildly. That was heathen superstition—preposterous—laughable. She could easily imagine what the Elways would say about such a notion, how entertained they would be as they made fun of yet another bizarre belief held by those they considered the most lowly of the King's new subjects, fit only to provide them with slave labor and to give them cause for amusement.

"Be strong," he said, and he let go of her arm and walked away.

Hannah stood for a moment looking after him. She still didn't know if he was trying to help her or hurt her. She didn't know, any more than she had known with Morgan.

She began walking in the direction the old woman had gone. Up ahead, something was lying in the middle of the path. She picked up her pace, but she still couldn't tell....

Wa-le-li.

Hannah hurried forward, still protecting the blackberries, and she didn't see the warrior hidden in the underbrush or the arrow in Wa-le-li's side until she had already knelt down by the old woman. A cracking branch made her look up. The warrior came running in her direction, screaming, war axe raised. By instinct and instinct alone, she raised the basket at the last moment and rolled away. It was just enough to keep the axe from hitting her directly. The blow scraped along her upper arm, bringing blood. The warrior wheeled around, intending the second time not to miss.

But the crack of a long rifle sent him sprawling on top of Hannah and the old woman both. Hannah struggled to get out from under him, then lay still at the sound of still others coming. They ran on past without stopping, their war cries making her blood run cold. Again she heard the long rifle fire.

Five Killer—

The old woman moaned, and Hannah reached out to touch her. Five Killer was there suddenly, dragging the dead warrior out of the way. He deftly broke off the end of the arrow in the old woman's side and forced it through.

"Take her, Hannah! Hide her!"

"Robert—"

"She is a 'war woman.' Her scalp will be a great honor to them—hide her—!"

He left them both, running in the direction the others had gone. Hannah tried to drag the old woman to her feet. The old woman was bleeding profusely from her wound, and the pain in Hannah's arm was excruciating. Finally, Hannah managed to get a good enough grip to pull the old woman over her shoulder. She staggered under the weight, but she turned off the path and into the woods. After a moment, she knew where she was.

She kept going, struggling hard to get through the underbrush and the briars and not be seen. Finally, she located the place—the ridge with the pine trees. She couldn't carry the old woman any farther, and she had to drag her by her arms the rest of the way, finally tumbling her bodily into the hidden depression beneath the pines and scrambling in after her.

Hannah lay there panting for breath. The old woman moaned.

"Shhhhh," Hannah whispered. "They'll hear you—"

The old woman struggled for a moment to sit up.

"No!" Hannah whispered, dragging her back down. "Be still!"

Hannah could hear the war cries coming in the direction of the village and beneath those, the screams of the women and children. She closed her eyes, still holding on to Wa-le-li.

Oh, God—

She kept listening for the long rifle. As far as she knew, no one else in the village had one, not even Maw. If she heard it, then she knew Five Killer was all right.

It sounded again—once—very far off. After that, there was only silence.

Chapter Nine

 F ive days—and still the Cherokee men had not returned. No one knew where they had gone, or if they still lived. All the children and the pregnant women had gone into hiding. Where, Hannah didn't know.

Wa-le-li had once told Hannah that keeping watch over the cornfield was dangerous, and so it had been. Nearly everyone who had been on the platforms that day was killed, including the young woman who had made Five Killer a shirt. Hannah was surrounded night and day by the wails of grief. Somehow she had thought—like all white people she knew—that the Cherokee were incapable of human emotion, that they weren't civilized enough to love someone and to mourn their loss.

With no children about, the village seemed eerily abandoned. Hannah was afraid all the time, constantly expecting the Shawnee to return. She still went about her business. She found it better to keep occupied than to be jumping constantly at every sound. She searched until she found some sacks of parched corn, and with her minimal skill, she tried to keep enough pounded into hominy to feed the ones who couldn't manage the chore themselves. Once, when Hannah carried some to a nearby hut, one of the women caught her hand and pressed the back of it to her cheek in gratitude.

But Hannah had no delusions that she was still here because she was being compassionate. And she hadn't stayed because she had nowhere to go. Yes, she knew she would be no better off returning to Morgan. And she knew that, if she could survive escaping into the forest, she could only expect to be taken by the Shawnee or Maw or perhaps another Hatcher.

There was only one real reason why she stayed. She knew beyond a doubt that, regardless of all those deterrents, she would have been long gone but for Robert McLarn.

Hannah had to know what had happened to him. It was as simple as that. Her mind simply wouldn't contemplate anything else. Sometimes when she closed her eyes, she could still feel his warm hand on her arm. Sometimes she couldn't even remember what he looked like—but she remained in the village with the survivors and the relatives who stayed behind to care for them. The wounded were all like Wa-le-li—hurt too badly to be moved.

Hannah kept a vigil by the old woman's bed, doing what little she knew to do to take care of the wound in her side. She knew that Wa-le-li was "Red Paint" and apparently a medicine woman, and she quickly found the numerous pouches of dried plants the old woman kept in her log hut. But Hannah could only guess as to their use. She had no idea which might heal an arrow wound or which might bind two souls together forever.

Once, Wa-le-li had a brief respite from her fever and delirium, and Hannah tried to her ask which of the pouches held the plant she needed. The old woman waved all of them away and pointed to a pot of honey instead. Hannah reluctantly followed her instructions to pour the honey into the wound.

"Do-sv-da-li," the old woman whispered. "Keep him...away."

"I don't understand," Hannah said.

"Ant—" the old woman said impatiently. "He will come for the honey. Keep him away!"

Hannah recognized that Wa-le-li's concern was reasonable, whether she was delirious or not. She found a piece of cloth and smeared it with bear grease before sliding it under the old woman's side as a barrier.

Hannah looked around at a small sound to find one of the women standing just inside the doorway, and after a moment of gestures and a string of Cherokee words, Hannah realized that she meant to stay.

"Ha-ni-gi," the woman said. She kept pointing at Hannah's filthy clothes and at the wound on her arm and then pointing toward the river. Finally, she shooed Hannah toward the door as if she were a chicken who had come to roost in the wrong place.

Hannah smiled and went gratefully. She was so weary, and she longed to be washed clean again.

The shadows were long, and a cool breeze came up from the water. She kicked off her shoes and stepped out onto the edge of a flat rock, its rough surface still warm from the sun. The numerous small splashes of the creatures she disturbed along the way gave her no cause for concern whatsoever. She stripped off her clothes and slid into the water, immersing herself quickly, forcing herself beyond the initial shock of the cold to the exhilaration she knew would follow. She began to glide back and forth, her eyes closed, fighting down the pain in her arm until it became a dull ache. Perhaps the Cherokee were right, she thought. Perhaps one could take strength from Mother Earth like this.

After a time, she returned to the water's edge to retrieve her clothes from the rock, and she began to wash them and herself. She was too tired to think, too tired to worry.

Hannah turned her head sharply at a sound from the village. A long wavering cry. She immediately pulled herself up onto the rock and began dragging on her wet clothes. Another cry came. And then another and another.

What is it! she thought, panicked now. *The Shawnee?*

She found her shoes and hurried up the narrow path toward the village, nearly stumbling on her clinging wet skirt. She stayed in the trees to keep out of sight. She could see people in the square and in front of the council house. Numerous fires had been lit along the edge of the swept ground.

Hannah stopped abruptly. The Cherokee men

were returning, some under their own power and some carried. They seemed to come from every direction. Joyful family members rushed past her amid cries of welcome—and of sorrow.

Hannah moved closer, searching the crowd, but she couldn't spot Five Killer anywhere. She stayed among the trees, trying to see into the open-sided council house where the wounded were being taken. She couldn't tell if he was among the men lying on the ground inside or not. She didn't dare go any closer. She was an outsider, and Maw was there.

Maw.

He seemed to catch sight of her, and she jumped violently as he suddenly let loose a war cry, both arms raised. The others picked up the sound until it echoed around the square. Clearly, Maw had been victorious.

There was a sudden commotion behind her, and Hannah turned to see. The children were coming—with Five Killer at their head. He carried a little girl on his shoulder, and it was all Hannah could do not to run forward to greet him. She knew perfectly well that she had no right to do that. She meant nothing to him, nor he to her. How could there be anything between them? She kept telling herself that it was just that she was glad he was safe—because he was Colm McLarn's son and because he had once saved her life. She felt...gratitude. Nothing more.

Nothing.

Thank you, she whispered in spite of herself and

without knowing whose deity she addressed—hers or his.

He passed by very near, and she shrank into the shadows. She didn't want him to see her, because if he did, he would surely know...

Know what, Hannah? she thought wildly.

That she longed for him? And what would Morgan and his kin say to that?

The drums began to pound, calling more people into the square to greet those who had returned. She slipped past them completely unnoticed, even when she turned abruptly and ran into the forest. She took no heed whatsoever of the direction. She just kept going, away from this place, away from the feelings that were forbidden to her. She had to run, now, before she made a complete fool of herself, before she let Robert McLarn see her behave as if she truly believed that her soul had been bound to his. He was safe, and that was all she needed to know. She belonged to Morgan Elway, for better or worse— no matter that he didn't want her, that he could use her for whatever purpose he wished. He could even offer up her life.

The moon was full and bright, lighting her way. The sounds of the night were all around her—frogs and cicadas and crickets. Something crashed through the underbrush nearby. Hannah kept running, mindlessly, until she couldn't run anymore.

She sank down on her knees on a carpet of pine needles, trying to catch her breath. It was all she could do not to weep.

A sudden night breeze whispered in the pine

trees above her. She abruptly lifted her head. She had heard nothing, no one, and yet...

She kept looking around her, staring into the shadows, listening, trying to find some reason for her sudden sense that she was not alone. It had been a long time since she'd experienced that sensation, but she was still certain.

"Where are you?" she asked quietly.

The wind sighed in the pines.

Hannah was afraid now. What if Maw had seen her go and had come after her? She stood and waited, still peering into the darkness. She could feel her heart pounding.

She turned suddenly and would have run, but she saw him, standing in the trees, watching. He began to walk toward her. It seemed a long time before she could be sure, before he stepped into the dappled moonlight and she could see his face. He stopped just short of reaching her, and still he said nothing.

They stood staring at each other.

"Don't run from me, Hannah," he said finally.

There was something in his voice, something she could not have named, and Hannah didn't need any more than that. She didn't hesitate. She flung herself at him then and held fast, burying her face in his shoulder. She heard him give a deep, wavering sigh as his arms went around her. He lifted her off the ground, crushing her to him. After a moment, he set her down again.

He moved her into the moonlight and stroked her wet hair away from her face. And he kept looking at her, caressing her cheek, as if he thought he'd never see her again and couldn't believe she was here. She could feel him trembling, as she was trembling. She had to lean into him, because she didn't think her legs would hold her.

She lifted her face and looked at him, her eyes searching his. She was so happy to see him.

She reached up and tentatively pressed a kiss at the corner of his mouth, and when his mouth covered hers, she couldn't hold back a soft moan. She had never felt like this.

Never.

He held her away from him, then took her by the hand, pulling her along after him into the shadows. She didn't ask where they were going. It didn't matter. Nothing mattered, except him. And she had no doubt as to his purpose. With his free hand, he pulled the powder horn and leather bag he still wore over his head.

He stopped in a small grassy clearing and let the powder horn and bag fall. He took off his shirt and spread it on the ground, reaching for her immediately.

Her—*his*—shirt was still wet and clung to her back as he brought it over her head. He tossed it aside, and he lay down with her, bringing her close to him and stroking her body. His hands were nothing like Morgan's. They were calloused, strong, and the feel of them on her breasts made her sigh with pleasure.

He spoke to her in words she didn't understand. She didn't have to understand. She could *feel* his desire and his need. She had never been touched like this—she hadn't even known that this kind of touching existed or that she would *want* it so. She couldn't get close enough to him.

I didn't know, she kept thinking. *I didn't—*

He sat up abruptly and moved away from her, leaving her abandoned and longing for more. He sat there, his head bowed, his breathing ragged.

"What is it?" she whispered. "What—?"

He didn't answer her. She lay in the moonlight, breathless, waiting. He finally looked at her.

"Hannah—"

Someone called out from the thicket behind them, and Hannah scrambled to cover herself. After a moment, the call came again.

This time Five Killer answered, then responded to whatever the intruder called back to him.

"Maw has sent for me," he said to her, taking up his shirt. "He is the war chief. I have to go."

Maw.

For a brief moment she had forgotten all about Maw and that Five Killer would defer to him.

"Wa-le-li lives?" Five Killer asked as he helped her get her wet shirt back on.

She nodded, not trusting her voice. She felt shaky, completely undone. Her body still ached with desire.

"Go to her and stay there until someone comes for you."

"No—"

"Stay with Wa-le-li!" he whispered fiercely. "Keep out of sight. It's the only safe place for you."

"What's happening?" she asked, clinging to his arm. "Tell me."

He didn't answer her question. "You have to trust me now," he said. "You have to trust me and do as I say."

She turned away from him, but he made her look at him.

"I'm not like your father. I'm not like Morgan."

She wanted to believe that. With all her heart she wanted to believe it, but she still felt abandoned.

He stood and took her by the hand to pull her to her feet. He led her in a wide path around the village so that he could leave her at Wa-le-li's hut before he answered Maw's summons. He gave her no words of farewell or encouragement, just one final look back before he disappeared into the shadows.

Hannah stood there for a long moment, then went inside. Wa-le-li was much as Hannah had left her—except that the other woman was no longer in attendance. Hannah bathed her and made sure no ants had breached her greased cloth. Then she roused the old woman enough to feed her a bit of cooked hominy. Wa-le-li was still burning up with fever, and if she knew where she was, Hannah couldn't tell. Five Killer had said that Maw was afraid Wa-le-li would ask to adopt her. Clearly, he wouldn't have to worry about that now.

Someone was coming. Hannah dared to look outside. There was a firelit procession of some kind coming up the path—old women and one man, who had a cloth decorated with feathers wrapped around his head. They came into the hut without prelude and took Wa-le-li, carrying her back in the direction they had come. None of them spoke to Hannah. None even looked at her. She might as well have been invisible.

Hannah took her place on the floor and sat hugging her knees in the dark, listening to the incessant beating of the drums and people chanting, wondering if Five Killer was among them. Once, she dared to look outside. She could see some of the men rushing from the square and running down the hill to leap into the river. In celebration? In grief? She didn't know.

Hannah gave a quiet sigh. When she closed her eyes, she could still feel Five Killer's mouth and hands on her body. She had no regrets about what had nearly happened between them. Her only regret was the interruption. She had wanted him. She still did. And as for trusting him, she only knew one thing. He had broken away from her *before* Maw's messenger arrived.

Hannah slept for a time, until she was awakened by a commotion outside the hut. She thought it must be Wa-le-li returning, but this group of women had an entirely different purpose. They were younger, and they had come for Hannah. They escorted her firmly to the river, as if they expected her to balk at any moment. But once there, she surprised them by going into the water willingly.

The sun was just coming up, and when she climbed out again, one of the women held out what might pass for a cotton dress. Hannah was loth to part with the shirt that had belonged to Five Killer, but she put it on. She was made to sit on a nearby rock, while another of the women raked her fingers through Hannah's tangled wet hair and then began to oil it with some concoction she had in a small clay pot. The scent of it was not altogether unpleasant. It smelled...green, like grass and hay. There was a great deal of discussion among the women about the entire process, and Hannah suffered it all in silence, even having her hair tightly braided.

Finally, the women urged Hannah to get up. She followed them back up the path from the river, but they didn't return to Wa-le-li's hut. They took her to the square instead—to the middle of it—where she was left to stand alone. After what seemed a long time, the people began to gather, silently, each one of them taking a seat on the step-like benches under the shelters that surrounded the square.

Hannah had to have been the very center of attention, and yet no one seemed to look at her. She continued to stand, to let her gaze move among them in search of Five Killer. She didn't see him. She glanced to her left as a number of elderly women came into the square, their feet shuffling across the swept ground. They were carrying fresh ears of corn in their arms. They were the same ones who had come for Wa-le-li. They walked by Hannah in the same kind of solemn procession, then took their places on a front bench. A man she knew to have some kind of authority followed them.

And then Maw.

Hannah waited, her mouth dry. The sun breached

the tree tops and beat down on her. She had been
standing a long time, and her body began to sway
slightly with fatigue. She hadn't eaten, and she had
barely slept, but she didn't dare presume. If anything she might have said in response to a proffered
basket of blackberries could have condemned her,
she didn't want to chance doing anything wrong
now.

Be strong.

The words played over and over in her mind.

I'm afraid of not dying well.

Where is he? Why isn't he here?

I should have run!

No, she thought immediately. It was too late for
regrets. Now she could only stand here and wait.
Perhaps Morgan hadn't survived his wounding after
all. Perhaps she had done murder, and she deserved
whatever would happen to her.

You have to trust me—

The drums began suddenly in an urgent and
frightening pounding.

Hannah took a deep breath, and Maw stepped
forward.

Chapter Ten

Five Killer watched from the sidelines as Maw prepared to speak against Hannah. He knew her well enough to know that she was afraid, but she was doing her best not to show it.

How beautiful she is, he thought. In spite of the cuts and bruises. In spite of everything.

Hannah had borne her captivity well, enduring her humiliations in silence—except when Goingsnake upset her hard-won basket of blackberries. He had admired her that day—and still did. She was worthy of adoption into the tribe, and there were none here who didn't know it. None except Maw.

Five Killer watched the faces of the "beloved" women as well. Everyone had a voice here, but they and they alone had the power to intervene on Hannah's behalf. Wa-le-li was conspicuously absent from among them, a fact that must surely please Maw. Five Killer had no hope that Wa-le-li would be able to help Hannah's cause. The old woman was already well on her journey to the Darkening

Land, and the real truth was that he had no hope at all.

No one remarked on his delayed appearance as he moved among the people to take a seat where Hannah could see him. Perhaps it was the only thing he could do for her—let her see that she was not alone.

Lying in the moonlight with Hannah Albrecht had not been part of his plan, yet she had come to be in his mind night and day—and he didn't know how or when it began. When had he stopped thinking of her only as something necessary for his son? When had it suddenly taken every bit of his self-control to feign indifference where she was concerned? She was a captive. He could have taken her, lain with her, any time he wanted. But, he had turned away from her even when she was willing. He had told her once there was no Cherokee word for guilt. Even so, he was well acquainted with that burden. He had struggled hard to overcome it after his wife had been murdered. He was struggling now.

Hannah's gaze met his. He had asked her to trust him. Her eyes told him that she was trying. Her father had left her to starve and her husband had given her up to be murdered. How could she trust an enemy?

He moved slightly so that he could rest his hand on the pistol he carried in his belt beneath his shirt. He had stolen it from the warrior who had brought Hannah here. It wasn't the engraved one that old man Elway wanted returned—he expected that

Hatcher had that one, or Morgan himself. But it would suffice. If worse came to worse, Five Killer would do for Hannah what she had not been able to do for herself. If he could not save her, he would not let her suffer.

The feel of her and the taste of her suddenly filled his mind. Her warm, soft body under his hands. Her willing mouth against his. He had wanted her with all his heart. He still did.

Hannah.

The sun went behind a dark cloud, and the wind picked up. A few scattered raindrops fell, then multiplied into a downpour. Hannah stood, unmoving. It was a good thing for her to do. The Cherokee had long marveled that the white people seemed to be at war with the rain, particularly their women, always running from it to stay dry. It was a peculiarity he had never heard explained. Perhaps Hannah—

No. He could not think of Hannah Albrecht that way. He could not think of her in *any* way except what she was—the means to an end, the price for his son's freedom. She could not stay in his life. She could not be his answerer of questions. She could not be anything. She was someone to be used, and he would use her, betray her to save his son.

Something was happening. One of the "beloved" women was standing, and not just any "beloved" woman. This one was the mother of Maw's murdered wife. She said something to him and to the peace chief, but a child nearby began to cry, and Five Killer couldn't hear her words. The old woman's voice was not strong—it was something about her murdered daughter coming to her in a dream.

The "beloved" woman began walking to the center of the square, her steps muffled on the swept ground. She carried a swan's wing, and when she reached Hannah, she began to pass it over Hannah's body, again and again. Then she turned and walked to the huge pot filled with the holy physic that had been prepared for the Green Corn Ceremony. To drink it was to have all one's sins taken away.

She filled a gourd and began to carry it to Hannah. When the old woman reached her, she offered Hannah a drink. There was not a sound now. No crying babies. Nothing but the wind in the tall trees. After a long moment, Hannah reached for the gourd and took a drink. Five Killer realized he had been holding his breath. This was the first stage of Hannah's being taken into the tribe, of having her past life stripped from her and being made "new." Her white name, even her marriage to Morgan Elway, would be taken away.

Maw had been standing without moving, seemingly indifferent to what was taking place. Five Killer had been able to see his face clearly, but now he suddenly turned and began moving rapidly across the square toward Hannah and his mother-in-law. Five Killer saw him reaching for the war club that dangled on a leather strap over his shoulder, and he realized immediately what Maw was about to do. Maw was going to make certain that Hannah did not escape retribution.

Five Killer hurled himself forward, diving head-long over the ground to topple Maw just when he was about to strike. Five Killer had the element of surprise on his side. Maw lost his grip on the war club, and they both fell. Maw struggled desperately to get out of Five Killer's grasp and reclaim it, his rage making him strong. Hannah snatched it away. The maneuver enraged Maw, but gave Five Killer just enough time to get the pistol from his belt. He brought it to Maw's temple and pressed hard, finally dragging him to his feet.

"Hannah! Go to the river!" Five Killer whispered fiercely.

She didn't hesitate, and he followed, forcing Maw to come along with him, the pistol still at his head.

At the edge of the square he stopped.

"Maw is brave in battle against the Shawnee!" Five Killer shouted to the people, most of whom were on their feet now. "But in this he is a coward! The red coat major—the murderer of his family—still lives. Maw knows where to find him, but he is too happy to have Jacob Albrecht's daughter handed to him instead. Jacob Albrecht brought medicine to the Cherokee when the smallpox came. He is a good man. He thought Morgan Elway was a good man and he gave his daughter to him.

"But Jacob Albrecht was fooled by the red coat major, and now Morgan Elway is using Maw to rid himself of the wife he has grown tired of. Maw helps him in this and Maw calls it justice for his dead ones! Cherokee people! Is she to be punished for her husband's evil, or rewarded for her father's good! I am Hi-s-ki-ti-hi! I am so called because I killed the soldiers who murdered my wife. *I* did not wait for her clan to carry out blood revenge for her. I did it—and by doing so I did not follow the Cherokee way.

"But only the murderers' blood could dry my tears. Theirs and theirs alone. Maw has asked me—am I white or am I Cherokee? In this, I ask *you* to tell me which I am!"

Five Killer didn't wait for an answer. He headed for the river, still dragging Maw. Hannah waited by the one dugout canoe left tied to the bank. The rest he had cut loose before he took his place in the square.

Five Killer forced Maw into the canoe. He took the canoe rope and quickly tied Maw's hands. Then he motioned for Hannah to sit behind Maw, and he handed her the pistol and positioned it with the barrel against the back of Maw's head. He looked briefly into her eyes. He didn't have to say what she needed to do. He had only to trust her to do it.

He quickly located his long rifle and his supplies in the underbrush where he'd hidden them, climbed into the canoe and pushed off. He paddled hard to get to the middle of the river where the strong current would take them more swiftly away. The Cherokee warriors were still uncertain of what he would do to Maw, but they were coming down to the river, some of the younger ones beginning to shout and run along the bank. One dared to shoot an arrow. Then more followed suit. The first volley passed well over their heads because of Maw's presence, but then several stuck into the side of the dugout as the young warriors' confidence grew or the rain caused their aims to deteriorate. Five Killer couldn't say which.

"If he moves, kill him," he said to Hannah more for Maw's benefit than hers. He had only the resigned rise and fall of her shoulders to tell him that she was bracing herself to do what he asked.

He kept paddling. An arrow grazed his shoulder, breaking his rhythm. But he kept going, in spite of the pain. He had to get Hannah away from here.

Finally, there were no more arrows. He dared to look back. The dugout was far enough away, and he dropped the paddle into the bottom. He put his hand on Hannah's shoulder, then reached for the pistol. She relinquished it gladly.

Still reaching around Hannah, Five Killer drew his knife and made a swift cut on Maw's forearm, drawing blood to show that he could kill him if he wanted. Then he cut the rope binding Maw's hands.

"Jump!" he said in Cherokee.

Maw hesitated, then went over the side.

"Tell the peace chief and the 'beloved' women you were not worth killing," Five Killer called after him. "Your death would do me no honor."

He handed Hannah the pistol and began paddling again. It was easier now. The current was taking them. But he had no doubt that they would be followed. He had insulted Maw, and there was not a man, woman or child in the village who would not know he had done it deliberately and with contempt. If he didn't drown, Maw would have to save face.

It was raining still, a steady, quiet rain now. Hannah sat with her head bowed. She had looked back at him only once. He didn't say anything to her. He had nothing to say. *This* had not been part of his plan, either. He needed to think about their situation and decide the best thing to do—only his mind would not take him where he needed to go. He kept paddling, focusing only on propelling the dugout forward. Maw and his warriors would come after them on foot. It would only be a matter of time until someone found the dugouts he'd let drift away—he'd had no time to sink or damage them. And with more paddlers, they would soon catch up.

He saw Hannah wipe at her eyes. She was weeping. Why was she weeping? Or perhaps it was the rain. He chose to think it was that.

The river began to run more swiftly. He paddled the dugout hard toward the bank. There was no flat ground anywhere along the river's edge, which is why he chose the spot. He grabbed onto a large overhanging limb to stop the canoe.

"Hannah," he said, and she looked back at him, settling his question as to whether or not she'd been crying. Yes. She had.

"Can you get up into the tree?"

She immediately began to look for a way to do it, and after a moment of struggling, she managed to climb up on the overhanging limb. When she had a secure perch, he handed her the long rifle, then placed the pistol against the bottom of the dugout and fired. The shot penetrated the wood, and water began to rush in through the hole. He stayed in the dugout as long as he could, using his weight to hurry the sinking along, then he swung up into the tree with Hannah, crawling past her to take the long rifle and get to the steep embankment. She followed him, nearly falling into the water once. He had no idea whether or not she could swim, and he had to let her hang on the barrel of the long rifle to finally get her to land.

He gave her no time to rest. He slung the long rifle over his shoulder and took her by the hand, pulling her up the bank until they reached the top. He could not let her rest then, either.

"Can you keep up?" he asked, and she nodded.

Five Killer pushed hard, trying to put some distance between them and the river. It would take Maw some time to realize that they had gone ashore.

He hoped.

Hannah was as good as her word. He stayed ahead of her, but he didn't have to wait for her. Whenever he looked back, she was there, trailing after him in the rain.

He stopped finally to read the signs, so that he could tell for sure in which direction they were going. Only then did Hannah fall to her knees in exhaustion. He let her rest as long as he dared.

"Let's go," he said.

This time, he helped her to her feet, and he realized suddenly that she was wearing the same leather shoes she'd been taken captive in, shoes that would leave distinct impressions in the wet ground for Maw to follow.

He bent down to take them and stuff them inside of his shirt. She made no protest. He took her by the hand, and he had to slow his pace in order for her to keep up barefooted. Once, he thought she would surely falter, but she didn't.

"Be strong," she said, as if she thought *she* needed to encourage *him,* and she forced herself over yet another obstacle of thickets and fallen trees.

Eventually, he had to carry her. Her feet were bleeding and leaving just as clear a trail as the shoes would have done.

When the daylight began to fade, he set her down again and pulled her along with him as he began looking for some kind of shelter for the night. He couldn't chance a fire, even if he could manage to get one started. The forest was dense, but they would still have to have a place well out of sight. He needed sleep, and he needed his back protected.

He spotted some huge upright stones, but they would be too obvious a choice for someone on the run. Finally, on a steep downhill slope, he came upon several flattened boulders, one upon the other. The one resting on the ground had a ledge, an outcropping, big enough and high enough for both he and Hannah to get under. He could see no evidence that this place was traveled by humans. There was no path visible, no trampled saplings or disturbed leaves.

"Here," he said to Hannah, pointing to the ledge.

She nodded. Her body swayed with exhaustion.

Five Killer found a long branch and ran it under the outcropping to encourage any creature who might have gotten there before them to vacate.

He sent Hannah in first. She looked doubtful, but she went. He checked the ground all around the boulders, trying to make it look as undisturbed as he could. The rain fell, pooled on the boulder then ran over the edge of the outcropping. But the ground sloped downward here, enough so that they would stay dry.

He scrambled under the ledge after her. She was lying face down on the soft dirt, her body shivering. He put his hand on her shoulder, and she immediately came to him, like a small child in disgrace, who had suddenly been forgiven.

Five Killer hesitated, then put his arms around her, holding her tightly. He could feel her warm breath against his neck. She said nothing, and neither did he. She was still shivering. After a moment, she lifted her head to look at him. Her eyes stared into his, her lips parted.

Her hair had come undone, and he reached up to brush the wet strands and the bits of leaf and dirt off her face. She closed her eyes when he touched her. Without even realizing it, he leaned toward her just enough to let his forehead rest against hers. Their breaths mingled. She opened her eyes.

And he was lost.

His mouth found hers and there was no holding

back. He wanted her too much, had waited too long. He would take her now.

Her body strained against his, needing this as he did. He rolled on top of her, fumbling for a moment between them to free himself from his breechcloth. Her dress was clinging and wet as he dragged the bottom of it upward out of his way. Then he entered her, hard and deep. She gave a soft moan, and he covered her mouth with his. She faltered only a moment before she returned the kiss, before her body rose to meet his in a struggle as old as time. To give. To take.

The pleasure burned in him and in her, brighter and brighter. Whatever else happened, he—they— would have *this*.

His hand clutched her breast. He wanted to look into her eyes. He wanted to see them, so that he would know her heart. But he had no time. There was no time for either of them.

At the end, he heard her whisper his name.

"Robert. Robert—!"

"What happened to your son?"

Hannah lay in his arms, waiting for him to answer, but no answer came.

"Did I...hurt you?" he asked, the question so unexpected to her that it took her a moment to reply.

"No," she whispered. There had been no pain— only joy. Didn't he know that? Hadn't he been able to tell? Perhaps not, she thought sadly. Perhaps men never knew, one way or the other.

"Sleep," he said. "We have a long walk."

"Where are we going?"

"Sleep, Hannah."

"Your wife—what was her name?"

"I don't want to talk—"

"Tell me something—anything—" she said, because she knew so little about him, and she was desperate for some detail to hold on to.

He sighed. "Her name was...Go-ge-yi," he said after a moment. "Summer. She was like the summer—bringing joy with her wherever she went. People were happy when she came. Sad when she left. I took her for my wife when I was sixteen. My son was born the next spring. He was almost six years old when the British soldiers killed his mother. They raped her and then they burned her. She was able to save the boy by letting them take her. Your father told me that men who murdered the innocent for hire were cursed. He showed me the passage in the Bible. He said they would be punished—if not in this world, then the next. But she was..." His voice trailed away.

Hannah didn't ask when he had spoken to her father—she thought she already knew. She said nothing. She waited. His words had been flat, toneless, but she could still feel his sorrow and his terrible sense of loss.

"A Cherokee marriage is different from your kind," he said finally. "If it's wrong, if there is no love between the two or if one of them is not a good person, then they can come before the people at the Green Corn Ceremony. The Green Corn Ceremony is the time for…beginning again. For righting old wrongs and ending unhappiness. For Goge-yi and me—there was no question of asking to be free of each other. But that didn't matter. The British soldiers ended the marriage for us.''

Hannah lifted her head so that she could see his face. "I'm sorry," she said.

"There was nothing I could do for her—''

He didn't say anything else, and Hannah moved closer to him. Her body had grown cold again, and she shivered. She didn't want to sleep. Maw would find them. She knew that. Nothing—*nothing*—would stop him. She pressed a small kiss against Five Killer's cheek. It seemed to take him by surprise, as if he had expected passion between them, but not tenderness.

"Hannah…''

She kissed the corner of his mouth, letting her tongue lightly touch as she did so. He turned to her. This time he went more slowly. He began to stroke her body, the way he had when they lay together in the moonlight. He touched her, tasted her. He suckled her breasts, and her head arched back in pleasure. This was not what she'd known with Morgan. This was—

She had no name for it.

Yes, she did. She had several. *Hi-s-ki-ti-hi.* Five Killer. Robert McLarn.

My father should have given me to you, she thought sadly.

It was incredible to her how strongly she needed to be with him, she who had always been so careful, worked so hard to never need anything beyond whatever life—her husband, her father—had given her. But now she needed this man. She had to take him inside her. She had to feel his weight on her body. She had to breathe his breath. Her soul had been put into the center of his soul. And for a brief moment perhaps, she could lead him away from his sorrow.

Wa-le-li had been right. Hannah did long for him, and would for the rest of her life. Now she gave herself up to him completely. Her eyes closed. Her body opened like a flower to receive him. She would wrap herself around him and she would never let go.

"Hannah!" he whispered, and she looked at him, into his eyes.

And it was herself she saw there. No one else.

The time for beginning again...

I will forget all that I was, and I will be his.

Hannah woke up alone. She lay under the shelter of the rock, listening, afraid to come out into the open. It was no longer raining. The sun was coming up. She could hear water dripping off the leaves, the sound waxing and waning in the early morning breeze. The birds were singing, a squirrel chattered somewhere in the branches overhead.

She closed her eyes and tried to sort through the last twenty-four hours. She hadn't understood precisely what had happened in the square yesterday. She understood only that Robert McLarn had saved her.

But where was he now? Her elbow bumped something. Her shoes, sitting neatly beside her, and the pistol. She felt the tears well in her eyes. Was this a gesture of kindness and concern for her safety—or a subtle indicator that she was now to go her own way alone?

She lay there, determined to wait for him, determined to believe that he would not have left her here without a word. Her belly rumbled with hunger. How long had it been since she had eaten? She couldn't remember. But hunger didn't keep her from seeing a kind of topsy-turvy irony here. She was indeed guilty of an illicit alliance with the Cherokee who had dared approach her father and ask for her—now.

But Morgan had thought her guilty before the fact, and he had punished her for it. She didn't think he would have given her over to Maw quite so readily if he hadn't believed Sibyl's tale. No doubt he had convinced himself that, in light of her deceit in the matter of her Cherokee suitor—someone he considered *less* than a man—he was perfectly justified in doing it.

Two birds with one stone.

He had rid himself of his sullied wife and he had pacified Maw.

Or so he thought.

Hannah wondered what he would think if he knew that her lover and his Cherokee slave were one and the same.

Hannah must have dozed for a time. When she opened her eyes again, it was full daylight, and she simply couldn't stay there any longer. She crawled out into the open. With some difficulty, she managed to get her shoes on. Then she limped painfully in an ever widening circle trying to discover where she was and whether or not there was anything edible in the vicinity.

She carried the pistol in her hand—she had no pocket in which to put it. The dress the Cherokee women had given her was more like a shift. She moved carefully from tree to tree, so as to never be in the open. The ground was wet. Decayed leaves stuck to her shoes and the bottom of the dress, as she tried to step so as not to leave footprints.

She couldn't find anything to eat. The blackberries were long gone. Once, she startled a flock of mourning doves, and they noisily took flight out of the underbrush. She knew them to be ground feeders, and she went looking for whatever they might have been after. She found nothing but a patch of tall grass gone to seed. She began to pull on the long shoots until they pulled free of the plant, then chewed the tender ends.

After a time, Hannah grew too weary to search anymore. She returned to the rocks. She was thirsty, and she took a long drink from a small pool of rainwater that had collected in a depression on the flat surface of the rock.

The shadows were growing long. She had been gone longer than she thought. She had to work hard to fight down her rising fear. What if she had wandered farther than she thought, and Five Killer had returned and found her gone? What if he never returned at all and never would?

No, she kept telling herself. *He wouldn't do that.* And, all the while, she knew that she should have no expectations regarding Robert McLain. If he had left her here and gone his own way, then she should not be surprised.

Hannah abruptly turned her head at a far off sound and she listened intently to identify it. The sound came again, much nearer. Some kind of animal. She stood poised to run.

Dogs, she suddenly realized. She knew the stories of what dogs gone wild could do to livestock and humans. They were more feared along the frontier than wolves and catamounts were. She had heard tales of settlers who had to shut themselves up in their cabin for days because of the dog packs. It was that rumor more than any that led her father to decide she should take up firearms, that and her stepmother's mounting hysteria.

The dogs were after something. She could tell by the baying. She turned and began climbing the pile of rocks, not realizing until it was too late that a man dressed in buckskin was her main concern. He came after her at a run, grabbing at her heels as she struggled upward. She dropped the pistol, and it clattered into a crevice below her.

"Wait!" the man yelled at her. "I'll not harm ye!"

Hannah didn't believe him, and the dogs were at the base of the rocks now, excited, barking loudly. Hannah dragged herself onto the next flat boulder to get higher still, using a sapling growing out of a crack for leverage. The man had her by her ankle, and he kept pulling. She kicked at him until he let go. The dogs jumped and nipped at her heels and skirt. The branch gave away, and she tumbled backward.

The man grabbed her and held her tight, forcing the wind out of her. She kept struggling.

"Here she is!" he yelled. "I got her!"

She fought to get away from him, hitting him hard with both fists. He jerked her around and shook her.

"Easy, mistress! It's rescued you are! I mean ye no harm!"

Rescued? she thought wildly.

Hannah didn't believe him, not for an instant.

He shook her again. "Are you understanding me, mistress! Try hard now. You wouldn't be the first gone addled by such an ordeal—" he began.

She shoved him hard in the chest, making him stagger backward, but he didn't let go. There were soldiers coming—British foot soldiers—and two officers on horseback. One of them was Morgan.

Hannah stopped struggling. She stared at him in disbelief as he approached.

"Bring my wife down gently, Willoughby," he said to the man who still restrained her. The man did so immediately, leading Hannah firmly by the elbow to where Morgan waited as if he were about to present her to her escort at a fancy dress ball.

Hannah continued to stare at Morgan, incredulous both that he really was alive and that he should have associated himself with anything even vaguely resembling her rescue.

"You'll not forget me, Major," Willoughby said. "Fair is fair, and you know that. You'll tell them I get the fee for finding her. You'll verify what occurred here to the gentlemen? You'll say that it was me and my dogs what found her?"

Morgan ignored him.

"Come, come Hannah. Be reassured. There is no cause for alarm," Morgan said. "You are safe now. Your captor can trouble you no longer."

Hannah looked past him. Five Killer was being dragged along behind two soldiers, who had him bound and tethered. His face was a mass of cuts and bruises. One eye was swollen shut. The leather strap around his neck was far too tight. He could barely breathe.

She took a step toward him, then faltered.

She would have gone to him but for one thing. Everything about him told her not to. It was the same as that time when Maw had offered her the blackberries, and she would have inadvertently given him exactly what he needed to expedite killing her.

No, Five Killer was telling her again. *No!*

He didn't want her to acknowledge him in any way or to react to what had been done to him. She knew that as clearly as if he had spoken. And it took every ounce of strength she had to turn away from him.

Morgan's eyes traveled over her. Even in her Sunday best, he and his family had always found her wanting. She could imagine what he must be thinking now. She couldn't have been more unkempt. She could feel the eyes of the soldiers on her as well, the speculation as to how many Cherokee bucks had taken her.

"Can you travel, my dear?" Morgan asked solicitously.

She looked up at him, wondering in whose nightmare she found herself. Did Morgan think she would not remember that *he* had given her over to Maw's minions? Perhaps her shooting him had addled his memory, and he really didn't recall the circumstances of her capture or that she had tried to kill him.

But how clearly *she* could remember. At the moment of her capture, she had had no thought of taking her own life. Nor had she had any thought of trying to save herself by taking aim at Hatcher when he was about to put his hands on her. Her only thought had been to injure the man ultimately responsible for her betrayal. It didn't matter that she also called him "husband."

"How did you find me, Morgan?" she asked.

"A reliable source was persuaded to reveal the village where you were held," he said.

"Persuaded? How?"

Morgan smiled—and ignored her question. "Of course, we arrived there a bit late. This slave here had already absconded and taken you with him. But no matter. I have him now. The bargain is off."

"What bargain?"

He was smiling again, but he didn't mean it.

"It's nothing you need concern yourself about." He lowered his voice. "Did he…harm you, Hannah?"

"No, he did not," she said, knowing exactly what he meant and knowing, too, that in spite of Morgan's discretion, his lieutenant had heard the question.

"Indeed?" Morgan said. "I must say I am surprised by his restraint. It really is the most amusing thing."

She gave him a quizzical look.

"That he is Colm McLarn's by-blow," he said pointedly. "It turns out that the Scotsman—for all his airs—is not at all particular about how and where he scratches an itch."

Hannah didn't respond to the remark. She could just see Five Killer out of the corner of her eye. He was on his knees now, and she drew an unsteady breath.

"Willoughby!" Morgan yelled. "Lead us out!"

He spurred his horse on, leaving Hannah standing, his token consideration for her abruptly vanished.

"Morgan!" Hannah called after him, and surprisingly he stopped and turned in the saddle to look back at her. Hannah walked closer.

"What happened to the village?" she asked.

He gave a half smile. "What village?" he asked lightly, spurring the horse on.

Morgan's young lieutenant rode up, and he was clearly at a loss as to what he should do. She couldn't help but feel a little sorry for him, she who had often found herself in a quandary where pleasing Morgan Elway was concerned. The young lieutenant obviously didn't want to leave an officer's lady to hobble along as best she could—even one taken by the Indians, and yet he couldn't give up his mount unless his commanding officer gave him leave to do so.

He abruptly spurred his horse and caught up with Morgan. It took him a moment to get Morgan to acknowledge his presence, then he put forth an urgent-looking question and gestured in Hannah's direction once. Morgan completely ignored him. The young officer persisted, and Hannah heard two words.

"She walks."

The lieutenant hesitated, then gave up, casting Hannah a look of embarrassment and apology before he took his place alongside Morgan at the head of the line.

But Hannah had no time for either of them. Her only concern was Five Killer and what they were going to do to him. And there was still the matter of Maw. Morgan was oddly...cheerful. Perhaps he had no reason to worry about Maw anymore.

She stood and waited, expecting Five Killer to be escorted past her. Two young boys were bringing along the dogs. The dogs were on leashes now, but they were still excited by her presence. The boys had to struggle hard to keep them away from her.

The soldiers who were guarding Five Killer followed, but the boys had stopped and waited for her to join the procession. She had no choice but to go on ahead of them. How hard it was not to look back. Sometimes she could hear some sound from Five Killer—when he stumbled or was hit.

Be strong, she kept thinking. *Be strong—*

She concentrated on putting one foot in front of the other, her eyes on the ground. She was afraid of the dogs, knowing that they still considered her quarry. Once, she looked up to find the man, Willoughby, at her side, when she had thought Morgan sent him on ahead of the column to make sure the way was safe. It startled her to see him there so suddenly, but she tried not to show it.

"How are you faring, mistress?" he asked. His tone was kindly enough, but she didn't answer him. She just kept going.

One foot in front of the other.

"Take the dogs to the rear," he said to the boys, and they struggled to get them past her.

"The major will be stopping soon," Willoughby said to her. "Ye can rest then, mistress."

This time, Hannah looked at him. Yet another of Morgan's subordinates feeling sorry for her, she thought. It was clear that they didn't understand the situation.

"You get a fee if I'm returned, is that right, Mr. Willoughby?" she asked quietly so that the soldier walking nearby wouldn't hear.

"Aye, mistress. It is."

"Who is paying it?"

"Your father, the Reverend Albrecht. And Colm McLarn. They heard the major was going out looking for you. The two of them sent me along because

I know these parts. The purse doubles if I bring you home safe and sound.''

"I see. It makes me very unhappy, Mr. Willoughby, that the Cherokee prisoner is being mistreated—perhaps on my behalf. I don't want that to happen. Do you understand what I'm saying to you, Mr. Willoughby?''

"Aye, mistress. I understand—but I've no influence in military matters. And your husband has good reason to want him punished if he had a hand in what happened to you—''

"Too bad, Mr. Willoughby,'' Hannah interrupted. "Of course, you know this prisoner is Colm McLarn's son. I tell you now, sir, there is *no* cause to injure him on my account. I would be burned, but for him. Perhaps McLarn won't be so interested in doubling purses if he thinks his son suffered unjustly on the journey back and *you* did nothing to stop it—''

"Mistress, how can I—'' he began in protest.

"On the other hand,'' Hannah interrupted again. "Perhaps he would…triple a purse if the opposite were true. Especially if someone told him of your…intervention.''

She glanced at him. She could feel how hard he was trying to weigh the consequences of whatever choice he made here. She had no doubt which alternative he would choose. Unless she was very much mistaken, well-filled purses meant a great deal to this man. The problem was how to get around Morgan.

Willoughby dropped back in the line. "Don't

worry, mistress,'' he said loudly for the nearest soldier's benefit. "We'll be stopping soon."

But Morgan didn't stop. Even when the sun disappeared behind the trees and there was barely enough daylight left to see by, even when his lieutenant had to get off his lathered animal and walk. Hannah could no longer keep up the pace. Her knees were beginning to tremble. She felt lightheaded, and it became increasingly difficult for her to think clearly. She kept stumbling over the rough ground.

One of the soldiers offered her his arm.

"The going is hard here, Mistress Elway," he said.

But Hannah didn't want his help. She wanted—

She didn't know what she wanted.

Yes, she did.

One foot in front of the other.

Her mind would not consider anything beyond that.

Be strong. Be strong!

Five Killer could barely see Hannah in the waning light, but he could hear her. She was humming. That same song that seemed to forever haunt his life. His white father had favored it. And one of Morgan Elway's soldiers. The first time he'd heard Hannah sing it was when he found her in the Cherokee village. She had been standing—then lying—dazed in the rain, and all the while singing snatches of that song. He tried not to think about that. He tried to think instead that as long as he could hear singing now, he knew she was all right.

He could feel someone close to him, and he turned his head painfully to the side, trying to see out of his swollen eye. The scout, Willoughby, who seemed to need to shadow him as the column moved along, was back again. Five Killer would have to say that the man was good at what he did— good at keeping arrogant and ignorant British officers like Morgan heading in the right direction and keeping watch for trouble. But Willoughby's dogs were the only reason Five Killer had been caught. They had cornered him, just as they cornered Hannah. Even now, Five Killer could hear the "huffing" sound they made as they strained their leashes at the sight of their master. Willoughby paid them no mind.

"So ye be Colm McLarn's bastard," he said when he was sure Five Killer had noticed him.

"Yes," Five Killer answered easily, refusing to take offense from the truth. The man smiled.

"I remember ye, Robbie. I remember seeing ye at Trading Ford on the Yadkin River. Always tagging along with McLarn ye were, big as ye please. Ye must have been no more than four or five—"

"Is there a point to all this remembering, Willoughby?" Five Killer asked, ignoring Willoughby's familiarity and the use of his white name. He kept his attention on Hannah. He could just barely make out her form in the darkness, and he thought for a moment she had fallen.

"Just passing the time, son," Willoughby said.

"I don't think the Major would like the sound of that," Five Killer said, still trying to see if something had happened to Hannah. He glanced at Willoughby. The man hadn't missed his interest in her, and this time, Five Killer didn't bother to hide it.

"Will the Major stop soon?" he asked quietly in Cherokee.

"No," Willoughby answered.

"Ask him."

"Elway keeps going no matter who asks. His woman is very tired. His men do not like to see the woman struggle to keep up. The red coat lieutenant tells Elway—let your woman rest, but he says no."

Willoughby was giving him far more information than he should have, and Five Killer knew he should be wary of the man—but Hannah faltered again, and then there was some kind of commotion surrounding her.

"Can you give her food?" Five Killer asked abruptly.

"Aye," the man said in English. "That I can do."

He left Five Killer and moved up the line to Hannah, but then the line abruptly halted. Willoughby came back almost immediately.

"Take him to the Major," he said to the soldiers guarding Five Killer.

The soldiers immediately jerked Five Killer forward by the tether around his neck. He didn't get his hands up in time to get a finger under it and he could barely breathe. The soldiers wasted no time going to see what Morgan wanted, pulling him hard all the way. He was leashed as the dogs were leashed—only he was less valuable.

They stopped just short of where Hannah lay on the ground, restraining him when he would have kept going.

"You—slave—" Morgan said, pointing at Five Killer. "Carry her!"

There was an immediate protest from the lieutenant and a murmuring among the soldiers in earshot.

"Sir, surely—" the lieutenant said.

"You interfere here and I will have you flogged, Lieutenant!" Morgan yelled. "Cut his hands loose!"

The lieutenant stepped forward and cut the rawhide binding Five Killer's wrists.

"Now carry her!" Morgan said.

The tether around Five Killer's neck remained, and he loosened it as best he could with his numb fingers. Hannah lay on the ground, not moving, and Five Killer bent down to get her. She made a soft sound when he lifted her, but did not rouse until he had gone a few yards.

"What—what is it—?"

"Be still," he whispered.

"I can walk—" she said, trying to get down.

"No."

"Morgan won't—"

"Morgan thinks to humble you by making you suffer this. Be still. Let me have you as long as I can."

She stopped struggling, and her head rested against his shoulder.

How good she felt to him. Five Killer had thought never to touch her, never to feel her body close to his again. And yet some part of him was glad that things had worked out the way they had. Morgan, by capturing him, by capturing them both, had saved him from having to make the most agonizing decision of his life. Now he would never know which of them he would have sacrificed— Hannah or his son.

Hannah murmured something, and his arms tightened briefly around her in the futile effort to make her feel all that she meant to him. Under the cover of darkness, she reached up and briefly touched his heart with the palm of her hand. Eventually, she would know of his bargain with her husband. She would know that he had intended all along to take her back to the man who wanted her dead.

And the reason wouldn't matter.

He became aware of someone laughing softly behind him.

Willoughby.

"Major's done put the fox in the hen house now, ain't he, son?"

Chapter Eleven

Hannah stood in the oppressive heat and waited, intensely aware of the smells around her.

Mud and manure.

Slops and garbage pits.

White people who didn't greet each day by washing themselves in the river.

Civilization.

There was no breeze because of the high log stockade. The sun beat down on her. She was so weary. It became harder and harder for her to stand without swaying. Her throat ached with unshed tears, and she had to bite down on her lip to keep her mouth from trembling. Sweat drenched her back and ran down her ribcage under her baggy dress. But she stayed where she was. She could feel everyone's eyes on her, feel them making their judgments about whether or not she could really be Major Elway's abducted wife. She knew how disheveled and wild she must look, and she had to work hard to seem oblivious to their scrutiny. She had only one concern. Five Killer.

Where is he?

Morgan stood impatiently in the shade of the fort watchtower, refusing to let his orderly placate him with something to drink. Why he and his soldiers were having to wait here, Hannah didn't know, but clearly there was not a person in the fort or camped around it who hadn't turned out to witness their—*her*—return. Even the Elway wives were in attendance—dressed in all their finery, as if they were spending the day picnicking on an English manor house green. They greeted Morgan with great show, but they made no attempt to acknowledge Hannah. They only stood and stared at her and whispered behind their fans, as if any overt contact with her might bring them bad luck and result in their being abducted as well.

Only "luck" had had nothing to do with Hannah's predicament. It had to do with her father's choice for her husband.

Hannah gave a quiet sigh. Whether the people here knew it or not, she deserved their judgmental looks—but not for the reason they supposed. They thought that she had been "ruined" and was therefore unfit for decent society. The truth was that she didn't feel ruined at all. She had sinned certainly, and sinner that she was, she needed her father's wisdom very much right now, the kind of wisdom he always had so readily at hand for other people. But, as always, he would be making his rounds among the various settlements, and even if he were here, perhaps he couldn't explain why she felt no remorse. The only thing she felt was longing for the man her husband must surely hold in chains.

She looked up as a ripple of laughter started with the Elway wives and traveled through the crowd. All eyes were once again riveted in her direction. Hannah stiffened her back and lifted her chin.

Let them look, she thought. She knew that only by satisfying their curiosity would she be able to find any peace. She had learned that in the Cherokee village.

Hannah barely remembered the journey to the fort, save when she was being carried in Five Killer's arms. That she remembered acutely. She had no idea how long they traveled before Morgan finally allowed them all to rest. When they stopped, Five Killer had been taken to the rear of the column, and it broke her heart to be parted from him. She couldn't see him when the line started up again, nor when they reached the main trading path. The going had been much less difficult along the path. Eventually, they reached the fort, and Hannah still didn't know what had been done with him.

"Mr. Willoughby," she said quietly, knowing he would be somewhere close at hand. He had taken the promise of the purse very seriously.

"Mistress Elway?" he answered almost immediately.

"Why is the general keeping us here?"

"Don't know, mistress. It ain't to the major's liking, I can tell ye."

"Can you find out?"

He looked toward an open doorway where the general must be, judging by the number of officers who came and went. "I'm thinking I can't get in there, mistress."

"I'm thinking you can get anywhere you please," Hannah countered.

Morgan's lieutenant abruptly appeared in the doorway. He stepped out onto the porch and then walked briskly across the compound to where Morgan stood. He saluted and said something to him, and Morgan immediately headed for the log building the lieutenant had just exited. Hannah expected the lieutenant to follow, but he didn't. He came to her instead.

"The general wishes to speak to you, Mistress Elway," he said, not quite meeting her eyes.

She glanced at Willoughby, afraid suddenly, afraid of what Morgan might have said happened the day she was captured.

"Very well," she said to the lieutenant.

The lieutenant offered her his arm, Hannah thought as much for the benefit of their audience as in the name of courtesy. Or perhaps she looked as unsteady as she felt. She took it, and he escorted her past the Elway wives to the same structure Morgan had entered.

"Can you tell me what the general wants?" she asked the lieutenant.

"It's not for me to say, Mistress Elway," he answered. "Please wait here."

He gestured to a half-log bench on the crudely done porch, and Hannah sat down, resting her back against the wall. The heat was a bit less oppressive here, but she soon discovered that she was all too apparent to the staring women. She had no place to look save her lap. She turned slightly, until she could see through the open door where Morgan and the lieutenant had gone.

There were several men in the room besides them—soldiers of varying rank—and a young Indian boy whose job, it seemed, was to keep the flies moving. Hannah had the sudden mental picture of Five Killer perhaps doing the same thing when he was a boy and still with Colm McLarn.

Two of the soldiers pored over a map hanging on the far wall. A small mouse scurried from behind a water bucket, down a table leg and into the corner.

She could see a ruddy-faced officer seated at an ornate mahogany desk. The desk was quite a fine piece of furniture and very out of place in a log fort—as was the man behind it. He was clearly miserable in the heat and completely unable to ignore it as the rest of the men were. She assumed that he must be newly arrived at the garrison since her abduction.

From her vantage point, Hannah had no difficulty hearing the conversation or seeing the only civilian in the group, Colm McLarn.

"I am telling you, Major Elway has no' kept his word, General," McLarn was saying.

"My word? And what *word* is that?" Morgan said. Even without being able to see his face, Hannah knew from his mocking tone that he was feigning his surprise—but not his contempt. He was very good at making anyone who dared oppose him feel stupid and small.

"Your word to my son! General, I can bring fifty men here who heard him."

"Your so-called *son* didn't keep his part of the bargain, McLarn," Morgan said.

"Your wife is returned to you—"

"Yes—but no thanks to your Cherokee bastard."

"He went after her—with your blessing—did he not!"

"It was Willoughby who found her and gave her over to me, McLarn. And if he hadn't, I have no doubt that I myself would have recovered her in good time. Your bastard—my slave—was to bring her back here before the spring. The fact is he didn't return her at all. He left her abandoned and starving in the back country. Whatever agreement we had is null and void on that basis alone. You can't expect me to honor something said to a savage—*your* son or no—when he didn't fulfill his part, surely. As far as I'm concerned everything is just as it was. Your complaint carries no weight with me, McLarn."

"Does your word mean nothing!"

"It was my father who struck the bargain! I was hardly myself that day. I had just been wounded. My father is old and addled. *He* wanted this Cherokee bastard of McLarn's to find his missing dueling pistol, for God's sake!"

"You, sir, are a lying dog—!"

"Gentlemen!" the general said, but Hannah was

no longer listening. She sat there, trying to understand. Old Mr. Elway had somehow appointed Five Killer to bring her back to Morgan?

No, she thought. Five Killer was the one who guessed—knew—what Morgan had planned for her. He was the one who—

It couldn't be true.

Of course, it could, she thought immediately. She had just assumed that he had escaped from Morgan's enslavement, but he had been sent to get her. He had fooled her from the very beginning, fooled Maw, fooled them all.

She understood that part of it, at least. What she didn't understand was why?

"Mistress Elway," the lieutenant said in the doorway. "Will you come inside now."

Hannah continued to sit on the bench. The lieutenant finally stepped forward and took her arm. She went with him, but her mind was in turmoil.

The room was more occupied than she had thought. Five Killer stood on the far side, near an opposite door, and she couldn't keep from faltering when she saw him. Somehow his being there made it all the worse.

It took a great deal of effort on her part to look at the men in the room. At Morgan, who took no pains to hide his annoyance. At Colm McLarn, who felt sorry for her. And finally at Five Killer.

She found him waiting for her to do just that. His hands were bound, and he still had the rawhide tether around his neck. For once, he held her gaze, but it was he who finally looked away.

"Mistress Elway," the general said. "Can you answer?"

But Hannah hadn't heard the question.

"Mistress Elway?" the general said again. He kept mopping his brow with a fine lawn handkerchief.

She looked at Five Killer. Never once had she felt she was being held against her will in the escape from Maw. Nor did she sense it when she had lain with him all night. She *was* still a captive, of course, and on her way back to Morgan, but she had been completely ignorant of that fact. She had never once suspected what he had been about. How easy she must have made it for him.

What was it Willoughby had said to her? She had been rescued? It hadn't been that at all. Robert McLarn had had his vengeance on Morgan Elway—and her. To return her, for whatever reason, was one thing. To make her love him in the process was unthinkably cruel. He must know that she had given him everything of herself she had to give— and all the while he had been working to keep his bargain. It wasn't for her sake that he'd saved her from Maw. It was for the sake of some kind of arrangement he'd made with the Elways. What could she have possibly meant to him when she lay in his arms if he had planned all the while to return her to Morgan?

Nothing.

Had it made his revenge all the sweeter?

"Forgive me, sir," Hannah said to the general. "I am most weary and I regret to say that I am...finding myself...near overcome by the heat." She licked her lips and tried to concentrate on what she wanted to say. "By your leave, sir, if I could just...go now."

"Yes, yes, of course, Mistress Elway," the general said immediately, seizing upon her request, almost in relief so as not to have to deal with the situation any longer. "And it is I who should ask for forgiveness." He looked at Morgan. "I was led to believe that you were up to this—but I see now that that is not the case."

The general waved the hand holding the handkerchief at one of his subordinates, a red-haired and freckled-faced boy corporal, who immediately snapped to attention. "Escort Mistress Elway to the surgery."

"No, please. I don't require a doctor," Hannah said.

"I insist, Mistress Elway. I regret our neglect of you and I must now be reassured that we have done you no harm, you see. You will be escorted to our doctor and with his approval you will then rest in your husband's quarters until such time as you feel up to discussing the matter of your return." He waved his hand again and the corporal took her arm.

The corporal was determined to escort her out the opposite door, directly past Willoughby, who she hadn't known had come into the room—and directly past Five Killer.

Hannah kept her eyes straight ahead, lest she betray how deeply she felt his duplicity. Indifference was the only defense she had left.

"Hannah—" he said as she walked by.

She kept going.

"Hannah!" he cried as she was about to go out the door.

She stopped, but she didn't turn around. He said something to her in Cherokee—something low and urgent. She looked at him finally, and he dared to take a step in her direction. His audacity sent the room into an uproar.

The corporal shoved Hannah through the doorway to the outside. She heard Colm McLarn swear and the sound of something overturning. She couldn't keep from stumbling against the wall.

"Don't you worry, Mistress Elway," the corporal kept saying, trying to keep her from falling and from seeing what was happening. "He ain't going to get loose again."

Hannah's hands were shaking, and it was all she could do not to cry. It was incredible to her that—in spite of everything—she didn't want Five Killer hurt.

What is wrong with me? she thought wildly. She had to think what to do. She had to get away from here—and she had absolutely no place to go. There was still the matter of how much Morgan remembered and what he had planned. It occurred to her that she was little better off now than she had been with Maw.

"Where is the surgery?" she asked abruptly.

"It's down yonder, mistress," he said. "That little building across the way."

"And the...necessary?"

The corporal blushed beet-red. "That way, mistress," he said, pointing in the same general direction.

"I can find my way alone," Hannah said. "To both places."

"The general was particular you should be escorted—"

"Please," she said. "I have been prisoner long enough. Allow me this small freedom."

He swallowed, then made up his mind. "Yes, mistress," he said and trotted away.

Hannah walked toward the surgery, but she didn't go inside. She went around to the back, looking for someplace to hide for a little while at least. She noted with relief that there were no windows on the back side through which she might be watched. A number of wooden wash tubs had been turned upside down on the ground to drain. She sat down on one and tried not to cry.

I will not remember. I will forget him. I will forget everything.

Everything!

Who had he been when she lay in his arms? Robert McLarn? *Hi-s-ki-ti-hi?*

She looked around sharply at a sound. Willoughby stood there with a bundle of clothes under his arm.

"Ye look...poorly," he said.

"I'm quite all right," she answered.

"I came to give ye these," he said, holding out the bundle. "Some of the women managed to come up with a whole set, I reckon."

Hannah looked at the bundle, but she made no attempt to take it.

"The sooner ye get the burrs out of your hair and get back to looking like a white woman, the better it'll go for ye."

Hannah glanced at him and then took the bundle, holding it in her lap as if it were a fragile thing she had to worry about breaking. She could feel Willoughby staring at her.

"Thank you," she said after a moment, hoping he would go away.

"It weren't no hardship," he said, and she nearly laughed.

"Not if you're the one with the musket," she said. She doubted that anyone here had contributed even a single article of clothing willingly.

"The women—they don't know what was done to ye," Willoughby said. "It makes them...scared. Ye are the living breathing proof of what could happen to them."

"Nothing was done to me," Hannah said. "I worked for the Cherokee from sun up to sun down—just like I did for Morgan Elway."

"They're waiting to see how he's going to be about this, too. By now they've already heard from his men how hard he treated ye on the way back. Ye understand everyone here will take their lead from the major."

"Yes, I understand."

"If he acts like he thinks ye be ruined, then ruined ye are."

"I understand," Hannah said again.

"I expect ye do."

They stared at each other.

"If you would tell the women I'm very…grateful for their…generosity." It was Willoughby's cue to go away, but he didn't take it.

"I was thinking ye might want to know what *he* said to you in there," Willoughby said quietly.

"No," she said. "I do not." Her voice wavered, in spite of all she could do.

He looked at her a long moment. "If I can see your true feelings, mistress, then so can the major. I'm telling ye now, if ye don't take care and keep 'em hid, Robert McLarn will suffer for them—"

"I don't want to talk about this!"

"It's a bad thing all the way around for Robbie," Willoughby continued anyway. "I reckon he's lost everything—except maybe old Colm McLarn's consideration. But he doesn't want that—or so he thinks."

Hannah stood, clutching the bundle of clothes now as if she could use them as some kind of barrier. She didn't want to think about Robert McLarn—or any of his other personifications. It hurt too much.

"I'll be going then," Willoughby said, but he hesitated a moment longer before he finally walked away. Hannah held back as long as she could.

"Mr. Willoughby," she called after him when he was about to disappear around the corner.

He turned and looked at her.

She took a deep breath. "Did they...hurt him just now, Mr. Willoughby?"

"Yes," Willoughby said. "Old Colm, too, I reckon."

Hannah looked away and struggled for control.

"Badly?"

"Don't know, mistress. I didn't hang around—lest somebody need another dog to kick. Ain't much honor in striking a man who's tied or one who's old, to my way of thinking. But neither one of them didn't get nothing they ain't suffered from British soldiers before, I reckon."

Willoughby stood waiting, and Hannah capitulated.

"Tell me what he said, Mr. Willoughby."

"He said, 'Your soul was put into my soul. I take your soul. Never will I turn away.'"

Tears spilled down Hannah's face. She couldn't keep her mouth from trembling.

"Put on the clothes, girl," Willoughby said. "Whatever you think you have to do now, it's best you don't go about it looking like you do. It's best you look like Mistress Elway."

No, Hannah thought. Too much had happened. She would never be "Mistress Elway" again.

Chapter Twelve

"What do you say now?"

Five Killer stood silent, passive, ignoring Morgan and his question. He had lost all track of time. How long had he been tied here? Days? It seemed days—but it couldn't have been.

He ran his tongue over his parched lips, willing his thirst elsewhere.

"Nothing?" Morgan said, startling him, because he had already forgotten the man was there.

"Where, oh, where has that irrepressible urge to speak to one's betters gone, I wonder?" Morgan said.

"You—are not—my—better—" Five Killer managed to say through his cracked lips.

It was all the provocation Morgan needed. He brought the riding crop he carried down hard across Five Killer's cheek, and Five Killer sagged in his bonds, head down. After a moment, he opened his eyes. He could see the blood, drop by drop, falling onto the dirt.

* * *

Hannah stood in the middle of Morgan's quarters. The corporal had found her behind the surgery and assumed that she was ready to comply with the second half of the general's orders. He escorted her here—and he'd given her no choice about coming.

The room was poorly furnished at best. There was only a primitive washstand, a field cot and one chair. It was hard for her to imagine Morgan living like this. It was certainly not in keeping with his idea of his social position.

She finally decided to take Willoughby's advice, and she set about bathing behind a blanket she hooked on two bent nails in the corner. Morgan's rank apparently permitted him not to have to share his living space, but there was no latch on the door. Her modesty had returned seemingly as strong as ever, and she had no wish to be caught naked. On the other hand, she would have dearly loved to have escaped the fort and made her way to the river for a long swim.

She took the time to wash her hair—and get at least some of the burrs out, as Willoughby suggested. He was right, she thought. She would do well not to remind the people here of what had happened to her.

And all the while, she was afraid that Morgan would come. She had no idea where he was or what he intended doing about her. She only knew that he would be doing something.

She gave a sharp sigh, remembering suddenly the look in Five Killer's eyes.

I take your soul. Never will I turn away.

She raked harder at the burrs in her hair and tried not to think about that or about the man himself. But even so, a plan began to form. She couldn't stay here. She had to know if he was all right, and she had to know badly enough to face the people outside. She would go among them, looking for the world like Mistress Elway, and as such, she would try to find out what was happening to him.

The set of clothing Willoughby brought her was a bit frayed, but it was complete—a linen shift and skirt, a lightly boned leather bodice, a pair of mended hose and a mob cap. The cap kept her from having to waste any more time on her hair. The shift was cut lower than she would have liked, and she had no linen to pin inside. But as Five Killer once pointed out to her, beggars could not be choosers.

She had no way to see the final result when she was at last ready. She had to rely on Willoughby's startled look when she stepped outside.

"Might I be asking what ye have in mind, mistress?" Willoughby said, clearly intending to accompany her wherever she planned to go.

"I'm going to talk to Morgan," she said, only that very moment making up her mind.

"And say what?"

"I don't know," she said truthfully, and he sighed.

"Ye can't go asking him about Robbie McLarn."

"Can't I?"

"No, mistress, ye can't. The major has had his fill of McLarns this day. Believe me."

"Perhaps you'll want to keep your distance, then."

"If I had any sense, I would," he assured her.

"Did you get your purse yet?"

"I will. As soon as Colm McLarn sells his tobacco and your father gets his wage."

She gave him a skeptical look, and he grinned.

"Now ye know why I'm not a rich man."

"Mistress Elway?" someone called, and Hannah turned to see who had spoken. A man came quickly across the compound. He had a slight squint, and he was barely as tall as she. He had more the look of a scholar than a soldier.

"John Henry Baines, at your service," he said when he reached her. "I believe you were to come see me. A very unhappy corporal tells me that the general insisted," he added, when she didn't immediately respond. "He was more than a little disconcerted to discover I have not yet made your acquaintance. How may I assist you?"

"In no way," Hannah said. "I have no need of a doctor." She knew perfectly well that what she said was true only at this moment. She was functioning on willpower alone, but how much longer she could continue to do so, without sleep, without hope, she didn't know.

The doctor looked at her closely. "Perhaps not," he said after a moment. "Very well. In that case, then, perhaps *you* could assist *me*. You have just come from the Cherokee. Perhaps you could tell me how to reach Major Elway's slave boy. He will not eat. If he dies, I believe the major will take exception. The other women here will not attend a savage. I was hoping...I believe you may already know the boy. Perhaps you could induce him to take some nourishment.''

Willoughby began to fidget, and Hannah looked at him. He studiously avoided meeting her gaze.

"Where is he?" she asked, in spite of what she took to be Willoughby's disapproval.

"He is kept in one of the cells. Will you see him?"

"All right. Yes."

"Good," he said. "If you'll excuse me, I'll go on ahead and make sure everything is...presentable."

"I don't know if I like the sound of that," Willoughby said as the doctor walked away. "That place ain't no place for no woman."

But Hannah was only half listening. She watched as the doctor disappeared into what must be the garrison jail. She glanced at Willoughby, suddenly realizing what might be the real reason for his protest.

"He ain't in there," Willoughby said without her having to ask.

"Are you certain?"

"The doctor is wanting ye to come along," he said instead of answering her. "If ye be set on going, that is."

"I'll go alone," Hannah said.

"You need someone who speaks Cherokee," he

said, walking along with her. "And ye need somebody to keep ye in line in case I'm wrong about where Robbie is. If he is in there, I'm expecting ye to keep your wits about ye. Ye go crying and making a spectacle of yourself and ye'll not be helping him one whit. Ye understand me?"

"I'm not going to cry."

"See that you don't."

"And I'm already a spectacle."

"That ye are."

"Why are you doing this? Why are you helping?"

"I respect Colm McLarn."

"And the purse?"

He gave her a half smile. "Maybe."

The doctor had to push the heavy wooden door hard to get it open so that Hannah could go inside. The jail area had two levels. The platform-like entrance with a table and a chair, and then some steps down to the jail proper. There was another table at the foot of the stairs with a lit candle on it. A soldier stood at the ready nearby.

The place was smokey and hot and still dark, in spite of the candle. There were few windows and they were small and high up. The air was thick and close and smelled of sweat, new wood and unemptied slops. Hannah expected cages, but there were a number of wooden rooms, each with iron bars and an iron lock set in a wooden door. Most of the cells seemed to be occupied. In spite of Willoughby's opinion, Hannah kept looking for Five Killer among the faces that stared out at her through the bars.

His face was not among them.

She peered in through the nearest door and saw a man lying on a pile of straw. She stepped closer to see. It wasn't Five Killer. It was his father.

"Why is Colm McLarn here?" she asked the doctor.

"I understand he…interfered with the King's business," the doctor said.

"Open the door," Hannah said. She glanced at Willoughby who seemed intent on making some remark, but didn't.

"I have no authority to—" Dr. Baines began.

"Open the door!" Hannah cried.

Willoughby coughed a warning, and she took a deep breath. He had been right to worry about her making a spectacle of herself. Her emotions were much too close to the surface.

"Please, sir," she said with a calmness she didn't begin to feel. "Colm McLarn was always kind to me. He hired Mr. Willoughby here to bring me back safe. I cannot bear to see him so."

The doctor still hesitated.

"Please," Hannah said again.

The doctor finally motioned for the guard to unlock the door. Hannah immediately went inside and knelt down in the straw beside the old man. Colm McLarn at first appeared to be sleeping. Hannah touched his hand. It was cold and clammy in spite of the heat.

"Sir," she whispered. "Mr. McLarn."

He wasn't sleeping at all. She looked up at the doctor.

"I believe he has suffered an apoplectic fit," he said.

"That and the broad end of a musket applied to his pate," Willoughby remarked.

"Surely, Dr. Baines, you can have him moved to a better place than this," Hannah said.

"He's better off here," the doctor said. "We are short handed because of the hostilities. There is no one to serve in the surgery. The turnkey sees to his needs."

"I will look after him," Hannah said, working hard not to criticize the present arrangement—when it was clear that the old man had simply been dumped here. "Please, sir. What harm can it do?"

Colm McLarn could barely tolerate being indoors. A jail cell and the turnkey's indifference would be a death sentence for the old frontiersman.

The doctor still hesitated.

"Sir," Hannah said, using every bit of self-control she could muster to sound reasonable. "This man has dined with more than one colonial governor and he is very welcome at their table. Do you not think *they* will take exception if—when— they hear how he was treated here? You must have the medical authority to see that an old man does not suffer needlessly."

Hannah's message was very clear—she hoped. Governors took precedence over British army officers anytime, anywhere.

"Yes, I see," the doctor said after a moment. "Very well. We will move him."

"Thank you."

She looked around at a noise behind her. The Cherokee boy stood in the opposite cell, his face pressed against the bars. He was watching her and McLarn, and he was clearly afraid and trying not to show it.

"I don't know his name," Hannah said to Willoughby, and he immediately said something to the boy in Cherokee. The boy made no attempt to answer.

"He's not going to help ye, mistress. He's not even thinking it over."

She stood and moved to the doorway where she could see the boy's face better. Not too close. She didn't want to chase him into a far corner. He watched her warily, and his eyes...

His eyes.

"Mr. Willoughby," Hannah said abruptly. "Ask him his father's name."

"Ye know his father's name," Willoughby said. "His grandfather's, as well."

Yes, Hannah thought. *Yes!*

All this time and it had never occurred to her that this boy was Five Killer's son—perhaps because of his age. It was only that last night before Willoughby found her that Five Killer had told her he was sixteen when he married and that the boy had been born a year later. How old would he be now? Eleven? Twelve?

Hannah was making the boy uncomfortable staring at him.

Oh, you have your father's eyes, she thought, and she walked to the cell door after all.

Did he speak English? She didn't know. And she didn't know how much she could trust Willoughby. His loyalty would surely lie with the nearest and fattest purse, and Colm McLarn would not be selling tobacco anytime soon.

The boy was thinner than she remembered, and hollow-eyed. His father's absence had not been a good thing for him. The doctor was right to be concerned.

"Do you know who I am?" she asked, deciding to leave Willoughby out of the conversation if she could.

The boy didn't back away, but he completely ignored her.

It suddenly occurred to her that when Five Killer and this boy had been taken, they had been serving the French—hence their having become Morgan's property. Morgan had remarked at great length how fortunate the two of them were to have been taken as slaves rather than scalped for the bounty. It occurred to her as well that the latter was still a definite possibility.

"Me connaissez-vous?" she whispered so that neither Willoughby nor the doctor could hear her. She hoped.

Again, the boy said nothing, but this time his eyes flickered.

"Il faut manger. Hi-s-ki-ti-hi—votre père a besoin de vous. Comprenez-vous?"

He dared to look at her.

"Comprenez-vous?" she asked again, determined to find out if he understood that he must eat, that his father needed him.

"Oui," he said faintly. He looked at Colm McLarn. *"Grandpèr est mort."*

"Non," Hannah said. Colm McLarn wasn't dead—yet.

The boy licked his lips and gave a quiet sigh.

"Soyez fort," she whispered.

Be strong.

Hannah looked around at the doctor. "I want him taken to the surgery as well," she said with an imperiousness that would have done the Elways proud. "I know what he will eat and how to prepare it. I can look after them both there. He can be tied so he doesn't escape."

"The major won't—"

"The major *will*," Hannah interrupted. "If he wants his property kept alive as you believe. I promise you this boy will die shut away here. He is a wild thing, Doctor. He is Cherokee. He will die because he wills it so. It may already be too late."

The doctor sighed. "I will go speak to the major. That is the best I can do."

He hurried off. Hannah stood there. She felt unsteady on her feet, lightheaded. The heat and the smell of the place was suddenly overwhelming. She moved blindly away from the cell, nearly colliding with Willoughby as she did so. She needed air, and she headed for the nearest door.

"Wait!" Willoughby said, but she plunged on. If she was going to faint, she preferred falling onto the dirt outside rather than the filthy floor in here.

She came out into the piercingly bright sunlight. Someone had placed a crude table with a water bucket on it just outside the door. She couldn't see after the dimness of the jail, and she stumbled into it. The water, warmed by the sun, sloshed over her skirt front and into her shoes.

She was now on the back side of the jail in a small fenced in space that butted up against the high log stockade. There was no relief from the heat here. If anything, it was worse. She closed her eyes, trying to adjust to the sunlight. When she opened them again, she could literally see the waves of heat shimmering around her.

There was a post set into the ground directly in front of her—and a man tied to it.

"Oh, dear God—!"

Five Killer—

Willoughby had already said that Five Killer had been hurt. Even so, Hannah wasn't prepared for the reality.

There were no soldiers around, and she ran forward. It wouldn't have made any difference if there had been. Nothing mattered—not his betrayal— nothing. The only thing that mattered was getting to him.

When she reached him, she knelt down in front

of him and gently lifted his head so that she could see his face.

"Five Killer," she whispered. "Robert—"

He didn't stir.

She rushed back to the oak bucket by the door and grabbed the dipper, scooping a dragonfly out of the water before she filled it. Then she hurried back to him, spilling water all the way. She poured some water into her palm and placed it against his lips, then again. After a moment, his eyelids fluttered.

"Robert—here," she said, trying to give him more to drink from the dipper.

He couldn't take it.

"Drink it," she insisted. She pressed the dipper against his mouth. How far they had come since the last time she'd done this.

He swallowed painfully and began to cough. The tether around his neck was too tight and she leaned into him to support his weight so that she could loosen it. She offered him the dipper again, and this time he was able to drink.

He tried to lift his head enough to see her. His face was so bruised and swollen she barely recognized him.

"Hannah—" he said through his cracked lips. "Get away from—here—"

"No!" she said. She was still holding the dipper, and she kept wetting her fingertips and putting them into his mouth.

She reached around behind him to try to get his

hands free, but she couldn't loosen the bonds. His head rested on her shoulder now.

"You—have much to—forgive," she thought he said.

"No, I don't."

"If I've gotten you—with child—"

"I will be happy," she said.

He moved so that he could see her face. His eyes searched hers.

For what? she wondered, reaching to touch his face gently so as not to hurt him.

The truth? It *was* the truth. Her own heart's truth. And she realized it the moment she said it.

He leaned his forehead against hers. "Go—before someone sees you. Morgan will kill you—"

"No—no! I have to get you out of here—"

"Hannah!"

Hannah looked around. Willoughby came at a run toward her. He grabbed her by the arm and pulled her to her feet.

"What did I tell ye!"

Hannah tried to fight him off, tried to keep him from dragging her away. "Let me go!"

"I will not!" Willoughby said, all but jerking her off the ground. "Ye cannot help him! Not now! Your husband is looking for a reason to kill him— ye already gave him cause to do *this*. Are ye listening to me?"

Hannah abruptly stopped struggling, but she had by no means capitulated.

"Ye get yourself calmed before that doctor gets back here. If he sees there's a reason ye want the boy and Colm out of jail—one that's got nothing to do with them—it will all come undone."

Hannah took a step in the direction Willoughby wanted, but then she whirled around and snatched the hunting knife out of his belt, swinging it in a wide arc when he would have grabbed her wrist.

She backed away from him toward Five Killer. In one quick motion, she cut the neck tether where it was anchored to the post. He slumped forward. His hands were still tied, and she cut them free as well. He fell onto the ground. She knelt down beside him, trying to turn him over.

"Willoughby—" he said, forcing himself painfully onto his side and then to his knees. "Take her—away—"

Willoughby grabbed her again, knocking the knife from her hand. It fell on the ground at her feet, and he jerked her upward when she would have retrieved it.

"Don't make me hurt ye, girl," he said. "I will if I have to!"

He held her at bay while he snatched up the knife, but he didn't put it back into its sheath. He threw it so that it stuck up in the ground inches away from Five Killer's knees.

"'Tis all the chance I can give ye, Robbie. If ye can get yourself over the wall, ye may make it," he said, dragging Hannah away. She fought him hard, finally digging her heels in when they reached the back door of the jail. She couldn't leave Five Killer like this!

Willoughby pulled her around and shook her

hard. "Ye know what happened to his wife!" he said. "Will ye let her die like that for nothing!"

"What do you mean?"

"She gave herself up for rape and burning—for that young boy in there. *His* boy. And it'll all go for naught if ye don't get yourself together. There's a chance ye will have his son and Colm put into your hands. Them ye can help—if ye will. Damn ye, woman, ye keep this up and ye are going to get us both hanged!"

The doctor was returning. Hannah could hear his voice, hear him coming in the other door.

"Make up your mind," Willoughby said. "Are ye going to give Robbie the chance to get away from here or are ye hell-bent on leading them right to him before he can get off his knees?"

"All right!" she whispered fiercely.

Willoughby shoved her forward and closed the door just as the doctor came down the steps. Apparently, the doctor's petition had met with Morgan's approval. Several soldiers were clambering down the steps after him and heading for Colm McLarn's cell.

Hannah looked back over her shoulder even though the door was shut, and she could no longer see Five Killer.

"He was raised up Cherokee," Willoughby whispered, pushing her ahead of him. "He'll make it over the wall or he will die trying. Now make a good lie. I've no weapon to give him the time he needs—thanks to ye."

Hannah realized that the doctor was watching her

closely as she approached. There was no need for her to feign unsteadiness.

"The heat," she managed to say. "I must—I need—"

"This way, Mistress Elway," he said, taking her arm.

She expected Willoughby to come along, but he didn't.

The doctor led her outside and then escorted her firmly all the way to the surgery. She resented every step. It was all she could do not to put up the same kind of fight she had with Willoughby. She kept listening for someone to have discovered that Five Killer was loose and sound the alarm.

The soldiers followed, carrying Colm McLarn and leading the boy, who had been firmly hobbled with rawhide and stones. A number of civilians and soldiers watched the procession from the jail.

The doctor had Colm McLarn put into one of the cots and the boy tied to a support post in the corner. Hannah stood waiting for them to get out of the way so that she could see to the old man, every nerve in her body taut. It was all she could do to concentrate on the matter at hand.

She went to McLarn immediately, seeing for the first time the injury done to him. She had missed it in the dimness of the jail cell. He had blood all through his hair. She thought that it must have happened just as Willoughby said. Someone had struck the old man with the butt end of a musket. She touched his hand. It was still cold in spite of the heat, but his breathing was deep and unhindered. She supposed that that must be a good sign.

Hannah glanced at the boy. He was watching with worried interest from the post where he had been tied. Their eyes met briefly. She wondered if he had any inkling of his father's situation.

"Do-sa," McLarn said abruptly, and the boy started.

But the old man was not awake. He slumbered on, deep in whatever place the blow to his head had sent him.

"Here," the doctor said at her elbow. He held out a tin cup for her to take.

"No, thank you—" she began.

"It's only a tonic. It will give you strength. It's my own concoction—and quite effective, if I do say so myself. You must not fall ill after I have insisted so earnestly on your behalf that you can manage the care of McLarn and the Cherokee boy."

Hannah hesitated, then took the cup, her mind immediately going to that last day in the Cherokee village. It was not the first time she had had no choice but to accept some unknown brew from a stranger.

She took a tentative sip. The doctor's tonic was slightly bitter, but reasonably palatable. She drank deeply.

"All of it, please," he said, smiling.

She drained the cup. It had been a long time since she'd eaten, and in only a few moments, she realized that the doctor's "concoction" had not been a tonic at all.

"What—? What did you do?" she whispered, reaching out blindly to keep from falling. The doctor held on to her by both arms.

"I haven't the brute strength required, you see," the doctor was saying from somewhere far away. "I cannot inspire enough fear to command people effectively. I must rely on my wits alone to accomplish what I know needs to be done. You will sleep now—"

"I don't want—to sleep—oh!"

"Nevertheless, sleep you shall. After which you will feel *much* improved. I am a physician, Mistress Elway. I have no difficulty seeing your present state is more than just the heat. Be calm now—and be assured that I have your husband's permission to do this. Rest and don't concern yourself about old McLarn. You were quite right to point out the governors' potential interest in his current situation. And the general very much appreciated my telling him, I must say—take her to Major Elway's quarters straightaway."

"No—" Hannah tried to say. She could hear something—muskets firing from the watch tower.

No!

Her body swayed, and someone lifted her off the floor and into a well of darkness.

Chapter Thirteen

You sleep too long.

Hannah stirred uneasily at the unwelcome intrusion. Her arms and legs, her eyelids felt so heavy.

Hannah! You must wake.

"I can't."

You can.

Hannah opened her eyes, and after a moment, she could make out the details of the room and then someone—a woman—no, a young girl—standing at the foot of the cot.

"Who are you? You shouldn't be in here—"

I can be anywhere—and here I am.

"No," Hannah said again.

Look! the girl commanded, and Hannah strained to see. The girl was holding something—a piece of paper. Slowly, she turned it over. Hannah blinked her eyes and tried to focus. It was…a watercolor. *Her* watercolor, one of many done in desperation and loneliness so long ago.

"Flowers that don't grow here," Hannah whispered.

You gave this to Hi-s-ki-ti-hi, is that not so?

"How did you know that?"

I know everything, Hannah, the girl said.

"Who are you?"

She didn't answer.

"What do you want?"

I told you. You sleep too long. You must wake up. You must stay strong. Eat—but do not drink—

"What are you talking about?" Hannah cried, suddenly coming awake and not knowing where she was. She lay there, heart pounding. She was afraid to move, afraid to even look.

Slowly, the room became familiar enough to reassure her. The blanket still hung on two bent nails in the corner—and she realized with certainty that there was no young girl at the foot of her bed.

It was raining outside, and she took comfort from the quiet, steady sound. The dream was fading, but not its aftereffects. She was still unsettled, and it didn't help that she had no memory whatsoever of how she had gotten here. She realized suddenly that she didn't want to remember, and it was at that very moment that the image of Colm McLarn, lying on a pile of straw, came into her mind.

And then the boy—Five Killer's boy—and the doctor and his "tonic."

And—

Five Killer.

She closed her eyes at the sudden mental image of him tied to the cedar post behind the jail. She remembered, too, the sound of muskets firing from the watch tower.

Oh, please! Please!

Had he gotten away?

She closed her eyes and tried not to weep.

"I should have told him," she whispered. She should have said the words, so that whatever happened, he would know.

No, she thought immediately. She had no right to say anything—and no reason, save Willoughby's version of what Five Killer's Cherokee words in the general's office had meant.

But she knew beyond a doubt that she loved this complex man who was both Robert McLarn and Hi-s-ki-ti-hi. There was no point in her pretending otherwise. Regardless of his betrayal and regardless of how wrong it was for her to have such feelings, she *loved* him. The seed for that love had been planted the day he first took one of her forbidden watercolors and left a seashell necklace in its place.

After a moment, she sat up and let her legs dangle over the side of the cot. Her head pounded from the effort, and her vision swam briefly. It was true. She had slept too long.

She frowned, thinking again of the odd dream, but beyond blaming it on the doctor's tonic, she took no time to dwell upon it. She had to find out what had happened to Five Killer.

It was raining harder now. She could hear it pattering on the porch outside. With some effort, she stood on the floor. Her legs felt weak and wobbly—she had no idea how long she'd been asleep. It was a great comfort to her that she was still dressed, still wearing the drab, brown linen skirt and the leather bodice Willoughby had brought her.

She moved to the washstand. There was water in the pitcher, and she splashed some on her face. Someone had left a meal of sorts on the small table. There was a wooden plate with a large chunk of bread and cheese covered with a piece of linen to keep the flies away, and something in a tin cup. She picked it up to sniff the amber liquid.

Cider?

Eat—but don't drink, Hannah thought, remembering the dream, but it was her experience with the doctor and his sleeping potion that made her so wary. The potion had apparently been given to her with Morgan's blessing. Who knew his reason for wanting to keep her unaware?

"Fool me twice—shame on me," she whispered, tearing off bite after bite of the bread and cheese and devouring them as if she thought someone might suddenly arrive to take it all away. She hadn't realized how hungry she was until she began to eat or that she had been so affected by her captivity. She was afraid not to eat when she had the chance.

She heard a great commotion outside—dogs barking and people shouting—and her heart sank. The dogs in the fort were kept specifically to give warning if Indians were near.

She moved unsteadily to the door, intending to open it enough to see, but she couldn't budge it no matter how hard she pushed against it. The door was now firmly bolted on the outside.

Panicked, she looked around the room. There was no other way out. She tried to concentrate. There had been no lock on the door before. She was certain of that. Perhaps she wasn't in Morgan's quarters after all. But for the blanket stretched on the bent nails in the corner, there was really nothing to indicate that this was the same place. She walked to the corner of the room and lifted the blanket. Someone had placed a chair and a chamber pot behind it.

She let the blanket fall. It was all she could do not to pace like a caged animal, in spite of her weakened state. If she called out, would anyone come? She abruptly moved toward the door again. Perhaps she could get someone's attention—someone who would find Willoughby. Surely he could tell her what had happened—what was happening now.

If Morgan hasn't hanged him.

She realized suddenly that Five Killer's escape— if he'd managed it—would likely be attributed to Willoughby's intervention, not hers.

She put her hands on the door again, then immediately stepped back. Someone was on the other side of it. The bolt rattled and the door abruptly opened. Morgan stood there, rain-soaked and visibly startled by the sight of her. Clearly, he hadn't taken into account that the doctor's brew might have induced such disturbing dreams as to cause her to wake well ahead of his schedule.

In spite of his obvious surprise at seeing her both conscious and on her feet, he recovered quickly.

"Hannah," he said easily. "How very much better you look."

His compliment rang so false that Hannah very nearly laughed. She felt no joy at seeing him. He was her handsome, highborn and well-placed husband, and she felt nothing at all, not even contempt. He avoided letting his gaze meet hers, and she realized that there must be some small part of him that could feel shame at what he had done. He had promised God and her father to love, honor and cherish her—but he had given her up to be murdered so that he could live. She could almost see the humor in their situation. In actuality, they were both thwarted murderers—and neither of them was quite sure if the other one knew it.

"Why am I locked in?" she asked.

Morgan made no attempt to answer her question. He closed the door firmly behind him, and Hannah suspected that it had nothing to do with the rainy weather. She could almost feel him trying to decide how the situation should be handled.

"Morgan, why am I locked in?" Hannah asked again.

"It is nothing for you to concern yourself about—"

"No? Are you planning to have Dr. Baines fool me into drinking another 'tonic' then?"

"That was for your own good," he said evenly. "As was having the door bolted. Patients under the influence of the good doctor's tonic sometimes wander. And you are being most tiresome—something, I suppose, we must attribute to the fact that you haven't recovered from the ordeal of your captivity.''

He walked closer, and he was looking at her so intently. It was all Hannah could do not to back away.

"What has happened to Colm McLarn?" she asked.

"Thanks to your meddling, the general decided it best that he be given private quarters. An Indian woman was found to look after him. She manages quite nicely, actually—as there is nothing to be done for him save trying to feed him and keeping his linens clean. His fate is in God's hands.''

"And the Cherokee boy?"

"There have been Indians skulking around the fort all day. Presently, I and my men will go out to engage them. I'm taking the boy along as a scout.''

"I think you mean a hostage," she said quietly.

"Call it what you will. He goes. His presence will be a deterrent."

Morgan was close enough now to touch her, and he reached out to lift a strand of her hair and inspect it.

"How is it you are more...comely under these circumstances, Hannah?" he asked.

Hannah ignored the remark.

"Is the Cherokee named Maw still alive?" she asked.

Something flickered briefly in Morgan's eyes. He let the strand of hair fall.

"Why do you ask?"

"Because if he is—and he is the one here now, that boy won't save you."

He forced a smile. "Your captivity has left you quite theatrical, Hannah."

"What about...the other one?" she asked, moving out of his reach.

"What other one?"

"The other Cherokee slave."

"The McLarn bastard? You needn't worry about him."

"You are...certain?" she asked carefully.

"Of course, I'm certain. His scalp is in a box in the general's office waiting to be turned in for the bounty."

Hannah turned away from him just in time.

Don't cry. Don't—cry!

She didn't think her legs would continue to hold her, and she willed herself to walk slowly to the one chair and gripped the back of it to keep from falling. She marveled at how prepared she had been to hear that Five Killer was dead—and without even realizing it.

But she would not give Morgan Elway the satisfaction of knowing that she grieved. Her sorrow was hers and hers alone.

It was all she had.

"I must go," Morgan said, coming to stand behind her. "It's a pity I don't have more time."

He reached out and stroked the back of her neck. Hannah held herself rigid, gritting her teeth to keep from jerking away.

He walked to the door. She heard him open and close it. She stood there, clinging to the back of the chair, listening intently for the sound of the bolt in the lock. When it came, she let her body sag.

Then and only then did she cry. She cried until there were no more tears left. She lost all track of time. Time meant nothing. Perhaps she slept. She didn't really know. She didn't even know what day it was, or if Morgan had actually gone on his campaign. She tried not to think about him. Or Five Killer. Or his son. She tried not to think about anything.

An Indian woman came again to empty the chamber pot. Hannah knew she was there, but she made no effort to speak to her. She lay on the cot, staring at the ceiling, earnestly seeking the same kind of oblivion her mind had afforded her after she had been taken by the Cherokee. She wanted to be in that safe cocoon of indifference again, but she couldn't manage it. The pain was too strong, the sorrow too great.

This time the Indian woman did not immediately leave. She came closer to the cot and stood there waiting. Hannah glanced at her. The woman was middle-aged. Her hair was streaked with gray, but she was still quite pretty.

"*Lv-la,*" she whispered, taking Hannah by the hand and gently pulling.

Hannah resisted briefly, then sat up. She was still wearing the same clothes Willoughby had found for her, and the woman looked at them and shook her head. She brought out a dress from a bundle lying on the floor. It was a Cherokee dress, much like the one Hannah had arrived in. Hannah understood that she was to change her clothes. She didn't object. It didn't matter to her one way or the other. With the woman's help, she put on the dress.

The Indian woman protested softly in Cherokee when Hannah would have lain back down on the cot. It was clear that she wanted Hannah sitting. When the woman was satisfied that Hannah understood, she went to the door and opened it slightly. In a moment, someone came in, someone in a hurry. The Indian woman quickly closed the door behind him.

Hannah turned away. She had no interest in whatever this might turn out to be.

"Hannah."

She looked at the new arrival in surprise, and she said the only thing in her mind.

"They killed him, Papa."

Her father hesitated, then came closer.

"He was the one who fed us, Papa. Did you know that? That time when you were gone so long. I gave him my watercolors for the food. Hi-s-ki-ti-hi. Five Killer. We would all be dead, but for him. *I* would be dead twice over. Maw intended to kill me, but he—" Tears streamed down her face. She couldn't stop them.

"Come, daughter," her father said. "Come. We go from here. Now. They will keep you locked in no longer."

"I cut him loose. Morgan would have killed him." She looked into her father's face. "But he killed him anyway, didn't he? He will kill his son as well, and I can't stop him. I want to save the boy. I don't want Go-ge-yi to die for nothing, but I don't know what to do, Papa—''

"You don't cry anymore," he said. "You come home to the family now. We will take care of you."

"Don't you see? I have to save the boy. I *have* to!''

Her father glanced at the Indian woman. "I don't know how the boy fares," he said. "I am not allowed to see him. I have seen Colm McLarn. There is nothing I can do for him. *You* are the only one I can help."

"It's too late, Papa. You should have let Five Killer marry me when he asked. You should have given me to *him*. Morgan is—"

She stopped and bowed her head. There was nothing she wanted to say to her father about Morgan Elway. She had already shocked him with her revelations. She could see it in his face.

"Come, daughter," he said again.

"No. I can't leave here. Morgan has to keep me where I am—until he can decide what is to be done with me. He put me into Maw's hands, but that didn't work out. Five Killer got me away from Maw—and then Willoughby found me. And I— I—" She gave a wavering sigh. "If you ask Morgan, he will say no."

"I don't ask. I do," her father said, and Hannah looked up at him.

I don't ask. I do.

It was the precept Jacob Albrecht lived by. When

she was a young girl and living in the cabin with her stepmother and the boys, she should have sewed that very sentiment into a sampler for him.

"Get your wits about you, daughter. Your husband has returned from his campaign. It's best we go while they are still celebrating his victory—before he remembers whatever his plans are for you. You must follow Ka-ti outside. You will get into the back of my wagon and you will sit there quiet and we will go from here, yes?"

She looked into her father's eyes. He was serious, and she wanted so much to believe that what he said was possible.

"Now, daughter," he insisted, helping her to stand.

"Papa, why—how did you come to be here?"

"The man Willoughby finds me in the wilderness. He says you and Colm McLarn and the McLarn grandson have need of my meddling. He thinks little of the clergy—but much of my daughter and my friend Colm McLarn. He was a good choice to go find you and bring you back. Let us go now."

"The boy," Hannah said. "You must find out what's happened to him."

"It cannot be done now, daughter. Later, we will see."

The woman, Ka-ti, opened the door a crack and peered outside. Then she motioned for Hannah to follow. The sun had disappeared below a brilliant orange horizon. There was a horse and wagon tied very near the door, and Hannah followed Ka-ti into it, squeezing into a small space near the seat.

There were still a number of wagons and carts inside the fort, and people milling about. Several of the men close by stopped and stared. Hannah's father mounted the wagon and sent the horse forward, driving in a wide circle over the muddy ground until they were turned around and headed for the gate.

Hannah couldn't keep from staring at the general's headquarters as they rode past. The door was open. She could see the mahogany desk and a silver candlestick sitting in the middle of it. A number of people milled around inside, one of them Sibyl Elway. Sibyl was laughing. Perhaps the general was entertaining his guests with the box of scalps he was keeping for the bounty.

Hannah looked sharply away. It would do no good to cry anymore.

The wagon creaked along, neither speeding up nor slowing down as they approached the gate. The gate was partially open.

"Halt!" the sentry cried, and her father let the horse crowd much too close for the sentry's liking before he stopped.

"Are you deaf, man?" the sentry snapped, and her father responded in lengthy German. He didn't lie precisely. He didn't actually *say* he didn't speak English—he only gave every indication that he didn't.

The sentry came to the edge of the wagon and peered inside. Hannah sat there, staring back at him. It was too late to try to hide her face.

"Get the major," he said to another soldier.

Hannah didn't hesitate. She stood and climbed over the edge of the wagon to the ground.

"Stop, mistress," the soldier said in warning. "I mean it."

Hannah put her hands on the gate and began to push with all her might, trying to get it open wide enough for the wagon to pass. She couldn't budge it. She leaned her back against it and used the strength of her legs for more leverage, but she kept sliding in the mud.

"Stop!" the soldier yelled, making the horse prance nervously.

"You will have to shoot me, Corporal," Hannah said.

Ka-ti got down off the wagon and joined in, but they still couldn't get the gate to move. A woman came running up to help.

"Eliza—" Hannah said in surprise, recognizing the indentured servant immediately. She had forgotten that the entire Elway household must be here somewhere.

"I'm sorry, mistress," Eliza whispered. "Truly I am. You were always kind to me."

"Sorry? For what?"

"For what I said. I had to say it. The major—he would have found a way to add years to my time."

"What did you say?"

"Mistress, I—"

"Tell me!"

"I said there was something sinful going on between the two of you—you and Hatcher—"

"What?"

"The major—he's given Hatcher money to accuse you—to go around telling people things happened."

"Hatcher is alive?"

"Yes, more's the pity. The major wanted it to look like you were running off with him when the Indians got you," Eliza said, still whispering over her shoulder because of the crowd that had gathered to watch. "And he didn't want anybody feeling sorry for you. I said what he wanted me to say. I couldn't help it, mistress. You know what he's like. You know he has to have his way—"

The gate creaked forward, only to stop immediately. A man stepped from the crowd to lend a hand pushing, and then another. Finally, it swung wide enough for the wagon to pass.

"Godspeed," one of the men said, and Hannah looked at him gratefully.

Eliza stood for a moment, then hurried away before any of the Elways saw what she had done. There was nothing left for either of them to say.

Hannah walked back to the wagon and climbed in. The people who had been celebrating in the general's headquarters were coming out onto the porch. Morgan was already crossing the compound, accompanied by the soldier who had been sent to fetch him.

"Reverend Albrecht," he called to her father. "What is this?"

"This," her father said, "is my daughter taking

her leave. On!" he said to the horse, snapping the reins sharply.

"You have no authority—"

"God is my authority, Major Elway. You have her locked away like a criminal."

"Perhaps she is," Morgan said.

"Then I want to hear what her crime is here and now."

They stared at each other, and, for whatever reason, Morgan backed away from the line he had just taken.

"You realize there are still hostile Indians about," he said.

"She will do better taking her chances with them than staying in here with you," her father answered within the earshot of any number of people. He urged the horse forward, forcing Morgan to step out of the way.

A soldier rushed up and grabbed the bridle to stop the horse.

"She must answer the charge of adultery," Morgan said. "What do you have to say about *that,* Reverend? She must confess her guilt and she must agree to the dissolution of the marriage. The circuit judge—the Chief Justice himself—will arrive at the Salisbury settlement to hear the case in a few weeks, after which he will put the marriage aside. *Then* you can have her and be damned."

Hannah could hear the murmuring among the onlookers, but she made no effort to look in their direction. She looked at Morgan instead. He was perfectly confident that he had everything well in hand.

"Hannah, get down," he said.

She made no attempt to do so.

He reached over the side of the wagon and grabbed her by both arms, hauling her out and setting her roughly on the ground. Her father moved to intervene, but the nearest soldier blocked his way with his musket and bayonet.

"This is the last humiliation I will suffer from you," Morgan said coldly. He was hurting her, but she didn't try to get away. She didn't even wince.

She stared into his eyes. "I confess my adultery, Morgan," she said quietly. "But it was *not* with the man you paid to accuse me."

His grip tightened, and this time she couldn't keep from crying out.

He abruptly let go, and she fell to her knees.

Chapter Fourteen

"I can't get to her," Willoughby said. "Nor the boy. Nor Colm. They're all three of them alive— or they was when I hightailed it out. That's all I can tell ye. Here—"

Five Killer gratefully accepted the pemmican Willoughby tossed him. He sat surrounded by Willoughby's damnable dogs. The pack had once again run him to ground. At Willoughby's command, however, he now seemed to be more dog bed than quarry. One slept contentedly under his left arm and another at his feet. The rest were scattered around recovering from the merry chase he had led them on. They were exhausted, and so was he, but they had won and he had lost. It was as simple as that. He supposed that he should be grateful that Willoughby had come looking for him before Morgan Elway conscripted him to go find his escaped slave, but, in truth, Five Killer still wasn't entirely sure that Willoughby meant him no harm.

Willoughby smiled suddenly. "Damned if I

thought ye would make it. They wasted a lot of powder and wad on ye."

"The sun was in their eyes," Five Killer said.

"You still took a big chance—with your life and the boy's."

"I took the only chance—for us both. I couldn't get him out where I was."

Willoughby made no comment and they sat for a time in silence.

"Does Morgan...know anything?" Five Killer asked.

"He don't know it was Hannah cut ye loose. I went back and got the rawhide so's nobody could see how it was you got away. I figured they could just think the rawhide broke and ye took it along with ye."

"I don't mean that," Five Killer said, and under the man's scrutiny, he didn't want to say exactly what he did mean.

"I don't know if he's figured out ye want his wife or not, son," Willoughby said. "If he understands Cherokee, I reckon he knows it. Ye did make that big declaration right there in the general's office, ye know."

"She's not his wife," Five Killer said. "Not by Cherokee law. At the Green Corn Ceremony, she drank the medicine the 'beloved' woman gave her. She became new. Everything that happened before, everything in her life with him, was taken away."

"Does she know that?"

"No," Five Killer said. Hannah didn't know what drinking the "physic" had meant—and would never have believed in the ritual even if she had. They had been on the run. He'd had no time to explain. He'd only had the time to lie with her and to feel such love for her and never once say so. He closed his eyes against the pain remembering caused him. He had to get her out of the fort, and he had no idea how.

He opened his eyes to find Willoughby watching him again, waiting.

"Well, even if she don't know, I reckon that explains why ye got so bold, why ye said what ye did to her. Maybe Morgan understood it—or maybe somebody else who was there did and told him. But I'm thinking it don't matter. Morgan Elway is a spiteful man, whether he knows about you and Hannah or he don't. It's enough to set him off she cares what happens to Colm and your boy."

"She thinks I betrayed her."

"Ye did."

"There was no other way to save my son. I gave my word."

"I know that. Maybe she will, too, if she ever gets the chance."

"Has he hurt her?"

"Well, he's keeping her locked up—"

"What do you mean—locked up?"

"So she don't get gone before the circuit judge comes around. He *says* it's for her protection—because people are thinking bad of her. *Somebody* put out the notion that a public whipping might be called for—her doing what Morgan wants folks to think she did and him being who he is—let me see them wrists, son.''

Five Killer reluctantly held out both hands for Willoughby's inspection. He wasn't concerned about the marks the rawhide bonds had left. He was concerned about Hannah.

''Them places need wrapping or else you're just going to keep breaking the raw spots open,'' Willoughby persisted. He reached into his pouch for a strip of linen and tore it in two. ''Your face ain't much better, but I don't reckon we can wrap that. Your ribs stove in?''

''No.''

''Bruised up like ye are and they ain't stove?''

''No,'' Five Killer repeated. Willoughby would have caught up with him long before he did if they had been.

The wrapping hurt, but Five Killer didn't flinch.

''I don't understand,'' he said. ''Why didn't Morgan let her go with her father? He wants to be rid of her.''

''It ain't that simple, son—not if ye be Morgan Elway and ye got to keep up appearances. Elway—see, he's an arrogant man. And somebody told him about ye asking the reverend for Hannah way back yonder—don't look at me like that. It ain't exactly a secret. The reverend told *me* about it when it happened. He was wanting to know who ye was and the like. He was worried about ye showing up some dark night and stealing her—which, if ye ask me, might have worked out better for everybody.''

''Morgan knows it was me, then.''

"Well, now, I'm thinking not. But he knows some one of ye did and by doing that—especially folks *knowing* it was done—it makes her..."

"What?" Five Killer asked when Willoughby didn't go on.

"Oh...not fit for the likes of him, I reckon. So then along came Maw and his blood revenge—and Elway, he's got a way to get rid of her for good—and get folks feeling all sorry for him while he's at it and maybe he gets Maw settled down, too."

"Yes," Five Killer said, still suffering Willoughby's attention to the raw cuts on his wrists. He remembered Morgan's speech on the front steps of his house after Hannah had been kidnapped. He wondered which had come first. Morgan's need to get rid of the wife he thought wasn't good enough for him or his need to pacify Maw.

"But here ye come along and mess up the whole plan. And Colm and the reverend had made sure I'm there so's she's brought back alive. All of a sudden it's folks feeling sorry for *her* not him—especially when they start hearing how he made it so hard on her on the march back. So there he is. He's still got his big problem—this here wife that ain't good enough for him.

"He went and sent word to the Chief Justice that he was wanting to divorce her, but the Chief Justice said he wouldn't let him, even if he is who he is—on account of how it would look to all the women brave enough to come and try to live on this land. Can't have them thinking their husbands could drop them like a hot rock if they was ever to get taken like Hannah was. So Morgan had to find himself another reason—one the Chief Justice could live with.

"He got that indentured man of his—Hatcher—to go around saying him and Hannah were adulterous together and they was trying to run off. He's telling the reason he happened to be there when Hannah got took was he was chasing after his stray-away wife—only he run into a pack of Indians bent on doing harm and stealing themselves some women. They took Hannah and he couldn't save her. No, sir. And he being the good God-fearing man he is, he don't have no hard feelings toward Hatcher—it was all Hannah's doing, you see, her being such a Jezebel."

"Jezebel?" Five Killer said, not understanding.

"A wicked woman what makes a man do wrong for her," Willoughby said, cutting a slit at the end of the linen strip so he could tie the bandage fast. "But all the time I'm thinking Hatcher's probably got Morgan's coins in his pocket for saying that Major Elway's wife seduced him—that *she* made him go running off like he did and take her along. He ain't exactly close-mouthed about what he's getting down the road, neither."

"What is he getting?"

Willoughby glanced up from binding Five Killer's wrist. "Hannah. I don't reckon she's got much say about it. And Morgan ain't going to stop him."

"Jacob Albrecht shouldn't have gone and left her there!"

"Well, he didn't have much choice, what with Morgan's foot on his backside all but shoving him out the gate. People ain't exactly pleased about *that*, either. It's one thing for the reverend to want to go putting himself in the middle of a Cherokee uprising—and something else for him to get more or less run out of the fort. But it's a good thing he is out. The fort Indians—they are all leaving. First one and then another so the British won't notice. And you know what that means."

Five Killer knew. The uprising was far from over.

"I reckon we're heading for another massacre like the one at Fort Loudon," Willoughby said. "You got to get Hannah and the rest of them out of there."

Five Killer didn't say anything for a moment.

"How much time have I got?"

"Not much, I reckon. That general at the fort—a lot is going to depend on whether or not he knows his business. If he don't, ye got a better chance of getting in and out again. If he does—well, then, who knows? I'm thinking he's a mighty high-ranking officer to be put in a fort with such a small garrison. Could be because he ain't worth a teat on a bull and they stuck him way out here to keep him out of trouble. Or could be he's good at his job—but he got caught with his hand up the wrong skirt and that's why he's stuck here. It may not matter, though."

"What do you mean?"

"It's Maw that's coming," Willoughby said. "I

reckon he'll get over the walls if anybody can—no matter what kind of general they got.''

''Anything else you haven't told me?''

Willoughby gave a sigh. ''Aye, there is.'' He cleared his throat and scratched the nearest dog on the head—but he didn't say anything. Five Killer supposed that it must make the man feel better if the information had to be pulled out of him.

''Well, what is it?''

''Your mother—she's in the fort, too.''

''What is she doing there!''

''Somebody sent her word about what happened to her husband—''

''He is *not* her husband anymore.''

''She drank the Green Corn Ceremony medicine, too, did she?''

Five Killer didn't say anything. The truth of the matter was that he didn't know. He'd always thought that his mother ended her Cherokee marriage to Colm McLarn, but he was by no means certain. The subject of his father had simply been too painful for discussion—for them both.

''Well, yea or nay, she come to see about him. They got her looking after Colm,'' Willoughby said. ''But nobody knows who she is. Colm don't know, either, if you get right down to it. She tried to get to your boy, but she couldn't—so she was going to leave with Hannah and the reverend—see if she could find some help someplace. Maybe go see Maw.''

''Enough!'' Five Killer said, holding up both

painful hands. His entire family was in peril. He didn't want to hear anymore.

Willoughby didn't pay him any attention. "There is one more thing that might be a problem."

"What is it?" Five Killer asked in spite of his reluctance to know.

"Hannah."

"What about Hannah?"

"She thinks you're dead, son."

Five Killer sat there. He was Cherokee. In his heart. In his soul. He believed in the ceremonies and the rituals. But there would be no time for him to make a warrior's preparations for battle. There would be no time for the period of seclusion and fasting and the careful attendance of the "beloved" women in the council house. There would be no time for taking the specially prepared black drink that would purge him of his fear and his unworthiness. He could not attempt this ordeal as Hi-s-ki-ti-hi. He would have to go as Robert McLarn.

He looked at the man who had brought him all this dire news, still not knowing if he was trustworthy. "I have to find Hannah's father."

The door was left unlocked.

Hannah dared to open it, but she was afraid to venture outside. A bright moon was shining overhead, and the air was full of the smell of wood smoke from the numerous campfires around the compound. The threat of a Cherokee attack had not abated enough for the civilians in the fort to return to their unprotected homesteads, but still they carried on with the business of living. She could hear laughter and conversation from time to time, neither of which she had ever had much occasion to enjoy.

Her father had long gone, encouraged in his departure by Morgan's insinuation that *she* would suffer if he remained. She was used to Jacob Albrecht's absences, and he was not the one she missed. Nor would he miss her. For all of Hannah's troubles, her father still had his church flock to attend to, and he was still the pragmatist. If he could not actively help her or Colm McLarn or the boy, then he must be about other things, and he would wait for God to provide.

Hannah had been able to glean some information about Five Killer's son. She prevailed upon the same Indian woman, who still came to empty the chamber pot every day, until she at least found out his name.

His Cherokee name.

Do-sa.

He was in a jail cell—again or still. Morgan hadn't been able to take him along on his forage outside the fort. His plans had been thwarted when the boy became too ill to make the march. She was able to get some food to him—she hoped. She gave most of her ration of corn to Ka-ti in the hopes that she could take it to him, but whether the boy would accept her charity or not, Hannah couldn't even guess. She remembered well his reluctance to drink the water she'd brought to him and his father that day in the fields.

She closed her eyes against the pain of yet another memory of Five Killer. So many of them, when she had been with him such a short time. They filled her waking hours. Sometimes she could feel him, taste him again in her mind. And he haunted her dreams. There, he was alive and whole again. She could talk to him, hold him, make love with him—but then she would suddenly awake and know that he was gone.

He had told her once that he didn't fear death— that the Cherokee believed that the dead went "west." She could barely look at a sunset without weeping. She wondered if Colm McLarn knew what had happened to his son. And Do-sa? Did he know? If she could just do something for them, perhaps it would give her some kind of peace.

But this evening there was the matter of the unlocked door.

She made no attempt to try to leave—yet. She stood in the doorway and savored the evening breeze, trying not to think of another warm, moonlit night like this when she had lain in Five Killer's arms.

Someone stepped onto the porch, and she jumped. The man didn't say anything. He just stood in the shadows. Even so, she had no difficulty recognizing him.

Hatcher.

"What do you want?" Hannah asked finally.

"Me?" he answered in mock surprise. "I only want what's mine, mistress. That big circuit judge will be coming soon. I'll go into Rowan County to the courthouse and say my piece and just like that, you'll not be Mistress Elway anymore.''

He stepped closer. She could see his face now. He was smiling.

"And we'll be on our way," he added.

"You are a very...simple man, aren't you?"

His smile promptly disappeared. "We'll see who is and who ain't 'simple'—"

"You've let Morgan take advantage of you, Hatcher. More than once. You think he didn't know there would be an ambush waiting in the woods that day? You're lucky to be alive—and especially lucky not to have been taken captive and sold to the tribes up north. And you are still doing him favors. His pockets are deep—or, at least, his father's are. I hope you're holding out for more than you got the last time."

His eyes narrowed. He stood there, clearly contemplating the possibilities.

"So simple," Hannah said, and he moved closer, crowding her so that she had no place to go except back into the room. She could smell the rum on his breath.

"I got my freedom. I am bondsman no more."

"Oh, well, then—"

He kept advancing. Hannah bumped into the chair and it fell over backward.

Hatcher stopped abruptly, and he seemed to be listening for something.

No, Hannah thought suddenly. He was listening for some*one*. Coming here—now—was reckless, even for him, and she immediately suspected the reason for the unlocked door. Hatcher had come here so that he could be seen leaving. Neither he nor Morgan was taking a chance that someone might believe her innocent.

But it was Hannah who left. She shoved Hatcher aside, catching him completely off guard and slipping past him and out the door. She pulled it shut and slid the bolt. She would let *him* do the explaining.

She stood there, her heart pounding, then stepped back into the shadows. As far as she could tell, no one in the compound took notice—and drunk or not, Hatcher had the presence of mind not to yell and pound on the door. She heard a laugh, and she recognized it immediately. Sibyl Elway was out for an evening stroll.

"This way," someone whispered.

Hannah looked around sharply. Ka-ti stood at the other end of the porch. Hannah asked no questions. She simply followed quickly.

Ka-ti took her toward the jail, then around to the fence on the back side. They walked along it, staying well in the shadows cast by the light of the moon.

"Here," Ka-ti whispered when they reached the stockade wall.

"What—?" Hannah began, because she didn't understand.

"We are going to get Do-sa out," Ka-ti said. "I was going alone, but as long as *you* are out, you can help. If we get caught, I will blame you."

Hannah stared at her for a moment, then nodded.

It sounded like a workable plan to her. And one more black mark by her name in Morgan's book of sins wouldn't make any difference.

There was just enough space left between the stockade wall and the last fence post for Hannah to stick her foot in. She was able to get a toehold long enough to hoist herself up, and after a minor struggle, she wriggled over the top and jumped to the other side.

She stood for a moment listening. No alarm had been sounded—yet. And when it was, she doubted that anyone would look for her here. She didn't wait for Ka-ti. She crossed the yard to the rear door of the jail, never once looking at the post where Five Killer had been tied. At first she thought the door was locked, but she pushed harder and it finally swung inward.

She slipped inside. There was a lit candle at the bottom of the steps and one on the table near a soldier who sat sleeping in a chair by the other door. The soldier snored loudly. Hannah could see the keys lying on the table in front of him, and she heard Ka-ti just as she was about to creep up the steps to retrieve them. She motioned for Ka-ti to stay where she was. If the soldier woke, there was no point in both of them being caught.

One of the steps squeaked loudly, and Hannah stopped short, but the soldier didn't stir. She waited a moment, then stared upward again. There were two sets of keys. One on the table, and one hanging on a hook just behind the soldier's head. Hannah was faced with the dilemma of trying to get both sets of keys. She immediately decided against it. She didn't want to chance waking him if she didn't have to. She would try the ones she could take easily first.

The keys jingled slightly when she picked them up off the table. Once again her luck held. She clutched them tightly against her bosom and crept back down.

She was about to look for the boy in the same cell where he had been kept earlier, but Ka-ti was motioning for her to come to the far end. Hannah had thought to find Do-sa ill, but he was standing by the door of the cell in front of Ka-ti, both hands gripping the bars.

He kept whispering urgently to her, and Hannah put her finger to her lips as a signal for him to be quiet. The first key she tried scraped loudly and wouldn't turn the lock. She tried another, and then another. She looked over her shoulder at the sleeping soldier to make sure he hadn't stirred. Do-sa waited, clearly full of youthful impatience, but he said nothing.

She tried another key. It went in easily, and just when she thought it, too, didn't fit, the lock scraped open. She pulled back the door and let him out. She had no plan beyond this, but Ka-ti apparently did. She went quickly to the back door and looked out. The boy stood with Hannah as if he wanted to say something, then he abruptly took a kind of bracelet from around his wrist and pressed it into her hand.

"Soyez fort," he whispered, then he went quickly to where Ka-ti waited. He turned to look at

Hannah once before he followed Ka-ti outside. He reminded her of his father. The McLarn blood was clearly in them both.

Clutching the bracelet in her hand, Hannah started to follow as well, but then she abruptly changed her mind. The boy had to have a chance, the best chance she could give him. She closed the cell door and locked it, then went quickly back up the steps, deliberately avoiding the one that squeaked. She laid the keys carefully on the table, and just when she was ready to congratulate herself that she had accomplished her goal, a dog erupted into frantic barking outside. She could hear it scrambling off the porch after something.

"What—?" the soldier said, sitting bolt upright. Hannah stood there, frozen.

"What the—?" the soldier said, lurching to his feet.

"I'm...looking for the doctor," Hannah said, because that was the first thing that came into her mind. She was not good at lying and never had been, but she was giving it her best attempt.

"Well, he ain't here," the soldier answered, clearly disgruntled at having his sleeping interrupted—or having been caught at it by someone who had no authority to do so.

"Are you certain?" Hannah persisted. She had to give Ka-ti the time to get Do-sa over the wall— and she prayed that *he* wasn't what the dog was after. "I can't find him anywhere else."

"I said so, didn't I? He ain't here—and you shouldn't be neither. Ain't nobody here but that Indian pup." He suddenly seemed to wake up enough to realize that Hannah was female, and he looked her up and down.

"Anything I can do for you, deary?" he asked. He grinned and winked. "I been known to fix what ails you."

"Nothing ails *me*, sir," Hannah assured him. "Well...perhaps..." she added, and her mind immediately refused to cooperate. She frantically tried to think of something intriguing, something on the order of what Sibyl or Charity would say.

The soldier waited expectantly.

"No, I suppose I really must find the doctor," she said sadly.

She could still hear the agitated dog, and the soldier came around the table.

"What ails that little beast!" he said, heading toward the door. He grabbed Hannah by the arm in the process, shoving her outside ahead of him. She could hear men shouting near the stockade wall.

The soldier whistled loudly for the dog, but it didn't come.

Hannah began walking away from him, slowly at first and then more swiftly. She kept expecting him to forget the dog and call her back, but he didn't. She kept carefully to the shadows. Staying out of sight was all she could do. She had nowhere she could go. Sooner or later, somebody would discover that she had gotten out and was roaming freely about the fort. She didn't mind being locked up again. Not if the boy escaped.

Something was happening. Two soldiers appeared across from her—and then two more off to the left. All of them were advancing in her direction. She looked around, trying to find a place to get out of their way. She tried to backtrack, but the private who was serving as the jail turnkey had returned. He, too, looked in her direction.

She stepped in between a wagon and a heavily laden cart, hoping to get lost among the settlers camping on the parade ground. She weaved in and out among them, as if she had some purpose, not daring to look over her shoulder until she was farther away. A woman with a baby at her breast looked at her curiously, but she made no objection when Hannah nearly stumbled into her cook fire.

Hannah kept going, dodging among the families sitting on the ground. A woman combed a little girl's hair. Someone began to play the fiddle, a lively jig and obviously a welcome invitation to dance.

"No, thank you, sir," she said to a young man who caught her by the hand and would have pulled her into the merry-making. She kept smiling and tugging until she was finally able to get her hand back. She nearly lost the bracelet Do-sa had given her, and she hastily wrapped it around her wrist in the same way he had worn it.

She stopped in shadows behind one of the wagons, looking for the soldiers who had seemed to be in pursuit. She could see one of them directly across from her—but his attention was taken by the lively dancing. She turned abruptly to run in the other direction—and collided with someone standing almost directly behind her. He grabbed her by both arms.

"Well done, Hannah!" Morgan said, smiling. "Is this some of that colonial ingenuity one hears so much about? I must say you have surprised us all—particularly Mr. Hatcher."

She struggled to get free of his grasp. "Let me go!"

His grip tightened, and he swung her around so that his face was close to hers.

"Did you imagine for one moment that I wouldn't guess what your inordinate interest in Cherokee slaves and Colm McLarn signified? Ah! I see you did. Well, my dear Hannah, I can assure you that that is not the case. How will you fare as bait, do you think? Will he come for you?"

"I don't know what you're talking about!"

"I'm talking about *Hi-s-ki-ti-hi*. Is that not how he is called? Hi-s-ki-ti-hi."

"He's dead! You said he was dead!"

"I think he *will* come," Morgan went on, as if she hadn't spoken. "After all, I have his son and his father, such as he is. And I have *you*. He'll have to come for you. It will be a matter of pride, don't you think? He can't just sit by and let me have you. Old McLarn isn't much of a lure, but the two of you and the boy he was so concerned about—"

"You said he was dead!"

"Of course I did. One does not want one's general in a constant state of dismay, especially in these perilous times. And especially one whose mental state is so fragile he must be posted with his personal physician in tow. But then you yourself sampled Dr. Baines's skill with hypnotics. The man is a genius. Anyway, at his advice, I told the general McLarn's bastard was dead. I gave him a scalp. And I thereby put his mind at rest. He had one less reason to worry about being murdered in his bed—and no responsibility for the disposition of an illegitimate, half-breed son whose father just might still have some small political influence."

They stared at each other in the moonlight. She didn't dare believe him. She *couldn't* believe him.

Oh, God, is he alive?

"I won't be bested by a savage," Morgan said, his voice deadly quiet.

"He is not a savage."

"Why? Because he has Scots blood as well? Believe me, I see little difference in the two breeds. Neither is civilized. And now, my dear Hannah, shall we set the trap, you and I?"

He forced Hannah to walk along with him.

"I won't help you!"

"Whatever makes you think I need your help?"

"He won't come," Hannah said—because she believed it to be true. She had heard no alarm. The boy must have gotten away. Five Killer would not risk coming here for her and Colm.

"He will. I will see to it."

"What are you going to do? Morgan—what are you going to do?"

He didn't answer her. He forced her to walk along with him, and no one noticed them because of the music and dancing. At one point, they nearly ran into the young man who had been so persistent about having her as a dance partner. Morgan's grip on her arm tightened. The boy looked at Morgan and then gave her a sheepish grin.

"Another one of your conquests?" Morgan said under his breath as he dragged her on.

There was no help for her here. Hannah knew that. There was no help for her anywhere.

Unless…

No.

Five Killer wouldn't come for her.

Hannah didn't ask where Morgan was taking her, because she could feel how much he wanted her to. She had to keep her wits about her. She would volunteer nothing. She wouldn't assume that Morgan already knew anything.

Be strong, she kept thinking. *Be strong!*

He kept moving her along.

"How is the family?" she asked, and he abruptly stopped.

She had meant to be insolent, and she had succeeded. He changed directions, taking her back across the compound toward the general's headquarters. When he reached it, he opened the door without knocking. The Elways were inside—all of them—and Dr. Baines. They were seated in mismatched chairs around the general's ornate desk, apparently having dinner. The only one missing was the general.

They all looked up in surprise. Hannah stood there, enduring their incredulity, marveling at their ability to drag their airs and pretensions with them wherever they went. It was very clear to her that neither Hugh and Doyle nor their wives had ever expected to enjoy her company again.

"What is this?" old Mr. Elway finally asked.

"Hannah wondered how you all were, Father," Morgan said. "I thought she should see for herself. Look closely, Hannah. This opportunity might not come your way again."

"Really, Morgan," Sibyl said. "You have been in this uncivilized country far too long. Why bring her here in the middle of dinner, for heaven's sake? It's most—inconsiderate." She looked Hannah up and down. "We have a guest, you know."

"Dr. Baines doesn't mind—do you, doctor?" Morgan asked.

"I—no," the doctor decided.

"How is Colm McLarn, Dr. Baines?" Hannah asked, as if she were playing hostess and trying to draw out a reticent guest.

"He is improved. He knows who and where he is."

"He will recover?"

"I believe so—"

"What have you done with my pistol?" the old man suddenly demanded.

"Yes, my dear Hannah," Morgan said, smiling. "What have you done with Father's pistol?"

Hannah stood there, looking back at him. He did remember the shooting and her part in it. She had no doubt about that.

"I expect you would know more about that than

I, Morgan," she said. His smile fell away, and he all but dragged her back outside.

"He's become an absolute barbarian," she heard Sibyl say behind them. "But of course, he did marry beneath him."

Guilty on both counts, Hannah thought, trying not to stumble.

This time Morgan took her back to her own quarters, ignoring the snap to attention from his soldiers along the way. The door was no longer standing ajar. He had to unbolt it to let her in. The room was dark, and Morgan gave her no time to light a candle before he slammed the door closed and slid the bolt.

It took her a few moments of fumbling in the dark before she realized she wasn't alone.

Chapter Fifteen

It took Five Killer the better part of two days to catch up with Reverend Albrecht. Knowing where to look was not difficult. The old man was driving a wagon and therefore could only travel from the fort via the trading path. Five Killer's progress was slowed by having to stay off the path itself so as not to encounter either the military or Cherokee scouting parties certain to be out. Even so, the old man made better time than Five Killer would have expected. He also expected to take the reverend by surprise, and so he did, bursting into his camp when the old man was about to rest himself by his campfire before he settled down for the night.

Five Killer didn't waste any time with amenities.

"I need you to get me into the fort," he said without prelude.

The reverend looked at him, but he said nothing. He was oiling a piece of harness, and he didn't stop.

"Did you hear me? I need your help. Everything that is mine is held in that place. My son. My mother and my father." He looked into the old man's eyes, because he knew this white man expected it. "And your daughter."

Five Killer waited for the argument that must come after his declaration of ownership. He had certainly gotten one the last time he had broached the subject of Hannah, when claiming her had only been a very remote possibility.

Jacob Albrecht bowed his head, and Five Killer realized after a moment that the old man was praying. He waited for the prayer to be over, but it was not easy.

"My daughter thinks you are killed," Albrecht said eventually.

"Yes," Five Killer answered.

"Perhaps that is best—"

"I'm going after her, old man," Five Killer said, and the reverend held up his hand.

"Perhaps that is best," he said again. "That way she cannot give anything away before we get there."

Five Killer looked at him. This was not the man he had encountered all those years before. He had expected this to be harder. He had been prepared to drag Jacob Albrecht to the fort gates with a gun against his head, to force the old man to get him inside if he had to. He had been prepared to do whatever it took.

But it was Hannah's father who was prepared.

He got up painfully from the ground where he'd been sitting and walked to the wagon, rummaging in the back until he came up with a bundle wrapped in cloth and tied with string.

"A tailor in the Salisbury settlement asked me to take this to the fort with me—but the man he made it for was killed in a skirmish with the French before I got there. He has no need of it now. I can see that it may be helpful to you."

He tossed the bundle to Five Killer.

Five Killer opened it. It was a new British army red coat and a white shirt with ruffles on the cuffs and a black strip of cloth to tie around the neck.

"If it is dark," the old man said. "Maybe they don't notice what else is missing. I want my daughter away from there—but I will kill no man to do it. And neither will you, if I can help it—I know what was done to your wife," he said when Five Killer would have protested. "And I can see with my own eyes what was done to you. I know you have reason to hate the British soldiers, but you will put all that aside. We will not have their blood on Hannah's head.

"This I will do. I will tie the horse to graze in the tall grass by the moat, and I will go into the fort on foot when the sun is nearly gone. I will tell them what I have learned about the uprising. Then I will leave, but I won't go far. I will get you into the wagon and I will return. I will say my heart is not in going because of my daughter's troubles— that will be the truth. Then, when we are inside, I will create the diversion, and you will get the others out—if you can."

"What kind of diversion?"

"I will preach," Albrecht said.

"You think that will…be enough?" Five Killer asked. Somehow one of Albrecht's sermons was not what came to mind when he thought of the word "diversion."

"There are people in peril there. They will want to hear me. And I will use my drummer tricks—eating the fire and thus. I learned these things when I was a boy," he added, apparently because of the look Five Killer couldn't help but give him. "They have served me well out here. If a shepherd wants to bring a lost lamb into the fold, he must first get its attention. Now. This you must know. Your father—and my friend—I fear you will have to leave behind, for he will not be able to go on the run with you. And I think your mother will not go without him."

"She was willing enough to leave before—with you."

"Before, she was going to seek help for your son. She couldn't get to him in the jail, so she was going to find someone who would pay ransom or trade a captive for him. She was desperate. If you can rescue the boy, she will have no reason to go."

"The man, Willoughby, says McLarn doesn't know who she is."

"That is true, I believe—but he still says her name."

The old man put the harness he was oiling aside. "My daughter—if you get her out, what happens to her then?"

Five Killer looked at him. "I will take better care of her than you ever did," he said.

Jacob Albrecht stared back at him and then nodded. He took his pipe from his pocket and lit it with a burning stick from his fire.

"I am an old man," he said after a moment. "I must sleep for an hour or so. Then we will go."

Five Killer moved to the edge of the firelight. The reverend might be at ease sleeping by a fire when there were war parties out, but he was not. When he reached the shadows, he stopped.

"Does Hannah know about this fire eating thing you do?"

"If I tell her that, then I have to tell her once I run away with the circus, yes?"

Five Killer nearly smiled, in spite of the dire situation. He had no idea if Albrecht was serious, but he still appreciated the notion that the stern reverend had a past. He shook his head and walked on, searching the perimeter of the camp for a vantage point from which he would watch over the old man during the night.

Hannah would laugh—

His amusement abruptly disappeared.

Hannah.

He looked back at Hannah's father. He was praying again, and so now would Five Killer.

He found a spot where he could still see the old man, and when he was certain that there were no enemies lurking in the darkness, he rested his back against a hickory tree.

And in his mind, in his heart, he began his war song.

* * *

Hannah waited in the darkness, afraid to move.

"Who is here?" she asked finally. "Hatcher?"

Her hand brushed the back of the chair, and she gripped it tightly. It wasn't much of a barrier and certainly not a weapon, but it was all she had.

Her eyes were growing accustomed to the dark. She could just make out someone standing on the other side of the room.

"Oh—no—Do-sa—"

He held up his hand for her to be quiet, but she didn't heed him.

"What are you doing here!" she said, forgetting to speak to him in French.

"I come for you," he answered her in English.

"What?"

"Can you climb?"

"I don't—"

"Hurry, woman!" he said. "Climb here."

He showed her the footholds in the log wall.

"The space is narrow at the top, but you must get through. Then down on the other side. That door we can get out—"

"What good will that do!"

"You can get out of here. Then I can take you out of the fort."

"But—"

"It's not safe here," he said. "We have to get out."

Hannah looked at him, but there was no more information forthcoming. It had never occurred to her to try to squeeze through that narrow space at the ceiling, and even if it had and she'd managed it, she would have had no place to go. That, it seemed, was about to change.

"Can you climb?" he asked again.

Hannah gave a quiet sigh. "Yes," she whispered. She had learned the art from his father.

Do-sa went first, and she followed—or tried. Her skirt kept getting in the way. She finally pulled it between her knees and tucked it into her waist— the way the cooks in the kitchens did to keep their dress tails from catching on fire. Her knees scraped the rough logs as she pulled herself upward. When she reached the top, her fingers slipped on the edge and she nearly fell. Finally, she was able to pull herself onto the top log. The space was tight, but she managed to wriggle through. She misjudged the drop on the other side, and her forearms scraped the logs all the way down.

"Come," Do-sa insisted, barely giving her the time to set her skirt to rights.

He cracked open the door and waited until the moon disappeared behind a cloud. Then he was off with Hannah right behind him. When the moon came out again, he scurried under the nearest wagon, and Hannah followed.

"We have to hurry," he said.

Why? she wanted to ask, but he didn't give her time. He was out from under the wagon and off toward the nearest building.

Hannah couldn't follow immediately. Someone—a man and a woman—came walking by. She couldn't hear their conversation well enough to understand the words, but she understood the intimate tone. She waited, willing them not to stop.

But they did stop—briefly. Hannah could hear the rustle of clothing and a soft sigh. Then they moved on. She waited for a moment, then rolled out from under the wagon and walked in the direction Do-sa had gone. She began to run as soon as she was in shadow again—but she had no idea what direction he'd taken.

Hannah finally saw him. He was standing at the corner of the surgery, motioning for her to hurry. She hesitated. She didn't want to chance running into the doctor—but she didn't have a choice. She kept to the shadows and caught up with him.

Briefly.

He was off again, this time toward the privies. He went around them and entered a lean-to shed built against the stockade wall.

When Hannah reached him, he was down on his knees, digging in the dirt floor. She knelt down to help, without knowing why. In a moment, they had uncovered several planks over a hole. He took them out and disappeared into it.

Hannah stood there, staring after him. He was a child—and yet he wasn't. And she was putting her life in his hands.

"Come!" he said, the sound of his voice muffled.

"Oh, Lord," Hannah whispered and crawled in after him.

"Hold on to me," she thought he said. She reached out blindly and caught his ankle. She could smell the damp earth all around her. Decaying roots slapped her face as she crawled along. At least she hoped they were roots.

When she thought she couldn't stand the confinement any longer, he pulled away from her. She lost her grip on his ankle. Suddenly, he wasn't there. She scrambled forward, trying to find him, trying to feel her way. She ran up against a dirt wall, and something thumped her on the top of her head.

Do-sa.

"This way, woman," he said. "Stand up."

He was out of the tunnel and kneeling on the ground. It took several tries for her to get her feet under her. When she stood finally, her head emerged from the hole. He reached and pulled her the rest of the way out.

"Now we wait," he said, still pulling her until they had their backs against the stockade wall.

"For what?" she whispered, trying to wipe the dirt from her face.

"We wait for our chance. The moat goes there," he said, pointing. "We will get into it and we will float along to the river. They can't see us here as long as we stay close to the wall—sit," he abruptly added, pulling her down to the ground.

"How did you know about this tunnel?"

"Tunnel?" he asked.

"That," she said, pointing at the hole.

"Ka-ti showed me. She—and the ones who

left—dug it. They worked at night. It is big enough for me—and you—but not *Grandpère*. No one in the fort knows."

"But how is it you return—?"

"No more talking," he admonished her.

Even so, she had one more concern. "You speak English."

"My father says to speak many white tongues, but don't let them know it—unless it suits you."

"My father, too," she said.

She could feel him looking at her in the darkness. Did he know what had happened to Five Killer? She herself didn't know for sure, and so she made no mention of Morgan's two conflicting stories. She could only hope—pray—that Five Killer was all right, and that he wouldn't fall into whatever trap Morgan would lay.

She wondered suddenly if she and Do-sa both were pawns in Morgan's deadly game. How easy it would be to get rid of her now. A well-placed shot from the sentry on the wall and he would be free—and blameless.

"The doctor says Colm McLarn is better," she said after a time, because she couldn't resist telling him. He had seemed so worried about the old man that day in the jail.

"He will die," the boy said matter-of-factly. "And Ka-ti, too."

Hannah intended to make some protest, but he held up his hand. He was in charge here—and he was clearly done talking.

She sat back. At one point she could hear one of

the sentries walking along the wall above their heads. The boy was right. Apparently they couldn't be seen here.

"Are you..." Do-sa began, but he didn't continue.

Hannah waited for him to say whatever he was of a mind to say, knowing that if he didn't, she couldn't persuade him.

"Hi-s-ki-ti-hi—you are his woman?"

Hannah looked at him, trying to see his face. She couldn't tell from his voice what he was feeling— and she couldn't see his eyes—the eyes that were so like his father's.

"Yes," she answered.

He didn't say anything. She looked toward the moat. The night had been alive with the croaking of frogs, but now it was suddenly quiet. She could feel Do-sa listening intently, as she was.

The wind picked up. A line of clouds slid across the night sky. The moment the moon disappeared, Do-sa jerked her arm.

"Now!" he whispered—and he was off running.

Hannah ran after him, falling to the ground on her belly when he did. Something was happening. Musket fire—but it was coming from somewhere else—the other side of the fort.

Do-sa was on his feet and running again. He waded into the moat and waited long enough for Hannah to catch up. Then he grabbed her by the hand and pulled her along, keeping near the bank.

The water grew deeper. Soon she could barely

touch the ground, and her legs kept tangling in her skirt. She was no great swimmer in the best of circumstances, and now she was struggling to keep her head above water. She could hear shouts and more musket fire. She dared to look back over her shoulder, but she couldn't see anything.

"Hurry!" Do-sa whispered fiercely, and she began to struggle forward again, trying to keep up.

Finally, he paddled to the far side and climbed out. Hannah followed him, but she was too winded to pull herself onto the bank. After a moment, Do-sa helped her, dragging her by the arm until she was on her knees in the mud.

There was a small sound in front of her, and Hannah looked up sharply.

Maw. She recognized him immediately. And he was not alone.

He signaled with his hand and two young men appeared out of nowhere—one of them the warrior Hannah had beaten with the blackberry basket. He dragged her to her feet by her hair and put the rawhide tether roughly around her neck, jerking it hard when she would have cried out. He bound her hands in front of her and then brought her to stand before Maw.

Maw gave a command, and the nearest warrior grabbed Do-sa as well. The boy struggled and protested, but it did no good. When he was firmly tied, Maw came closer.

"Well done, boy," he said in English.

Chapter Sixteen

Something was happening at the fort. Five Killer could hear the musket fire long before he could see it. He pushed hard, leaving Jacob Albrecht to catch up as best he could. He moved quickly, but with care, every sense, every muscle in his body alert. The moon was bright—whenever it escaped the cover of the clouds—and he traveled accordingly. He didn't want to be seen. He had no weapon save Willoughby's hunting knife. He didn't want to run into the reason the fort was up in arms.

The musket fire stopped abruptly. Five Killer's heart sank—not at the ominous silence, but at the war cries he could hear now in place of the guns.

He could see the fort. Some part of it was burning. He heard someone off to his left, and he whirled around, ready to do battle.

"It's me!"

"Willoughby—?"

"Aye! And don't go thinking I'm going to let ye gut me with my own pig-sticker."

Five Killer peered into the shadows. Almost immediately Willoughby stepped into a clearing and ran forward. Five Killer hadn't expected to see him again. The man was out of breath from running.

"Hannah and the—boy—" he said, sliding to his knees in the underbrush near Five Killer.

"What about them?" Five Killer demanded, grabbing him by his shirtfront.

"Maw's got her—or had her. She was out of the fort—her and—Do-sa both."

"How do you know that!"

"I seen them! They was outside—they waded the—moat—right into Maw. But then—all hell broke lose. The moon went behind—the clouds. When it come out—again—I could see where they *was* all right—Hannah and the boy—but they were gone. And two of the braves that held them were on the ground. Then that damn fool Morgan—he come marching his men out of the fort. The musket fire was so heavy—and the moon was gone. I didn't see them again—don't know which way they went."

"There are still soldiers in the fort?"

"Aye—"

They both turned at another sound. A wagon. Jacob Albrecht.

Five Killer swore, using the English words he'd learned following McLarn in the white settlements. Only the reverend would drive so blithely into the middle of a war. Five Killer circled around to head him off. When he got the old man stopped, he told him what Willoughby had seen.

"I don't know if she's outside or in. I'm going to go see what I can find. You stay here. The red coat will get me into the fort if needs be. And if you've got any pull with the god you follow, you better use it."

He retrieved the leather pouch that now carried the red coat from the back of the wagon where he'd left it.

"Here," the old man said, throwing him a powder horn and a long rifle he had hidden under the wagon seat.

Five Killer looked at him, then put the powder horn over his shoulder.

"I do not want my daughter to suffer, Robert," the old man said quietly, and Five Killer nodded. He was certain only of one thing. Whether Hannah and the boy were with Maw or not, he would find them.

Five Killer traveled the rest of the distance to the fort at a run with Willoughby right behind him. The bodies still lay on the ground between the woods and the fort wall, but everything was silent.

"Where did you see Hannah last?" he whispered to Willoughby.

"They came from along the wall there to the left of the tower and down to the moat. They got as far as that clump of cane growing yonder. That's where Maw and some of his braves took them—tied them. I didn't see them left laying nowhere around there."

"I'm going to look anyway," Five Killer said.

He took the red coat and the shirt from his pack

and put it on. He could feel Willoughby's interest immediately.

"I don't want the sentries to shoot me," he said, and Willoughby nodded.

"You better be hoping Maw didn't leave any warriors behind with long rifles."

"That's what you're here for," Five Killer said.

He didn't hesitate. He emerged from the cover of the trees and made his way along the edge of the moat, stopping at each body for some sign of Hannah and the boy. He found no one alive.

He kept going, zig-zagging across the open ground, still checking bodies. He made his way into the moat and across to the other side. He wasn't exactly sure where Willoughby had seen Hannah and the boy last and there was no moonlight for him to search for signs. He kept going as far as the wall. No sentry hailed him. In fact, there was nothing coming from the fort at all.

Five Killer stood for a moment, then began to backtrack, crossing into the moat again, but this time he continued to wade along the bank, meticulously looking for something to tell him what had happened here.

The moon came out. He could just make out footprints in the mud. There were two bodies nearby—the two braves Willoughby had seen lying on the ground, he thought. He came out of the water and knelt down to inspect them more closely. Both were dead.

He moved to where he could see the footprints— small footprints among the larger ones. This was where Do-sa and Hannah had come on to the bank. He recognized the marks left by Hannah's shoes.

The moon went behind a cloud again, and he had to wait. He looked at the fort, listening hard for a sound from the inside. Whoever was on the ramparts must see him, and their restraint must indicate one of two things. They were fooled by the red coat or they were seriously low on powder.

There was a break in the clouds. Once again, he inspected the ground in the bright moonlight. Both sets of smaller footprints led away from the fort, and after a short distance, one of them showed signs of being dragged.

The sun was coming up. Hannah stood waiting, trying not to show her fear. Maw approached her with his knife drawn.

I'm afraid of not dying well, she thought, and she looked directly into the eyes of the man who meant to kill her. Would anyone know what had happened to her—or would she be one of many on the frontier who simply disappeared?

A tear slid down her cheek. She couldn't help it, but she made no move to acknowledge it. She waited.

Maw reached out to grab her bound wrists. She didn't cower, even when he raised the knife. He swiftly brought it down and cut her hands free.

He stared at her, his eyes as cold and unforgiving as she remembered. Then he turned away, moving swiftly into the woods. The others followed. Do-sa looked back at her once before the warrior leading him pulled him along.

"Wait," she said, as he disappeared among the trees. She took a step forward. "Wait! The boy—"

She stood there, alone and still disbelieving. How silent everything had suddenly become.

No, she thought. It wasn't silent at all. She could hear animals from time to time in the underbrush. And birds singing. It was the sudden absence of other human beings that made this place seem so empty. She couldn't hear Maw and his warriors at all now, when they must still be near.

She had no idea which way to go or what to do. Her knees suddenly grew weak, and she fell to the ground. She didn't understand.

Unless—

She closed her eyes. Perhaps the object of Maw's revenge had changed. Perhaps it was no longer Morgan. Perhaps it was now Five Killer.

She rolled onto her back and looked up at the sky. It was going to rain. She would have to find shelter. She forced herself to get to her knees, then stood. There was still plenty of daylight. She could see where she was going. If she followed the obscure woods trails her father called "the traces," perhaps she could even find something familiar. She had learned a few things in her time with the Cherokee. To keep a steady pace when traveling. To go around an obstacle, if at all possible, rather than wasting time and strength trying to climb over it.

But following the traces was harder than she

thought. There were times when she wandered aimlessly and times when the trail was clear to her.

The rain began to fall, but she didn't stop. At one point she came to a clearing. She watched from the cover of the trees for a moment, then continued on, and she picked up the pace. She knew where she was. She had been in this place before. She had come into the meadow from the opposite side—with Five Killer—when they were on the run from Maw.

She saw the boulders up ahead and the overhanging ledge, but she didn't stop there. She began to climb the rocks, retracing her flight from Willoughby and his dogs. It took her several minutes of searching, but she finally found it. The crevice where she had dropped the pistol Five Killer left with her.

The gun was still there. Willoughby hadn't seen it fall. She lay on her belly and tried to reach it. Her fingers just brushed the barrel. She kept trying and trying, but she couldn't get a good hold. She abruptly got up and went looking for some kind of stick or branch she could slide under it and raise it enough so that she could reach the barrel.

She searched under the trees, finally choosing several limbs that might do. The first one she tried was too short. The second, too big around to get under the pistol. The third one slid under it easily. She pushed down on the other end. The weight of the pistol caused the branch to bend, but she was able to raise the pistol slightly.

She put her knee on the limb to anchor it and

reached into the crevice again. The pistol slid off the branch just as her fingers closed over the barrel. She had it—but not securely.

She rested for a moment, then carefully pulled the pistol upward, catching it with her other hand, just as it cleared the boulder. She sat there, hanging on to it for dear life. She had no idea if it would still fire. It didn't matter. She had it. She had *something*.

The rain came harder, but she made no attempt to get out of it. She knew there would be shelter under the ledge, but she couldn't bring herself to go there. Not yet. She just sat, letting the rain beat down on her.

Something caught her eye on the far side of the meadow. She looked more closely, but she couldn't see anything—anyone.

She stood to get a better look. This time she saw a brief flash of red, so brief that she nearly convinced herself that she had been mistaken.

After a moment, she sat down on the boulder again, not out of choice—out of necessity. She just couldn't go anymore. She sat with her head bowed and the pistol in her lap.

"Hannah?"

She grabbed the pistol and swung it around, pointing it dead center at a red coat.

"Hannah, it's me—"

"Five Killer—oh—" She let the pistol fall, and scrambled to him. He lifted her down off the rock and held her close, leaning back to look at her once and wiping the rain from her face. But she couldn't bear to be apart from him, and she clung hard, pressing her face into his shoulder.

"Are you all right?" he said against her ear, and she nodded.

"I don't know why he did it," she said, still clinging.

"What?"

"Maw. He let me go—he kept Do-sa, but he let *me* go—"

"He's wanting to slow ye down," someone else said.

Hannah looked around. Willoughby stood close by, his long rifle ready.

Hannah leaned back to look at Five Killer's face. Now she understood. Willoughby was right. Maw had deliberately left her alive for Five Killer to find so he would have to take care of her. Even if he continued the pursuit with her in tow, she would only slow him down. She reached up to touch his face, looking deeply into his eyes. He was in such pain and she couldn't bear it. She would have to make the decision for him.

"Hannah—"

"Go," she said, kissing his mouth gently. "Find him. Find your boy."

His arms tightened around her.

"Go," she said again. "Mr. Willoughby?"

"Aye?"

"My father's old cabin—is it there yet?"

"Was last time I was by that way."

"And no one lives in it?"

"No."

"Will you take me as far as the trading path? I can find my way from there."

"Aye, Hannah. That I will do."

"Morgan won't look for me there. If the cabin is gone, I'll find my father. If I'm not there, you look for me with him. I have the pistol. I know what to do—" She abruptly stopped because she could feel her eyes welling with tears. The last thing she wanted to do was weep. She hugged him tightly so that he wouldn't see.

"You wait for me," he whispered, kissing her hard. "You wait!"

She nodded, not trusting her voice.

He said something to Willoughby in Cherokee, then his mouth came down hard on hers one last time.

"Your soul is in my soul—" he said, and he left her there.

Hannah stared after him, long after he'd disappeared into the line of trees on the other side of the meadow.

"Ye ain't going to cry, are ye?" Willoughby asked as she retrieved the pistol.

"I am, Mr. Willoughby," she answered, the tears already streaming down her face.

"Well, just so I know."

Hannah looked at him, and he winked.

"We best not hang around here. Your former husband is still lurking about."

"Former?" she asked.

"Ye got to be careful what ye drink at them

Cherokee ceremonies," he said. "It'll get ye married and unmarried before you know what hit ye."

Willoughby started out, and Hannah followed, still crying in spite of his attempt at levity.

"What was that?" she asked, stopping to look over her shoulder.

"Nothing," Willoughby said.

"It's musket fire—"

"Mayhap," he said, still walking on.

"Mr. Willoughby!" she cried. "Stop! You have to go see!"

"He charged me not to leave ye no matter what."

"You won't be leaving me," she answered, heading in the direction Five Killer had gone.

"Wait! Hannah! Damn it all. He'll have my hide—" He caught up with her and grabbed her by the arm. She brought the pistol up level with his chest.

"I have but one shot, Mr. Willoughby. I don't want to waste it on you."

After a moment he let go of her arm.

"The two of ye are more trouble than I ever wanted, I'll tell ye that," he said, striking out ahead of her. "Keep up or get left behind—here," he added, tossing her one of his powder horns. "I trust ye know what to do with this."

"I do, Mr. Willoughby," she answered. "And I will keep up."

The sound of musket fire was louder now, closer. Willoughby took off into the woods, and Hannah followed him tree to tree. The rain drumming on the leaves overhead drowned out the sounds of their movement, and Willoughby picked up the pace. From time to time, Hannah could see puffs of smoke from among the trees up ahead. At Willoughby's signal she dropped down behind a large tree. He indicated that he was going on and she was to remain. She nodded to show that she understood, and she took the time to reload the pistol with the powder from the horn he had given her.

She could hear war cries now—the kind she had heard in the woods when she was first taken, the kind that made her blood run cold. A musket fired very close at hand, but she didn't show herself to look. She could hear the sounds of a struggle—and finally a shriek of...

What? she thought in a panic.

Not pain—triumph.

Someone was coming, his progress irregular like a drunken man trying to find his way home from an evening at the tavern. She sat perfectly still, the pistol ready, but she misjudged which side of the tree he would pass.

He was there suddenly, behind her. She cried out as the man fell face first at her feet.

Willoughby.

She couldn't see a wound, only the blood. He reached out to grab her skirt, and she bent down to him, trying to turn him over. He managed to say one word before he lost consciousness.

"Run—"

She hesitated only a moment, then took his remaining powder horn, his knife. She would get his long rifle as well, if she could find it.

She began to move from tree to tree again, going in the direction Willoughby had gone. She found his rifle where he'd dropped it, and she dragged it behind a tree to reload, then slung it over her shoulder by the strap. Her heart was pounding. She couldn't stay here.

She heard someone running in her direction, and she pressed her back against the tree, the musket on her knees. A warrior ran past her, but he saw her immediately and whirled around, his axe raised. Hannah pulled the trigger, the delayed report loud enough to make her ears ring. The warrior crumpled on the ground.

She took no time to think about what she had done. She began to reload the musket, but her hands trembled too much for her to pour. She wiped the sweat from her eyes with the heel of her hand and tried again.

"Do it!" she whispered.

There was musket fire all around her now—and then it suddenly grew quiet.

"Hi-s-ki-ti-hi!" someone called. Then again, "Hi-s-ki-ti-hi!"

She moved to the other side of the tree, trying to see.

Maw stood in the open with Do-sa. The boy couldn't stand. He hung limply by the rawhide tether around his neck, his hands still bound.

She heard the response off to her left. Five Killer answering in Cherokee.

Why is Maw daring to show himself like this?
she thought frantically. It could only be for one
reason. Five Killer couldn't do anything to him, and
he knew it. She tried to tell where his voice was
coming from, waiting impatiently for him to speak
again.

He did finally, and she immediately lay down on
her belly and crawled in that direction. There was
enough underbrush to hide her—she hoped.

A scream pierced the air, but she didn't stop.

Do-sa.

He wasn't dead. He was being tortured.

Five Killer was behind some large rocks. She
could see him now. She didn't call out to him. She
crawled around so that she could sit up with her
back against a tree. He was wounded. One arm was
completely useless. Do-sa screamed again, and
Maw would be certain now that he had nothing to
fear.

Hannah began crawling again, dragging the musket with her. She had to stop several times to decide
which way to go. Five Killer had seen her now. She
could hear him.

"No," he said. "No—Hannah—"

She reached him without being seen, and she
dragged the musket into the shelter of the rocks.

He reached out to her with his good hand. She
tried to see to the wound in his arm, but he
wouldn't let her.

"You have to help me, Hannah," he said, trying
to get to his knees. "I can't do it alone—"

The boy screamed again.

"He is already dead. It's only his agony that still lives. Do you understand, Hannah? Ah, God!" Tears streamed down his face.

Hannah took a quiet breath. His right arm was useless. He couldn't manage this, and they both knew it.

"I'll do it," she said. She brought the musket around and propped it on the rock. Her hands shook. She bowed her head and clenched her fists for a moment, then she picked up the musket again.

"Please..." she whispered, knowing that such a prayer must be an affront to God.

Sight and pull the trigger. That's all she had to do. The rock would keep the musket steady.

Maw had no fear now. He no longer used the boy as a shield. Two other warriors held Do-sa, and Maw's knife flashed. This time the boy made no sound. Maw looked at him incredulously. The two warriors let his body fall.

Later she would think about how easily she shifted from an act of coup de grace to an act of revenge—but not now.

Forgive me.

She squeezed the trigger. Willoughby's long rifle was meant for distances far greater than this. The musket ball passed through Maw almost at the same instant of the musket's report. The sound echoed in the woods, echoed in her head. Then there was a stunned silence. No birds. Nothing—except the rain.

Hannah looked at Five Killer. He was no longer conscious. An unnatural calm seemed to have descended upon her. She reloaded the musket, then moved to his side, tearing strips of her skirt to bind the wound in his upper arm.

And then she sat by him, holding him and keeping vigil, waiting for the inevitable to come.

The silence went on and on.

Where are they? Why don't they come? she kept thinking, but she made no effort to look. *He* was the only thing she wanted to see. She leaned down and pressed a kiss against his cheek, the sorrow she felt on his behalf nearly unbearable.

Your soul is in my soul.

She had no idea how long she waited. Time meant nothing when one had no time left. Once, she thought she heard voices. She turned her head, listening intently.

There were voices. Women's voices, coming closer.

Someone made a soft hailing sound, and she held Five Killer closer. She didn't dare answer. She held the long rifle on her knees again—ready.

A woman was there suddenly, holding up her hands and making soothing motions. She called over her shoulder to the others, and another woman appeared—Ka-ti.

"Don't shoot me," she said, maneuvering to get close so that she could see Five Killer.

Other people appeared—several more women and an old man.

"I will take him now," Ka-ti said, trying to help Five Killer up.

"No—" Hannah protested. "No!"

"I will take him," Ka-ti repeated. "You cannot make him well. Your English husband will kill him if he finds him."

"I'll come with him—"

"No. If you are disappeared, your husband will use it as an excuse to burn more Cherokee towns. There has been enough killing. Go. The old man will take you to your father. If my son lives, he will come for you."

"Your—?"

Hannah stared at her. *Of course*, she thought. The woman had not been "found" to look after Colm McLarn. She had placed herself there willingly so that she could help her husband.

Hannah was moved bodily out of the way. The women lifted Five Killer and put him on a litter. He cried out in pain, but he did not wake. Hannah knelt down beside him and took his hand, pressing a kiss on the back of it, before she let him go.

"Be strong," she whispered.

She looked to where Do-sa had fallen. He was still there. Women were taking him onto a litter as well. There was no sign of Maw.

Hannah stood in the rain, watching them go.

"Lv-la," the old man said, but Hannah had one other thing she had to do. She had to find Willoughby.

But the women had taken him, as well. His body had been draped over the back of an aged horse.

"They will take him to his woman," the old man said. "Lv-la."

He began walking, and Hannah followed—because there was nothing else she could do.

Chapter Seventeen

Hannah sat alone and motionless on the flat boulder near the water's edge. She could feel the sunlight on the top of her head. She kept listening to the silence that was not silence at all. Birds singing. Insects buzzing. The quiet rush of the water. The wind in the treetops.

And nothing—no one—else.

In spite of everything she chose not to stay at her father's house. The Reverend Albrecht had learned one lesson from all that had happened to her, it seemed. He no longer left his family alone on the frontier to fend for themselves while he ministered to his scattered flock. Now they lived in the Salisbury settlement. His young wife was still sad, but his boys thrived. And his daughter...

She gave a quiet sigh. His daughter endured. Five Killer was never far from her thoughts. Her longing for him was almost unbearable, and being around so many people seemed to make it all the worse. She had had no news of him. Nothing. Her father made inquiries, but without result. No one would speak of Ka-ti's whereabouts, and Colm McLarn had recovered enough to disappear as well.

Morgan was still attached to the garrison at the fort. She had seen him once, from a distance, when he came to file his request for a divorce at the county courthouse. She herself did not attend the session. It wasn't required of her. Her father went in her stead, and what was said there, she didn't know. She suspected that the people in the settlement knew, but out of respect for her father she was never snubbed outright when she dared to intrude among decent folk. There were stares, of course, and whispers. How could they help it? She was the woman taken captive by savages, the woman who was so "changed" upon her return that her husband had no recourse but to divorce her.

For all of Morgan's earlier machinations, he didn't dare accuse her of adultery, because he was afraid she would tell the truth. He accused her of leaving the marriage bed instead, which she had done with alacrity. His pride could stand that more than her public confession that she loved Colm McLarn's Cherokee bastard. By the time the leaves had turned she knew that she couldn't stay in the settlement any longer. She had to have time to come to terms with all that had happened. She would always bear as much blame for Willoughby's death as for Maw's.

And she had to be where Five Killer could find her.

She returned to the lonely cabin—without her father's blessing but with his understanding and a generous donation of dried meat and fruits, onions and cabbages, and cornmeal to get her through the winter. No one would hear her cry here. No one would intrude upon her thoughts. Her days were solitary, but she was not lonely.

And now spring had come again. With the arrival of warm weather, she went every day to the rock by the water's edge, as she had all those years ago. To sit. To listen.

To wait.

Before, she had always known when he was near, and she longed to recapture the sense that he was somehow there and watching. It never came, and she tried not to despair.

One warm May night, she woke abruptly without knowing why. She lay in her narrow bed in the loft, listening. She heard a faint rustling at the door and she reached for the pistol she kept near at hand. After a moment, she got up and quietly climbed down the ladder to the room below.

The noise came again, and she stepped closer, pistol ready. She could see something stuck under the door, and she bent down to touch it.

A wild flower, freshly picked.

She slid back the bolt and cracked open the door. A bright moon rode high in the night sky. No one was there, nor could she see any movement outside. She looked down. A leather pouch lay on the rough stepping stone. She picked it up, still on guard for some sign of whoever had left it. She opened the pouch and gave a soft cry. She recognized the contents immediately.

Her Psalmody.

She looked wildly around, but she still didn't see anything. She stepped outside and stood there in the moonlight. A faint breeze lifted her hair. She didn't call out.

After a moment she began walking toward the river, slowly at first and then faster, until she was running and running. She didn't stop until she reached the flat rock, and she stood in the middle of it. She was out of breath; her eyes kept searching in the patches of moonlight that filtered through the new leaves.

She saw him then, as he stepped out of the shadows. Her heart leapt with joy, but she didn't go to him. She waited, watching as he walked closer.

He came down the path and onto the rock, and he stopped a few feet away. His face was in shadow.

"Are you all—?" she began.

"I came to tell you not to wait anymore."

She stared at him in the darkness, not knowing what to do. He was here. He was alive.

And he was a stranger.

"I see," she said after a long moment. "Do you think it's as simple as that? Do you not care enough to even ask if it's the same for me?"

"*I* am not the same."

She kept looking at him. She could see it now, the odd angle he had to carry his right arm. She came closer.

"Can you not hold me now, Robert McLarn?" she asked. "Is that it?" She stepped closer still.

"If I come to you in the night, my body hungry for yours, can you not lay me down and give me pleasure?" She pushed hard against his chest.

"If I am angry, and I raise my hand to you—" She did just that, and she would have struck him—hard—if he hadn't caught her wrist.

She could feel *his* anger now. She didn't care. How dare he throw it all away after all they had been through?

Her face was close to his. She could breathe his breath.

"Hi-s-ki-ti-hi—" she said, her pronunciation perfect. She let her mouth almost—*almost*—touch his. "If I run away," she whispered. "Can you not catch me?"

She jerked free of his grasp and ran to the edge of the flat boulder, stopping to look back at him. Then she grabbed up the hem of her shift and began to run again, into the night, not knowing if he would follow.

"Hannah—!"

"You think you are the only one who has any say in this? I don't want you!"

She did not make it easy for him; she ran as hard and as fast as she could, but he caught her finally in a small grassy clearing. He lifted her off the ground, in spite of his lame arm, and crushed her to him.

"I don't want you!" she said again, hitting him with her fist.

"You are mine—"

"No," she answered, turning her face away.

"Your soul is in my soul—"

"No—!"

"Yes!"

His mouth found hers, his kiss full of hunger and pain. She turned her face away and still tried to break free.

He tumbled her into the grass and rolled over with her until his hard body lay on top of hers. He held her face, making her look at him.

"Tell me," he said. "Is it the same for you?"

She struggled harder.

"Is it!"

"Yes!" she cried, tears streaming down her face.

"Even now? Even the way I am?"

"Yes!" she said again.

She stopped struggling, and he stared into her eyes.

"Hannah..."

He began to kiss her gently, her mouth, her eyes. His hands trembled as he touched her. Her arms slid around him, and she kissed him in return, softly at first, and then harder and harder, as her body began to burn with her need for him.

Then he was on his knees straddling her, as if he thought she still might try to get away. He pulled his hunting shirt over his head in a practiced move he must have had to learn to accommodate his injured arm. He stripped off his leggings. When he was free of his breechcloth, he knelt over her again.

"You are my woman," he said, raising her shift

to stare down at her. He reached down to boldly caress her breast. "Mine—"

"Yes," she whispered, completely vanquished now, her body restless with desire.

Moonlight. Night sounds. His body entering hers.

She clung to him, wrapping her legs around him to take him deeper, possessing him as he did her. The joy of it was nearly unbearable. Her body rose to meet his, trying to make the pleasure last forever and yet driven to make it end. She couldn't keep silent and she felt no shame that he would know his power over her.

Her need for him grew with every thrust of his body into hers, and with it the craving for more. She was awash in pleasure, mindless with it. There was nothing in her existence but him.

The pleasure peaked suddenly in a white-hot rush of sensation, and she cried out. And, slowly, so slowly, she began the long fall to earth.

"What happened to them?"

Hannah lay along his good side, and Five Killer turned his head to look at her, not knowing what she meant.

"The sketches of the flowers," she said.

"I gave them to Ka-ti," he said. "McLarn always told her he would take her to his country—to Scotland—to see the heather growing. The flowers in your pictures—I didn't know what they were. I thought maybe they were the kind that grew across the sea where he came from, and she would like seeing them. It had been years since she left him, but she was still sad."

He could feel the sadness in Hannah as well, and he reached up to touch her face.

"Is it too late for us?" she whispered. "Has it cost too many lives? Do so he tried to save me. He was so brave—and Willoughby. I made Willoughby go back that day. If I hadn't—"

"He lives, Hannah. They both live."

"Both?" she asked, trying to see his face.

"Both."

She moved closer to him and hid her face in his shoulder. They lay in the moonlight with the sounds of the summer night all around them. He suddenly thought of the song McLarn used to sing to Ka-ti, and perhaps now he understood what the words really meant.

All that I hae endur'd
Lassie, my dearie,
Here in thy arms is cured,
Lassie, lie near me...

He tightened his arms around her.

"Hannah, you know, don't you?"

She lifted her head. "Know?"

"That I...love you. Your soul *is* in my soul. I believe this with all my heart—"

She pressed her mouth against his, and how good it felt. He gave a contented sigh. He didn't know what would happen. Perhaps they would stay here, or perhaps they would go to one of the Cherokee towns deep in the mountains and well away from the Morgan Elways of this world.

"Come," he said, sitting up and pulling her with him. The sun was rising and they must go to the river. They would enter the lifeblood of Mother Earth and wash away all sins and all doubts, and they would emerge new again, with only their love for each other remaining.

Later he would tell her that she was called "war woman" among the Cherokee. For her bravery in trying to save his son and for killing Maw, who had let his hate twist him until he became a renegade among his own people.

He would watch her eyes and he would tell her that they—and he—called her beloved.

* * * * *

Back by popular demand are

DEBBIE MACOMBER's

Hard Luck, Alaska, is a
town that needs women!
And the O'Halloran brothers
are just the fellows
to fly them in.

Starting in March 2000 this beloved series returns
in special 2-in-1 collector's editions:

MAIL-ORDER MARRIAGES, featuring
Brides for Brothers and *The Marriage Risk*
On sale March 2000

FAMILY MEN, featuring
Daddy's Little Helper and *Because of the Baby*
On sale July 2000

THE LAST TWO BACHELORS, featuring
Falling for Him and *Ending in Marriage*
On sale August 2000

Collect and enjoy each MIDNIGHT SONS story!

Available at your favorite retail outlet.

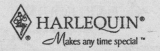

HARLEQUIN®
Makes any time special ™

Return to the charm of the Regency era with

GEORGETTE HEYER,

creator of the modern Regency genre.

Enjoy six romantic collector's editions with forewords
by some of today's bestselling romance authors,

**Nora Roberts, Mary Jo Putney,
Jo Beverley, Mary Balogh,
Theresa Medeiros and Kasey Michaels.**

Frederica
On sale February 2000
The Nonesuch
On sale March 2000
The Convenient Marriage
On sale April 2000
Cousin Kate
On sale May 2000
The Talisman Ring
On sale June 2000
The Corinthian
On sale July 2000

Available at your favorite retail outlet.

HARLEQUIN®
Makes any time special ™

CHERYL REAVIS

Cheryl Reavis is an award-winning short-story and romance author who also writes under the name of Cinda Richards. She describes herself as a "late bloomer" who played in her first piano recital at the tender age of thirty. "We had to line up by height—I was the third smallest kid," she says. "After that, there was no stopping me. I immediately gave myself permission to attempt my *other* heart's desire—to write." Her Silhouette Special Edition novel *A Crime of the Heart* reached millions of readers in *Good Housekeeping* magazine. Her books *The Prisoner*, a Harlequin Historical novel, and *A Crime of the Heart* and *Patrick Gallagher's Widow*— both Silhouette Special Edition books—are all winners of the Romance Writers of America's RITA Award. *One of Our Own* received the Career Achievement Award for Best Innovative Series Romance from *Romantic Times Magazine*. A former public health nurse, Cheryl makes her home in North Carolina with her husband.

HH512IBC

Robert McLarn Had Killed Five Men For Vengeance—

and so was named by the Cherokee "Five Killer,"
a man doomed to live life armored in grief. All that
mattered to him was the safety of his son—until the
day he met Hannah Albrecht, and their destiny
was forever sealed…!

Capricious fate had bound Hannah Albrecht to half-
breed Robert McLarn, a man who was slave to one
people and hero to another. And in his arms, she had
opened to love like a flower in the sun, for
McLarn had captured her heart….

HARLEQUIN®
Makes any time special™

Visit us at www.eHarlequin.com

ISBN 0-373-29112-4

29112

UPC

0 65373 00499 4